MAGES & MONSTERS

A MONTAGUE & STRONG DETECTIVE AGENCY NOVEL
BOOK 27

ORLANDO SANCHEZ

ABOUT THE STORY

We all contain mages and monsters within.

As they faced and defeated Emissary Salya, Tristan Montague and Simon Strong found a path to increase their power.

Monty must now go home.

Home to Shadowpeak, the ancestral home of the Montagues—a location which has been cloaked in mystery and death for centuries.

Shadowpeak, which is currently protected by Guardian Monks from the Order of the Sky, has killed every Montague Mage that has set foot on the property in the last three centuries.

Until now.

When the mutilated bodies of the Guardian Monks are discovered, word is sent to the remaining living members of the Montagues.

Each Guardian Monk was the victim of high-level magic. A level of magic that hasn't existed at Shadowpeak in centuries.

Now, Monty and Simon will venture to Shadowpeak,

discover how the Guardian Monks died and who, or what, killed them.

What they discover will challenge every belief they hold regarding magic and those who wield it.

Three new worlds. Download three novellas for free.
https://BookHip.com/PZWGAVV

"Darkness, true darkness, corrupts, then kills."
-Byron Montague
Archmage of the First Order

"You can never go home again."
-Thomas Wolfe

Sicut intra, ita extra
sicut supra, ita infra.

DEDICATION

For our light to shine, we must confront our darkness.

This is for those who face the darkness and hold firm against it, knowing that to surrender is to lose yourself.

Let your light shine.
Conquer your darkness.

ONE

Dex glared at Monty.

We sat in the newly remodeled conference room in the Moscow. Olga had dropped by earlier to give her approval of the renovations and, I think, to warn us about any more destruction to the property.

Monty had assured her that there wouldn't be any more destruction taking place. I kept my opinion to myself. If the Fifth Pillar or any of the multitude of the '*Crush Monty and Strong*' Fan Club decided to pay us a visit, Monty would have to eat those words.

What she really wanted to know was about Cece and her preparation for her upcoming examination. I still felt it was wrong to put Cece through this, but I wasn't an expert on Jotnar culture. It wasn't my place to contradict their traditions.

That didn't mean I was okay with it, just that I would be nice until it was no longer time to be nice. I really hoped it didn't come to that, but I would be ready for it.

We had just finished speaking to Olga when Dex came into the space from his room. Apparently Dex could sense when Monty was home. This was news to me, but it didn't surprise me; Dex was beyond ancient—not that I would say that out loud. It was usually the extremely old mages that were touchy about their age. That and the fact that Dex was old but he wasn't powerless. Annoying him was a recipe for pain, and I had had plenty on our recent trip to Iron Fan.

It seemed that the responsibilities of the Montague School of Battlemagic had Dex in some high-powered meetings. He wasn't doing casual Bohemian today. Today, he actually looked like he belonged to the official mage class—with his own flair, of course.

He was actually dressed, which was a surprising change from his usual half-naked method of fashion. He was wearing what I considered a typical mageiform. It was a black runed Zegna bespoke suit with dark green accents. On anyone else, it would have looked gaudy.

Dex made it look stylish and understated.

The shirt he wore was a deep green, almost black. If I focused, I could see the runes that flowed across the fabric. Since I had recently acquired the ability to read runes, I tried to decipher the ones on his shirt. I was still getting the hang of it, which meant I couldn't read them easily.

From what I could make out, anyone attacking Dex while he was wearing this shirt was in for an agonizing time. Then again, with or without the shirt, anyone insane enough to attack Dex was looking to shorten their life expectancy in a hurry.

His mostly grey hair was pulled back, away from his face and held in place with a large, dark green raven pin. It wrapped around the bulk of his hair, forming a loose ponytail while keeping the hair in place.

The only thing that was typical Dex were his bare feet and the set of softly glowing rings which adorned his toes.

He tapped his feet as he gazed at Monty.

It was not a happy tapping.

In fact, if I had to define the tapping under the conference table, the only word that came to mind was menacing.

Only Dex could make something as mundane as foot tapping into something that conveyed an undercurrent of barely controlled menace and anger.

Everything about him today whispered a promise of maiming. He had just gotten here, so I had to assume that whatever meeting he had just come from, did not go as expected.

The energy around Dex was on the lower end of the mangling spectrum, and his expression was not happy as he focused on Monty. Every so often, he would glance my way as if to say 'don't think you're off the hook'.

Every time he looked my way the temperature in the conference room dropped a few degrees, making me wonder if Olga had snuck back into our space.

I almost checked the walls for frost as I remained as still as possible, hoping that my statue imitation would hide me in plain sight.

It didn't work as he turned his glare from Monty to me. Only my hellhound was spared the level two Clint Glint.

Dex was not pleased at Monty's latest suggestion, and after hearing some of the details, I had to say I wasn't thrilled either.

Peaches whined under the table, and for a brief moment I wished I could join him under there, if only to get away from the 'angry uncle' vibes Dex was giving off.

We sat around our newly purchased, rune-inscribed Buloke conference table in the freshly runed conference room in the Moscow.

Monty figured that the best way to prevent future destruction—and unneeded future run-ins with our landlord

Olga—would be to systematically begin to reinforce all of the defenses in our space.

He started in the conference room, but was working his way around our space. I think he was going to work on the kitchen area next if only to prevent any hellhound-sized disasters from happening there.

From the way Dex was looking at us, we were a few wrong comments away from needing to flip the table over and hiding behind it.

Which is why I opted to remain silent...for now.

Elder Han and his learning pebbles had taught me that silence could prevent unnecessary pain. Then again, we weren't getting anywhere with this high-level staring contest.

Sometimes mages took themselves way too seriously.

"Rough day at the school?" I asked, to break the tension in the room. "You're looking very official today."

"Aye," Dex said, with a sigh as he ran a hand through his hair, dislodging the raven pin. He took it and put it inside his suit jacket pocket. I figured it was a gift from the Morrigan. "Some of the sects sent over a delegation of representatives to inquire about my *intentions*."

"Your intentions?" I asked, still treading carefully. "The relocation of the entire Golden Circle wasn't clear enough?"

"You'd think," he said. "It was a scouting mission. They wanted to gauge how powerful the defenses were at the school. Since they were so curious, and in the spirit of diplomacy, I did the most courteous thing I could—I let the Head Dean give them a tour of the campus grounds."

"Wait...the Head Dean?" I asked. "You don't mean—?"

He gave me a wicked smile and nodded.

"Mo gave them an excellent tour," he said. "So excellent in fact, that they chose to end it early. I wonder why."

"That was cruel," Monty said, shaking his head. "You know it won't deter them. They will be back...eventually."

"I know," Dex answered with a growl. "I just gave them something to think about, while they plan on how to remove me and recapture the Golden Circle."

"Can they?" I asked. "Remove you and recapture the sect?"

"I suppose anything is possible," he said, rubbing his chin as he considered the Sect Elders removing him. "I never expected my nephew to actively seek to end his life, but here we are."

The glare returned, focused directly on Monty.

I had to give Monty credit—he took Dex's glare and appeared to be unbothered. He was either incredibly brave, or woke up today choosing violence for breakfast.

It had been some time since our recent mountain retreat at Iron Fan, and I, for one, was glad to be in a city, not having to climb murder stairs every morning.

I grabbed my enormous mug of Death Wish and took a long sip as Monty stared back at his uncle. He took his cup of tea—Earl Grey, of course—and took a small sip before methodically placing the cup back in its saucer.

There would've been less tension in the air if I were color-blind, and trying to defuse a bomb with only red and green wires to cut.

Peaches rumbled again under the table.

<Do you think the old man can make me some meat?>
<Now may not be the best time, boy. He seems angry.>
<Why is he angry? Is he not eating enough meat?>
<I don't think it has anything to do with meat.>
<Everything has to do with meat. If he ate more meat, he would be happier.>

Of course, zen bliss could only happen with large portions of meat according to my Zen Meat Hellhound.

<He's angry with Monty.>
<Is it because the angry man doesn't eat meat?>

<Really? Not everything has to do with meat. It's not that.>

<Then why is he angry?>

<Monty volunteered us for something dangerous, and I think Dex is upset because Monty's suggestion makes sense, not that I think it's a great idea.>

<What did the angry man suggest?>

<That we go to his ancestral home. It seems his home is filled with traps and failsafes.>

<If he ate meat...>

<I know—he could deal with the traps and failsafes easily. I wish everything could be solved with meat, I do, but I don't think this is one of those situations.>

<When you become mighty, you will understand.>

<Can hardly wait. Now be still, I need to get the details on this ancestral home of the Montagues.>

He chuffed in response and angled his body next to my feet, getting comfortable by crushing my legs.

TWO

"I don't understand your reaction," Monty said, refocusing my attention as he faced his uncle. "My suggestion solves both our problems."

Dex gave him another glare.

He took a deep breath and let it out slowly as he shook his head. He slowly placed both hands on the table, and I could sense him restraining himself from strangling Monty. If he was reacting this way, then the dangers at this ancestral home were major.

Dex had sent us on any number of operations that were potentially dangerous and life-threatening. Somehow, this was different. I didn't know how yet, but I knew he was concerned more than usual.

I looked down at Dex's hands as they rested on the surface of the table and saw that they were glowing with a soft green energy that was outlined with traces of black.

That can't be good.

I was thankful the table was Australian Buloke, because the energy radiating from Dex was reaching dangerous levels. A normal table would have probably been reduced to splinters. Dex rolled his shoulders and turned his head to both sides, cracking his neck.

"Aye, what part of 'deadly failsafes' did you not comprehend?"

"They can be circumvented," Monty replied, keeping his calm in the face of the growing storm that was his uncle. "*You* said Shadowpeak needs to be investigated."

"I never said that *you* need to do the investigating."

"It needs to be someone from the bloodline," Monty said matter-of-factly. "The ancient failsafes are still in place, all the more now that the monks are dead. You need a Montague."

"Actually, I said the property *near* Shadowpeak needs to be investigated," Dex answered with a growl. "Elder Han wants to know what happened to his monks."

"And I need to access more power."

"Not *that* power, you don't," Dex snapped. "Shadowpeak kills. It's...evil."

Monty narrowed his eyes at Dex. I could tell he didn't believe his uncle, but had too much respect for him to blatantly refute his claim.

"Evil?" Monty said, keeping his tone even. "If this is true, why haven't you destroyed it?"

"Aye, I was about to, some time back," Dex said with a small head shake. " I was younger then, full of myself. I learned then, I'm not meant to face every foe. Some entities must be faced and destroyed by others...this is one of them."

"Are you saying it's too strong for you?"

"This has nothing to do with strength," Dex said. "Anymore than your ability has to do with being a mage. Which it doesn't. Byron designed that place to kill mages...especially Montagues."

"Which it will if we don't secure it," Monty said. It may only allow Montagues normally, but now...any mage who can find it—"

"Aye, and there are a few," Dex finished. "Some of them twisted."

"Precisely," Monty said. "The normal deterrents are gone with the loss of the monks. If not arrested, the power inside Shadowpeak will begin to kill indiscriminately."

"Excuse me?" I said, raising a finger and risking my life. "Shadowpeak kills? Is this a figurative thing, or are we being literal here?"

"What do you think, boy?" Dex said, glancing at me. "That place is beyond cursed—it kills."

Monty shook his head.

"You realize you're anthropomorphizing a castle?" Monty asked. "According to my studies, it only kills those who fail the gauntlet. Montague or not."

"The gauntlet?" I asked. "What gauntlet?"

"The one neither of you are going to run," Dex answered. "And it's not just the gauntlet you need to worry about. Byron's essence guards the place. You can't face him."

"That's a myth," Monty said. "Byron Montague has been dead for centuries. He was ancient when you were born; do you really expect him to be alive currently guarding Shadowpeak?"

"Are you calling me old, lad?"

"I'm merely pointing out the obvious," Monty replied after taking another sip. "It would be impossible for Byron to still be alive, much less guarding Shadowpeak. He was powerful, but he wasn't immortal."

I didn't think it was possible to irk Dex further, but Monty proved me wrong. Dex narrowed his eyes at Monty, and I felt the energy signature of the room increase.

"I didn't say Byron, lad," Dex said with a growl. "I said his *essence*."

"Monty..." I started, but he held up a hand to stop me.

I immediately became silent.

I slightly pushed my chair back, giving myself some maneuvering room in case we needed to make a quick exit or dodge away from some teleportation circles of pain.

"You know I'm right," Monty continued. "You obviously can't go, due to your responsibilities at the school. You yourself said it needs to be a Montague—a direct bloodline descendant, and after Iron Fan, I need to pursue my next shift—this is a case of killing two birds with one stone."

"With the emphasis on the *killing*," Dex snapped. "You're not listening, lad. Just how hard did Yat hit you on that mountain?"

"My mental and physical faculties are in full working order," Monty said. "Elder Han wants—and deserves—an explanation. He lost how many monks at Shadowpeak?"

Dex looked away for a few moments before nodding.

"Twelve," Dex said after a pause. "Guardian Monks are some of the best fighters in the Order of the Sky. One monk dead, I can see, maybe even understand— Shadowpeak *is* dangerous. They could have tripped a failsafe or triggered one of the lethal defenses, but to lose all twelve? That's unheard of."

"How strong are these Guardian Monks?" I asked. "And what could take out twelve of them?"

"*That* is what I'm trying to explain to my very dense nephew," Dex said, before taking a pull from his massive mug of inky black Death Wish. "Anything that can eliminate all twelve Guardian Monks needs to be left alone for now. Neither of you are strong enough to deal with it."

"I disagree," Monty answered. "Perhaps not alone—"

"No, not alone *or* together," Dex said, cutting Monty off. "Shadowpeak has been killing primarily Montague mages for the last three centuries. It stands undefeated. No one has been able to disable it or has had the desire to take it on."

"Primarily Montague mages?" I asked. "There have been other kinds of mages?"

"Of course, child," Dex snapped. "Montague mages are not the only mages on the planet. Shadowpeak doesn't care, you go in, try to access the power and fail...you die. It's too dangerous."

"Even for you?" I asked, glancing at Dex. "Are you saying it's too dangerous for *you*?"

"No," Dex said. "I—it's complicated. If I were to shut that place down...it needs finesse. I can't just destroy our ancestral home, which would be my way of solving this particular problem."

"You have to preserve the property?" I asked. "The murderous magekilling property?"

"Aye," Dex said. "It has the history of the family. Destroying Shadowpeak would be unforgivable. It's why I've stayed away from the cursed place. That and did I forget to mention it's been killing mages for three centuries?"

"Three centuries?" I said, glancing at Monty. "This is where you *want* to go? Deathtrap Central?"

"*Must* go, not want," Monty said. "This is my home and currently, if the monks are gone, that means it's unprotected. An unprotected Shadowpeak is a danger we can't afford."

"Why would this place need protection?" I asked. "Seems like it has the whole deterrence to breaking in thing down to a science. Talk about the ultimate security system. No one will want to set foot in a place that kills you just for visiting."

"You have it backwards," Dex said, shaking his head. "The power of Shadowpeak will attract mages who want that power. It's the Guardian Monks that were the deterrent."

"But now they're gone," I said. "Which means?"

"Other mages will try to access the power," Monty said. "Mages who will use the power to destroy."

"Can't we just get more monks?" I asked. "I'm sure if we ask Elder Han nicely, he—?"

"He won't send any monks until we determine what killed the twelve that were guarding the property first," Dex said. "Preferably removing the threat too. You're right about one thing—twelve dead monks is no light matter."

"Until then, other mages, ambitious mages, will try to break into Shadowpeak," Monty said. "It will end badly for them, fatally so."

"This Shadypeak place will kill them," I said. "Isn't that just this house handing out Darwin awards? I mean, if they are crazy enough to go for the power and get iced in the process, isn't that a greater good for the world?"

"No," Monty said, glancing at me. "There are several scenarios you are not considering. The low-level apprentice who hears about Shadowpeak, allured by the power, thinking this is the perfect opportunity to acquire that power for themselves. A fast track to increasing their greatness."

"That sounds like a bad idea."

"Because it is," Monty said. "They will most certainly die. Then there's the other, more devastating scenario: the mage who actually succeeds in accessing the power and using it for evil. Even if it's a short-lived reign of terror, it will still be catastrophic."

"Can that happen?" I asked, looking at Dex. "Can someone access the power?"

"Hasn't happened in three hundred years," Dex said, but I heard the hint of uncertainty in his voice. "Doesn't mean it can't. Even if they do, the power will burn them out, cooking them from the inside out."

"That sounds—lethal...and disgusting."

"The power in Shadowpeak will destroy the mind and incinerate the body," Dex said, his voice hard. "Usually takes a few days, but it can't be stopped once it's started."

"It's irreversible?" I asked. "There's no way to stop it?"

Dex shook his head.

"The power in Shadowpeak is part of the Montague familial line," he said. "Any other mage not of the bloodline trying to harness *that* power is asking for a gruesome death. That little detail hasn't stopped them, though."

"But you said it killed Montague mages?"

"Primarily Montague mages," he said. "There have been others, power full mages that have tried to access the Well."

"The Well?"

"A repository of power within Shadowpeak," Monty said. "Any mage that embarks on the gauntlet will have to face the Well."

"Aye, those were the ones who underestimated the traps and failsafes," Dex said. "They died in the gauntlet, Montague mage or not. You fail the gauntlet…it's over."

"You're serious?"

"Regarding Shadowpeak?" Dex said. "Deadly serious. That place will kill you both." He glanced down at my hellhound. "The pup too."

"What?"

"What my nephew is failing to explain is that, yes, Shadowpeak contains unfathomable power," Dex said. "It also contains failsafes designed to eliminate with extreme prejudice, any magic user that steps onto the property."

"I'm not—"

"That includes *any* kind of magic, like *your* darkflame and dawnward." He looked at Peaches again. "Your hound's very existence makes him a magical being. It also includes a particularly mule headed mage nephew of mine, who wields magical orbs."

Monty crossed his arms and stared at Dex.

"Very well, how soon before *you* or someone you approve of can be sent to Shadowpeak?" Monty asked. "I would imagine this situation requires immediate attention. Don't you agree?"

"Don't you think I know that?" Dex said with another growl. "It's not like Montague mages, or anyone powerful enough are falling over themselves to go investigate Shadowpeak. Not everyone is keen on rushing to their deaths like you two."

"Imagine that," Monty said before taking another sip of tea. "A singular opportunity like this."

"I wouldn't exactly say *keen*," I pointed out. "This does seem like it needs to be addressed as a high priority."

"How could they refuse?" Monty asked, ignoring my suggestion. "This is their chance to step prominently into our family history and make a name for themselves, how can they not?"

"Because they enjoy breathing," Dex answered. "Shadowpeak is the product of a twisted mind. You studied this, you know the history. They aren't too eager to visit, much less deal with it in any meaningful manner."

"I'll agree, Byron Montague was somewhat unstable, yes."

"*Somewhat* unstable?" Dex said, incredulous. "Don't be daft. Before he disappeared, Byron was barking mad. A powerful Archmage, but by the end he had completely lost the plot and his mind."

"He went mad?" I asked. "Did you say he disappeared?"

"Caught that, did you?" Dex asked. "Yes, no body was ever found. He was *presumed* killed by the very house he created."

"*Presumed*," I echoed. "You don't believe he's dead?"

"I don't believe Shadowpeak could have killed him," Dex said. "He created the place, set every failsafe and rune in the place. I find it unlikely he would be defenseless against it."

"Plenty of mages have met their end due to arrogance," Monty said. "It's that overconfidence that kills them."

"Wait, this Byron person was an Archmage?" I asked.

"Another little tidbit my nephew conveniently omitted," Dex said, shooting Monty a glance. "Byron Montague was the strongest Archmage of the First Order. Then he lost his mind, becoming the greatest threat of the First Order."

"You want to go to this Byron's house?" I said, looking at Monty. "You know, when I suggested a vacation, this is not what I had in mind. Can we pass on visiting the family asylum?"

"Shadowpeak is *not* an asylum," Monty corrected. "Yes, it's dangerous, but a Montague mage *must* go."

"Dangerous is what you just did—going up against an Emissary of the Grand Council," Dex said. "Stepping into Shadowpeak is beyond lethal, not dangerous."

"Are *you* going to do it?" Monty asked, his tone a little softer this time. "Will *you* go?"

"No," Dex said. "The school needs me right now. The runic wards that are being put in place need my presence."

"Maybe we can wait?" I said. "At least until the runic wards are done?"

"By then it may be too late," Monty said, looking at Dex. "You know I'm right."

"That doesn't mean I have to like it," Dex said, running his hand through his loose hair again with a scowl on his face. "Fine, lad. You may go, but only to investigate what happened to the monks. You are *not* to run the Gauntlet. I'm going to say it again, so that you understand. Do. Not. Run. The. Gauntlet."

"I wouldn't dream of it," Monty said before taking another sip. "My entire purpose is to secure Shadowpeak and find out what happened to the Guardian Monks."

"You cannot access the power of Shadowpeak," Dex said, giving Monty a hard look. "You are vulnerable. It *will* destroy you."

"Investigate the deaths and secure the location," Monty said with a short nod. "Anything else?"

"Yes," Dex said. "You *will* take this with you."

Dex gestured and formed a thick, rune-inscribed bracelet that appeared to be made of white crystal. He handed it to Monty. It shrunk and fit snugly around his wrist.

"And this is?" Monty asked, raising an eyebrow as he lifted his wrist to admire the bracelet. "Some sort of tracking device?"

"Hardly," Dex scoffed, pointing at the bracelet. "That is a Radiant Star, because I know you. You will be tempted to try the Gauntlet—the power will call to you, like it does to every mage, Montague or not, that enters Shadowpeak."

Monty looked at the bracelet with some surprise in his eyes.

"A Radiant Star?" Monty said. "I've never seen one in this configuration, does it—?"

"Yes," Dex said, cutting him off. "You shouldn't need it, but if you do, I'd rather you have it and not need it, than need it and not have it. If you stick to investigating only the monk deaths and securing Shadowpeak, you won't need it."

Monty nodded.

"I shall do my utmost not to need it, then," Monty said. "Thank you, Uncle."

"You can thank me by getting out of Shadowpeak in one piece," Dex said, getting up. "Secure Shadowpeak, find out how those monks died, and get out. Do not spend a second longer on that property than you have to—understood? Not a second longer."

"Understood," Monty said. "Is a teleportation circle out of the question?"

"Yes, it's out of the question," Dex said. "Shadowpeak is locked down tighter than a hangman's knot. I couldn't even teleport you *close* to the property. It has an area denial cast placed on the entire estate."

"The entire estate?" I asked. "Is it a null zone?"

"No," Dex answered. "Casting is possible; the results, however, may be mixed."

"Mixed results?" I said. "Why does that sound bad?"

"Because it is," Dex said. "Ach, most of the Black Forest is a mess when it comes to casting, because of Shadowpeak's presence."

Monty nodded as if making a mental note.

"Not a fan of the imagery there," I said. "Really? You had to go with a hangman's knot?"

"Got your attention, didn't it?" he said, then looked at Monty. "Call Cecil, use the Shrike and get there the old-fashioned way. There's a private airport not too far away from the property where he can land that thing."

"Are you sure you can't help?" I asked. "I mean, it would be excellent to have an assist, you being a Montague mage and all."

"My presence there would only muck things up worse," Dex said. "I'll be going to England and give you a hand from there. Hopefully, things won't spiral out of control, but with you two involved...you can never be too sure."

"England?" I asked. "What's in England? How are you going to help us from there?"

"It's too complicated to explain," Dex said glancing at me. "Shadowpeak exists both in the Black Forest *and* in England. The family would stay at the England site since the Black Forest location was too dangerous."

"You realize that's impossible," I said. "It can't exist in two places at once."

"Like I said," Dex answered. "It's complicated. I'll deal with what I can from the English side, while you three are in Germany. Just give Cecil my regards."

"I shall."

Dex paused at the doorway and turned to face us.

"Do not lose your way, nephew," Dex said before heading out of the conference room. "Not all of the dangers of Shadowpeak are external. The power will call out to you. You cannot answer this call, remember that."

"I will remember."

"For all your sakes, I truly hope you do."

The way Dex said those words filled me with a cold dread. He turned and left us alone in the conference room.

THREE

"Have you ever been to Shadowpeak?" I asked. "Have you felt the call of this power? Do you think you can resist it? I only ask because I really don't want to be trapped in some castle estate with you losing your mind."

"Alone never, twice as a child with my family."

"What happened?"

"Considering Shadowpeak has been killing Montague mages for over three centuries, it's safe to assume visiting was not encouraged," Monty said, glancing his tea. "Also, I think most of the reports regarding Shadowpeak have been exaggerated."

"Exaggerated how?"

"Do you really think my family would allow a murderous estate to exist for centuries without taking some kind of steps to secure it?"

"They had the Guardian Monks on site," I said. "Are you saying Dex was lying?"

"No," Monty said, shaking his head. "I wouldn't go *that* far, but I do believe something has been deliberately obfuscated regarding the true history of Byron Montague and the Shadowpeak estate."

"If Dex didn't share all the details, don't you think he has his reasons?" I asked. "Maybe this place *is* too dangerous for us?"

Monty raised his arm and looked at the Radiant Star around his wrist.

"And yet he gave me this," Monty said mostly to himself as he examined the bracelet. "As a precaution? Unlikely. If it was really too dangerous, why would he agree so easily? No, there is something else at work here."

"That was Dex agreeing easily?" I asked. "Did you not sense his energy signature?"

"Did you?" Monty answered. "Think back—how menaced did you feel? Now compare that to your first run-in with my uncle holding Nemain."

I thought back to the first time I faced Dex wielding Nemain and shuddered.

Monty was right.

"It seems like he was putting up some resistance," I said, "But it was half-hearted. That time I faced Nemain...he felt like death."

Monty nodded.

"He wasn't thrilled with the idea, but he wasn't entirely against it either," Monty said, rubbing his chin. "The real question is why?"

"I have a better question."

"Which is?"

"Where exactly is Shadowpeak?" I asked. "I mean, where in England?"

"It's not," Monty said. "Shadowpeak is not in England."

I did a double take.

"What?" I asked, surprised. "Your family, the Montagues *are* English?"

"To our very core, yes."

"And Shadowpeak is the *ancestral* home?" I asked, trying to figure out the logic. "I do have the meaning of *ancestral* right, in this case? The home of your ancestors, not some other obscure mage meaning where the ancestral home is the home your ancestors used to grow in mage power or something strange like that, right?"

He gave me a sideways glance that caught me off-guard.

"There are times where your intuition is quite accurate," he said. "Geographically, Shadowpeak is located in the Black Forest."

"Geographically?" I asked. "What does that mean?"

"It means pack for rain and cold as we are heading into the mountains," Monty answered after finishing off his tea and pulling out his phone. "I'd better call Cecil."

"You know what I meant."

"I did," he said with half a smile. "It's complicated. The actual estate exists in the Black Forest which is in Germany, however, Shadowpeak also exists in England due to the fact that it rests on a nexus of power."

"How?" I asked, expecting another convoluted magespeak answer. "How is it in both places?"

"Byron was an extremely powerful Archmage," he said. "Probably the strongest in the family line."

"Until he went insane."

"His insanity did not diminish his power," Monty said. "Some family historians say that his power increased after his schism."

"He had a schism, like yours?"

"Beyond whatever I experienced," he said. "His schism fractured his mind permanently. He was never the same after that event. In the process of that schism, he created a space which allowed Shadowpeak to exist simultaneously in two locations."

"This is where the explanation gets magey," I said. "You do realize that a solid object can't exist in two places at once."

"Until things get very small," Monty answered. "Since I don't want to risk melting your brain, I'll keep it simple. The best way of explaining it would be by applying the laws of quantum physics. Two objects can, through superposition, exist in two places simultaneously. Byron just managed to expand the scale."

If I was going to encounter mind-melting conversations, I was going to be ready. In an effort to keep up—and protect my brain from spontaneous combustion—I had been brushing up on my quantum physics.

"Quantum physics says no two objects larger than an electron can exist in two places at once," I said, confident in my information. "I'm going to go out on a limb and guess that Shadowpeak is considerably larger than an electron."

He nodded in approval.

"You've been studying, good," he said. "Normally I would agree with you, but remember, I was giving you an example you could comprehend and relate to."

"Thank you for preventing my few brain cells from melting."

"Of course," he said with a short nod. "What Byron did with Shadowpeak has not been replicated by anyone in the family. I daresay there is not a mage on the planet that could pull it off successfully."

"Not even Dex?"

"If he could, he would have moved the Golden Circle—a feat unto itself—*and* simultaneously left it where it was," Monty said. "That would have avoided needless conflict, don't you think?"

"Knowing Dex, even if he could, I think he would still move the whole thing, just to spite the Sect Elders."

"True," Monty said. "In any case, what Byron managed to

do with Shadowpeak was a product of his damaged mind, staggering power, and the First Order."

"You never brought the First Order up before," I said. "Family secret?"

"More like family curse," he said with a dark expression. "I suggest you get ready. Like I mentioned earlier, pack for rain and cold. Whether we are on the German or English side, the weather will be similar. However, the actual entrance is in the Black Forest."

"We can't attempt an entry from the English side?"

"We can," Monty said, and something about the way he said it set my hairs up on end. "The few mages who tried were shipped to their respective sects in boxes—small boxes."

"German side it is then."

"You will get to experience the Rhine Valley, the Danube and an assortment of mountains, hence the cold weather gear," he said. "Though I doubt we will have much time for sightseeing."

"How exciting and non-tropical," I answered with a growl. "Why don't we ever go somewhere warm?"

"We could always visit your home in the Elysium Fields?"

"That is Hades," I said, serious. "Not the person, the place."

"Which from my recollection has seas of lava, mountains of flame, and an enormous, murderous hellhound guarding it," Monty said. "That sounds quite warm; in fact, some would even call it...hellish."

I glared at him.

"Your mage humor, all mage humor in fact, is broken," I said, getting up from the table and waking my semi-dormant hellhound. "How do you even make that leap, from some place warm to hell?" I tapped the side of my head. "That's not normal."

"Define normal," Monty said, following me out of the

conference room, turning down the hallway which led to his bedroom. "Besides, I hear normal is overrated."

"I left normal long ago," I grumbled as I headed to my room. My hand dropped to my side and brushed my holster holding Grim Whisper. I looked down and realized that most of the enemies we were facing these days laughed at my use of a gun. "Why do I even use a gun these days? As a distraction?"

I poked my head out of my room.

"Do I need to bring Grim Whisper?" I called out. "It's not like it's much of a threat these days." I looked down at my gun. "Not unless I physically throw it at someone."

"Yes," Monty replied. "I have something that will make it, and by default you, more intimidating, but it will take some time to enact."

"Really?" I asked as I looked through my closet for thicker woollen suits Piero had made for me. "You have special monster-killing rounds? That would be excellent. I would consider *that* intimidating. One shot for an ogre. Now we're talking."

"Monster-killing rounds are not a thing," he answered, as Peaches jumped up on my bed and proceeded to turn in a circle a few times, before plopping down in the center, taking up all of the space, and sending small tremors through my room. It was a good thing my bed frame was made of titanium. "This will transform your weapon into something formidable."

That sounded dangerous.

"Exactly *how* will you do that?" I asked warily, picking out a thick shirt, a suit jacket, and an overcoat, vetoing all the suits. I wasn't a mage and even though I could use energy and owned some amazing suits thanks to Piero, I would never take myself seriously enough to start dressing like one...ever. Besides, all my clothing was as heavily runed as any of Monty's suits—just less fashionable. "How, as in details."

"I will show you once we are in transit," he said. "The Shrike MKS actually has a casting lab which should suffice for this."

"Of course it does," I said under my breath. "Why would that surprise me? It's Cecil after all. I'm sure Ian Fleming consulted with him for his books and devices."

I changed into my warmer winter gear and found that my body adapted immediately. I'd expected to be sweating up a storm, but found myself actually comfortable.

I wonder if this is a side-effect of the curse or part of my growth as the Aspis?

Monty appeared at my doorway.

His hair hung in typical Monty-style—which meant no actual style, just let it hang loose and wherever it fell, it fell. For someone so meticulous about the rest of his appearance, the state of his hair had always been a mystery to me.

He was dressed in a black, rune-inscribed Zegna which was covered by a Kiton Blue Vicuna Peru overcoat, also rune-inscribed. His pale gray shirt was offset by a blood red tie. The multitudes of runes on his clothing were amazing to see.

They slowly traveled across the fabric of his clothing in pale blues, reds, and greens, barely visible except for the fact that my recently awakened ability to read them, had made me more sensitive to their presence.

"For the record, Cecil never consulted with Ian Fleming," he said. "It's not something he would have pursued."

"Heard that, did you?"

"We have extraordinary acoustics in here."

"I have a few questions," I said as he stood there like a renegade BMA model, admiring his Patek Philippe Sky Moon Tourbillon. It was a move he used, to let me know he wanted to get moving, without saying so. I ignored him. "How do you get your clothing rune-inscribed? What happens if they make a mistake?"

He raised an eyebrow in my direction.

"A mistake?" he asked, looking down at his clothing. "On *my* garments?"

I could almost hear the runic tailors in House Zegna gasp with indignation that I would dare to even utter the word *mistake* in the presence of one of their *runed garments*.

"Yes, on *your* garments," I said. "What happens if they inscribe the wrong rune? You know, instead of a rune of protection they mistakenly put a rune of distraction, or something?"

"The runing process of my clothing is performed by masters of their craft in House Zegna," Monty said, brushing off his sleeves. "Mistakes of any kind are *unheard* of."

"They don't happen?"

"No," he answered. "If they did, the House of Zegna would procure an identical garment, inscribe it correctly and provide it without my knowing. Mistakes are not made public, if they ever happen—not that they ever occur."

"Right, no mistakes or errors...ever. Got it," I said, raising a finger. I knew he wasn't going to elaborate on the runing of his clothing, so I dropped the subject for now. "One more question: what are we heading into that you need this many runes on your clothes?"

He looked down at his clothing again, this time lingering over some of the items more than others.

"What do you mean?" he asked. "This is what I usually wear."

"No," I said, pointing at the overcoat. "Most of the runes on your overcoat are for defense against"—I focused on his coat, narrowing my eyes—"shadows? Do I have that right, defense against shadows? We're facing shadows?"

"Spectres," he clarified with a slight shake of his head. "It seems your ability to decipher runes *has* improved."

"The runes on the Zegna are your typical indestructible type, though I have to wonder how effective they are, considering how many suits you go through on a regular basis."

"I wonder the same thing at times," he said. "These are considerably more potent, or so I'm told."

"We'll see," I said, examining the runes on his clothes. "You're expecting ghosts?"

"Spectres, yes," he said. "Especially at Shadowpeak and the Black Forest in general. Robert will be waiting for us downstairs; we can address this in the car."

"You don't want to take the Dark Goat?"

"To the Black Forest?" he said. "I think not. We need a vehicle for rugged terrain. Cecil will have one for us, I think you will approve."

"SuNaTran has a vehicle for outrunning ghosts in rugged terrain, right," I said with a knowing nod. "Something built for mountains and monsters. Totally understand."

"Somehow I doubt it," he said, glancing over at my snoring hellhound. "Is your creature joining us, or is he taking an extended nap?"

"Wherever I go, he goes," I said, rubbing my hellhound's oversized head. "Let's go, boy."

Peaches bounded out of the bed and followed us out of the loft.

FOUR

Robert was waiting for us in front of the Moscow in what could only be described as next-level automotive art. He stepped out and opened the door for us, waiting a few extra seconds for my hellhound to bound into the vehicle.

This vehicle didn't so much as shudder as my hellhound bounded in and sprawled on the seat opposite the rear. The air suspension must have been incredible.

I took a moment to absorb the transport.

We were sitting in the latest SuNaTran tank disguised as a vehicle, with Robert behind the wheel. This version was a Bugatti Galiber, a sedan in black with silver accents, and was a considerable upgrade from the Phantoms I was used to from SuNatran.

I was thoroughly impressed as I sat in the back.

"Welcome, Mr. Montague, Mr. Strong," Robert said with a tip of his cap. "I will be your driver today."

"Robert, it's been too long," I said, leaning forward and clapping him on the shoulder. "How have you been?"

"Well," he said, glancing back at us in the rear-view mirror.

"It appears your companion has grown some since I saw him last."

I looked down at my hellhound and nodded.

"He's still growing, you know," I said, looking at the interior of the Bugatti. "But he fits fine in here. What happened to the Phantoms? Did Cecil decommission them?"

Robert started the engine to a low roar, which let me know this may have been outfitted as a four-door sedan, but it sounded like a rocket on wheels.

"Not at all," Robert said, running a hand admiringly along the wheel. I figured he loved vehicles as much as I did or more, considering that working with Cecil, he must have encountered, created, or driven some of the strangest vehicles in existence. "The Phantoms have been reassigned to other clients—those with lower security concerns."

"*Lower* security concerns?" I asked, incredulous. "They were tanks that looked like cars. Are you kidding? Lower security concerns like what—random attempts of explosion?"

"I do not kid, sir."

"Wait, what are you saying?" I asked. "Are you saying that *our* security needs have increased?"

He nodded.

"Quite," he said as he pulled away from the Moscow and headed up the West Side Highway. "You've been upgraded to Level Black by Mr. Fairchild."

"Level Black," I said. "I didn't realize there were actual security levels."

"For the clients, vehicles and drivers," he said. "It's why I'm your driver today. I specialize in Level Black clients."

"I see," I said. "Is this a recent thing?"

"Yes," Monty said. "I advised Cecil to create the level system to keep his drivers safe and to minimize the damage to his inventory. Pairing the right vehicle to the right client keeps his vehicles in working order with less wear and tear—"

"Or destruction," I added, with a nod. "Makes sense."

"It also keeps the personnel safe," Monty continued. "Robert and Ayrton, I believe, are two of the best Level Black drivers SuNaTran has in their driver pool."

"Only two Level Black drivers?"

"No," Robert answered. "We have many more, but I'm not at liberty to share exact numbers for operational security."

"Understood," I said, thinking it over. "I realize we have been hard on SuNaTran vehicles—"

Robert covered his mouth and coughed in response.

"You could say that, yes," he said after his short and polite bout of coughing. "I do know that Mr. Fairchild had the Aventador—or what remains of it—moved to his personal office. Says it keeps him focused."

"Focused?" I answered indignantly. "Blow up one Lamborghini, and Cecil never lets you forget it. He keeps it there to rub it in my face, that's why it's there. Did he put up the pieces of the Duesenberg in his office?" I glanced at Monty. "I bet you he didn't. Anyway, tell me Robert, why are we *now* Level Black? Tell me it's not because of the Aventador?"

"Not at all, sir," Robert said without taking his eyes off the road. "You have recently been declared outcast by the Grand Council. In addition, you were both instrumental in the deaths of two Grand Council Emissaries. Mr. Fairchild felt it was prudent to introduce the Strongmonte prototypes to serve your travel needs."

"The Strongmonte," I said, glancing at Monty, who rolled his eyes at my expression of satisfaction. "See? That's how you title a work of automotive art like this. Did you notice it's Strong, then Monte?"

"I am acutely aware of the ordering of the name," he said. "I should be, I was the one who gave it to Cecil."

"You what?"

"I was not going to have another vehicle with the 'Montague Package', it sounds crass," he said with a huff, pulling on his sleeve. "If Cecil was going to go so far as to name a car's defensive package, it would include both our names and it would have some dignity—Strongmonte fit nicely. Don't you agree?"

I had to admit he was right.

Plus, it was a Bugatti, and once Robert got us on the highway and opened up the engine, she took off.

"How many of these Strongmontes did Cecil make?"

"I commissioned three vehicles," Monty said. "Two are Strongmonte prototypes, this one and the other, a Lamborghini, will be waiting for us in the Shrike MKS, and the last, as repayment of my debt to Cecil, was a new Duesenberg—for SuNaTran."

"That must have cost a fortune."

"Any one of these vehicles cost a small fortune," Monty answered. "All three were a sizable investment. However, we have specialized needs that commercial, even extremely skilled and qualified professional automakers would find impossible to meet."

"True, few automakers build cars that are ogre and magic resistant," I said. "How far did these prototypes set you back?"

"No distance is too great when our lives are on the line," Monty said, deflecting from the subject of his wealth. "Suffice to say, we should refrain from destroying them for as long as possible."

"Ouch," I said. "That much?"

"More," he said, waving my words away and turning to look at Robert. "Is the Shrike MKS ready?"

"Yes, sir, Mr. Montague," Robert answered. "Take-off is scheduled once you arrive and get settled."

"I remember the Shrike," I said, leaning back in the ultra comfortable seat. "JFK isn't going to be happy with something that size parked on their runway waiting for us. Can Cecil even get clearance for his plane at a commercial airport? Wouldn't he be better off someplace military?"

"Ideally, the Shrike is designed for a military airport," Monty said. "However, Cecil appears to have all the clearances he needs to access whatever airport he requires at the time. I believe we're heading out to the new LaGuardia facility he recently acquired. Robert?"

"Yes, sir, Mr. Montague," Robert answered as we crossed the city on 34th Street and headed to the Queens Midtown Tunnel. "The new facility is open for operations, and Mr. Fairchild will be on site to greet you."

"Cecil is going to be on site?" I asked. "Doesn't he have people for that sort of thing? Or does he want to see us to remind us not to break his plane?"

Robert smiled and refrained from answering as he drove us into the Midtown Tunnel. He raised the partition, obscuring the driver's section of the vehicle and giving us privacy.

"Cecil is there to debrief us on the other prototype which will be on the flight with us," Monty said. "And probably to give us a stern talking to about keeping the vehicles intact. He was quite upset after the Duesenberg."

"You brought him back a mangled steering wheel," I said, giving Monty a look. "He gave you—*loaned* you—a work of automotive art, a masterpiece, and you returned with a mangled steering wheel as a thank you. I would've strangled you with the wheel... to start with."

"I don't recall him being that upset when you rendered the Aventador into abstract art," he said. "In fact he even put it up as a piece of focusing art. Quite the compliment, if I do say so."

"Two things," I said holding up two fingers. "I didn't explode the Aventador, that was a troll trying to obliterate me and get my attention in the most violent way possible. Also, I didn't explode the Aventador. That was completely out of my control."

"Much like the Duesenberg's destruction was out of my hands," he answered. "Wouldn't you agree?"

I just shook my head as Monty leaned back and smiled.

"He *was* quite...upset."

"I don't know how you convinced him to ever give us another SuNatran vehicle," I said. "I mean I get the histories your family share, but the Midnight Ghost was rendered to a memory."

He glanced at me and rested his head back for a few seconds before looking at me again.

"We've been through life and death," he said. "Our bond of friendship, of being brothers, has weathered all of the enemies we've faced, yes?"

I didn't understand the sudden line of questioning, but I did my best to follow. He rarely spoke of our bond, usually bringing it up when we were facing a life threatening situation or enemy.

The question set my radar off.

"Yes," I said cautiously. "That's sort of pointing out the obvious. We're only here because we've faced enemies and survived."

He paused before continuing.

"What could I do to betray that friendship, that sense of brotherhood?" he asked, completely throwing me. "What action could I take that would betray your trust?"

"Seriously?"

"Yes, seriously," he said. "What could I do that would make you stand against me?"

"Where is this coming from?" I asked. "How dangerous is Shadowpeak exactly?"

"Humor me."

I paused and thought about the question.

What could he do to make me stand against him? Why was he asking? Was he planning on taking an action that would turn us against each other?

"If you betrayed your principles," I said after a few moments of thought. "If you embraced darkness and let it consume you. I would *have* to stand against you, because I know it wouldn't be you, it would be whatever corruption you allowed to take over."

"Have you ever wondered why I stayed in this city after that first case?" he asked. "Why I stayed to fight alongside you?"

"You mean aside from my phenomenal wit and world-class detecting skills?"

"Not to mention that incredible sense of humility you possess," he added. "Yes, aside from the wit and your skills as a detective."

"I figured you had a sense of what was coming," I said, growing serious. "You knew I couldn't do it alone. So you stayed."

"You're partially correct," he said, looking away for a moment. "I had chased Shiva and his operation all over the globe, before I ran into him here alongside you. Like you, I was mistaken and misread the situation. Like you, I followed the wrong lead and we nearly failed. We certainly cost Kali a five thousand year plan."

I nodded.

"She was a little pissed about that, in case you hadn't noticed."

"I noticed."

"So why *did* you stay?"

"I made an error, nearly a fatal one," he said. "You helped me when so many wouldn't, at great risk, and later at great cost to yourself."

I nodded.

"You didn't *have* to stay," I said. "We solved the case and I made a new best frenemy in Kali, the Goddess of Destruction. It was more than I bargained for, but it wasn't all bad. I mean even though cursed immortality is a long term thing, obviously. It has a definite upside in the short term."

"Nevertheless, I stayed," he said, nodding at my remark. "By staying, I knew we could stand against the forces I was fighting, together. I knew it wouldn't be easy—you're not exactly educated as a mage—but I knew it could work."

"And it has," I said. "I mean, true, the Grand Council wants us dead, and the list of enemies we have after us is probably as long as my arm, but we have faced them and survived, learned along the way, and have grown stronger. What's going on? Why are you bringing this up?"

"Two reasons," he said, holding up two fingers. "One, if I ever make that choice and step into darkness—"

"You're not going to—"

"Hear me out, Simon," he said, raising a hand. I became silent. "Did you know I have a kill order for the Night Warden?"

"You what?" I asked. "From who?"

"From Grey," he said. "If Grey ever loses control and surrenders to the being in his blade, he has instructed me, in writing, to end his existence. This final request is shared by everyone in his immediate circle."

"All of them?" I asked, surprised. "Frank, Cole, and Koda?"

"I don't think they could do it," he said. "At least not Cole and Koda. I don't know if Frank would be strong enough to stop a fully surrendered Grey. They're too close to Grey and he considers them his family. If the time ever came, they would hesitate."

"Even Frank?"

"Even Frank."

"They would pay for that hesitation with their lives."

"I think Grey understood this, which is why he approached me," Monty said. "He made the request, and then bound me to it."

"He *bound* you to it?"

"I agreed," he said, raising a hand. "He wanted someone who would take the ultimate step, someone who wouldn't hesitate to act decisively."

I took a moment to consider Grey losing control and having him on the loose under the control of his sword, or better said the bloodthirsty goddess in his sword.

I shuddered the thought away.

"Grey under the control of his sword is not good," I said. "That's me being generous in the most apocalyptic way possible."

"Agreed," he said. "I recently asked Cecil for the same thing."

"To destroy Grey if he loses control?"

"Stop being obtuse," he said with a scowl. "You know what I mean."

"I do, but I'm me, so it's sort of the default."

"Which I accept," he said and paused before sighing. "Cecil turned me down. He said he couldn't do it, that our families share too much history for him to take that step."

"Shouldn't it be the other way around?"

"It should, but I respect his position on the matter."

"You're basically asking him to be your *kaishakunin*," I said. "I can imagine him not wanting to do it?"

"*Kaishakunin?*"

"Most samurai didn't die from their self-inflicted wounds

during seppuku," I explained. "They died from beheading, which was done by their second, their *kaishakunin*."

"An apt definition," he said. "Cecil chose to not accept this role, citing he would find it impossible to fulfill the responsibility required."

"You're asking him to act as your executioner," I said. "That's no light matter. I can understand why he turned you down."

"Can you?"

"Of course I can," I said, pausing for a moment. "Should you be telling me all of this?"

"Yes, do you know why?"

The realization hit me gently, like a cinderblock to the head.

"Shit, you're going to ask me the same thing, aren't you?"

He nodded slowly.

"Yes, I am."

FIVE

"No," I said, raising a hand when he made to speak. "Hear me out."

"Go on."

"Not without conditions," I continued. "Ironclad ones."

"Conditions?" he asked. "If I have embraced darkness, do you really think you will have time to consider *conditions*? Your life may very well be in danger."

He had a point, but still I needed this to be ironclad.

"If this really happens, the first conversation I'm going to have after dusting you, will be with a murderous Dex, who will want to know what happened and how," I said, keeping my voice calm. "I've already faced him holding Nemain, I can guarantee he'll be holding it when we have the conversation about why I needed to remove you from existence."

He nodded.

"Fair enough," he said. "What are your conditions?"

"You have to have gone full darkness for me to even consider this," I said. "Not semi-dark. This is jet-black, deepest pit of the outer darkness, kind of dark."

"You realize that's not even a thing."

"I don't know, some of the beings and mages we've faced definitely fit that description," I said. "Emissary Salya was the poster child for a mage dwelling in outer darkness."

He gave me a look and sighed.

"There is no such mage classification as 'dwelling in outer darkness'," Monty pointed out. "Dark mage should suffice."

"Not for some of our enemies," I said. "In any case, you know what I mean."

He nodded.

"Darkness without any question as to how deep—understood," he said. "Just to satisfy my personal curiosity, how exactly will you determine this *ultimate* darkness? Do you happen to have a darkness meter hidden on your person somewhere?"

"Amusing, but no," I said. "And you can't just face me. You have to face me, your uncle, and…Roxanne."

He became pensive for a moment and raised a finger before continuing. I had a feeling he was about to slip into professor mode as he went all Spock on my request and tried to deconstruct it into its logical components.

"So if I understand the terms of your conditions, I am to wait until you convene all the parties mentioned *before* my darkness is determined?" he asked. "That ranges from difficult to impossible."

"If you go *that* dark, trust me, I *will* convene whoever needs to be convened," I said. "Those are my conditions. You do realize that as your Aspis, this is the exact opposite of what I have sworn to."

"I know," he said. "Also as my Aspis, your job, your purpose, is to protect those your life touches."

"In case you haven't noticed, that includes *you*."

"Not if I become the threat," he said. "Your purpose dictates that you protect *everyone* your life touches. If I go dark, that means everyone your life touches is in danger. It means you *must* remove me as the threat that impacts everyone else in your life."

"Your loopholes suck."

"Not a loophole, a fact," he said. "Do you agree, as my Aspis and brother?"

"Only if you agree to my condition."

"I agree," he said. "If you can somehow manage to get Dex and Roxanne in proximity, to analyze my condition while I am in the midst of succumbing to ultimate darkness, and together face and end me, then I accept. Otherwise you will have to do it on your own—yes?"

I paused for a few seconds.

The chances of locating both Dex and Roxanne in time to deal with and stop a Dark Monty were slim to none. He knew it and I knew it. Worse, I knew that he knew that I knew it.

Still.

I didn't have a choice.

As his Aspis, I had to stand for him, even when it was against him. If he surrendered to darkness, he would be the first to demand that I stop him, even if that meant ending him.

I would expect no less from him if I somehow became a Dark Aspis and surrendered to darkness.

It still concerned me that Grey had bound him to a similar agreement, but I understood Grey's position. There was no way those closest to him would agree to ending him, except maybe Frank.

I had a feeling Frank would hate to do it, but he wouldn't hesitate either. I think being trapped as a lizard gave him a unique perspective on Grey's situation.

"Do you think Frank would do it?"

He gave me a perplexed look.

"I'm not asking Frank, I'm asking *you*."

"Not that," I said, waving his words away. "You know I

don't have a choice, and before you tell me there's always a choice—no, there is not in this situation. As your Aspis, the only acceptable choice was made for me before you ever asked the question."

"Yes," he said, "to your question about Frank. As for your choice, you can still choose not to act. That, in itself, is a choice."

"Not one I can live with," I said, still pensive. "Thanks to Kali, that's going to be a long time to consider that specific choice—no, thanks."

"True," he said. "You would have to exist several lifetimes with the knowledge of failing to remove me as a threat. I would not relish your position."

"Don't rub it in or anything," I said. "No matter how you frame it, the choice sucks. I accept it. Just make sure you do everything in your power not to surrender to darkness."

"I have no intention of doing so," he said. "This is merely a precaution."

I nodded, still pensive about Frank.

"Why would Frank do it?" I asked. "I have a feeling he's the closest one to Grey out of that group."

"A few reasons, I think," Monty said. "Because he's the closest to Grey, he also understands what it means to live with the consequences of actions, of a cast gone wrong."

"What does that mean?" I asked. "You mean the fact that he ended up trapped as a liz—dragon? A *tiny* dragon?"

"Good save," Monty said, raising an eyebrow at me. "If Francis as a mage had succeeded in his self-cast, he would have pulled off a successful transmogrification, from human to dragon. The power output to get even as far as he did, to survive, not only with his intellect intact, but his ability to cast undiminished is staggering."

"You make it sound like he pulled off the impossible."

"In many respects, he did," Monty said. "I don't know the

inciting incident that acted as a catalyst for him to undertake such a risk, but he should have died a deformed and mangled mess as soon as he lost control of the cast."

"Can't you argue that in a way—he did?"

"Frank should have never survived the initial cast," Monty said, glancing at me. "The fact that he's still a formidable mage in a slightly different body, speaks to his immense power."

"Slightly?" I asked. "He was human and now...he's not."

"But he's *still* Francis," he said. "You're right, he should have died but he didn't. A lesser mage would have been rendered a bloody, indistinguishable, gory pile of flesh. He wasn't."

"Has anyone done it?" I asked. "The cast Frank attempted? Has anyone turned themselves from human to dragon?"

"Dragons are considered an origin species when it comes to magic and energy manipulation," Monty explained. "Many mages believe our ability to cast came from them."

"Many dragons believe that too," I said. "Can we say superiority complex? Is that true? Magic started with them?"

"I think the truth is probably a little more complex," Monty said. "Dragons may have played a part in humans acquiring the ability to cast, but I don't believe they are solely responsible. There are too many variables."

"Variables like?"

"Take you for example," Monty said, glancing at me. "Which dragon was involved in your acquisition of power?"

I gave him a look.

"You know there were no dragons involved, though I have met a few after the fact who wanted to end my existence."

"Yet you can wield energy in your way," he said. "Without a dragon imbuing you with this ability."

"I had divine help," I said. "I never cast anything before Kali cursed me."

"My point exactly," he said. "There are other methods, sources, that exist for humans to have acquired the ability to learn to cast and manipulate energy."

"Does that mean it's been done before?" I asked. "A human to dragon cast?"

"I've never met any who have, but that's not to say it hasn't happened," Monty said. "Everything I have heard or read about that cast implies that the risk outweighs the benefits—as you can see from the results."

"I wonder why Frank tried it?"

"You could always ask him," Monty said. "You have mentioned several times you'd like to have a conversation with him. I think that would be an ideal opening."

"Sure, I could just open with: Hey Frank, so about that cast you tried, you know, the one that trapped you in this dragon—miniature, but still a dragon body—what made you try it?"

"I would amend the opening somewhat," Monty said, shaking his head slightly. "But if you really want to know why I think he would fulfill Grey's wishes, I think the answer lies with him attempting, failing that cast, and having to live with the outcome of that failure."

"No one likes to be reminded of their failures," I said. "He has to live with his every second of every day. There's no way I'm going to ask him about something like that. It feels too personal."

"Perhaps Grey knows," he said. "Not that he would share that information with you, or me for that matter."

"Doubt it," I said and asked the question I'd wanted to ask all along. "Why did you make this request? Are you planning a scheduled dive into darkness I don't know about?"

"Hardly," he said, glancing away for a moment before

turning back to face me. "Even though I've studied Shadowpeak—every Montague mage is required to do so—I still don't know what I'm going to face. That uncertainty makes me wary."

Before I could say anything, the partition dropped and Robert looked at us in the rear-view mirror.

"We've arrived," Robert said from the front. "Have a good trip."

SIX

I looked outside of the vehicle. We seemed to be in an abandoned part of the airport. There was no traffic, pedestrian or vehicular, as we drove through the employee parking lot.

To my right, I noticed most of the airport proper, complete with planes and bustling traffic. Directly in front of us, where Robert was heading, sat what appeared to be an unused or abandoned terminal.

Right before the entrance to the terminal, I noticed the tall, solid industrial gate, with razor wire covering the top and edges. As we approached, a low hum filled the air, and I realized that along with the deterrent of the razor wire leaving you sliced and diced, the gate itself was electrified to barbecue you in place if you felt bold enough to scale its height.

Robert slowed as he approached the entrance checkpoint. He showed the heavily armed guard at the gate an identification. The guard peered at Robert for a few seconds before waving him on.

There was only one road with a nondescript terminal

building sitting at the end of it. This building was unlike most of the terminals in the rest of the airport in that it lacked any windows.

This building wasn't built for its aesthetics.

It was a solid, squat, gray block of a structure with one side being a hangar. At the moment, the hangar doors were open, allowing a visual of the interior of the building.

Inside, I saw what appeared to be a variation of a B-2 bomber, except that it was smaller than the usual bomber and had ample cargo space.

It was the only plane in the entire hangar.

I examined the rest of the hangar from where I sat and noticed the Shrike was missing. It seemed to me to be a waste of space to have only one plane in the oversized hangar. It could easily hold whatever this futuristic B-2 copy was with room for three more Shrikes side by side.

I looked at the plane sitting in the hangar, a dark shadow looking ominous as we approached, its sleek, futuristic, stealth design definitely drawing my attention.

It wasn't the Shrike.

"Where are we?" I asked as Robert headed to the unnamed terminal building. "Since when does LaGuardia require a hardened, electrified, armed checkpoint, leading to...where exactly is this road leading?"

"We are not exactly in LaGuardia Airport," Robert answered as we headed to the unnamed terminal which was farther than it appeared. "This is SuNaTran Terminal X."

"Terminal X?" I asked, surprised. "What exactly does that mean? SuNaTran *owns* this terminal?"

"Yes, sir," Robert answered. "We have several properties for our aircraft. This is our most recent property acquisition, purchased specifically for this type of aircraft."

"This type of aircraft," I asked. "What type is that?"

"The classified kind, sir."

We exited the Strongmonte and I looked around.

"You're telling me SuNaTran bought all of this just to house one plane?" I asked. "Seriously?"

"Very much so," Robert said. "I'll let Mr. Fairchild explain the rest. It was good to see you all again, I'm certain you will have a safe flight."

He tipped his hat in our direction and drove away.

We stood on the tarmac as the sun began to set, and I realized this whole setup reminded me of a black ops military base. Except that instead of being in the middle of a desert, or some isolated mountain range somewhere, we were on the outskirts of Queens, New York.

Talk about hiding in plain sight.

"Did you know about this?" I asked, turning to Monty. "How extensive *exactly* is Cecil's network?"

"The recent acquisition?" Monty answered, looking around the property. "I seem to recall him mentioning it recently in one of our conversations."

"You *seem* to recall?"

"We *have* been away on urgent matters," he said. "Besides, Cecil doesn't need my approval for SuNaTran matters. I'm certain the purchase was shared with all the members of the company's leadership."

"You didn't know?" I asked. "About the purchase of an airfield along with the creation of some next gen stealth fighter?"

"I don't make it a point to keep abreast of SuNaTran's or Cecil's activities," he said. "As long as I know he's at the forefront of SuNaTran, I know everything is running smoothly."

"He bought an entire terminal and you're unfazed?"

"Should I be fazed?" he asked. "If SuNaTran made this purchase, I'm sure Cecil has a reason."

"Are you certain Cecil isn't raising a small, well, not so small, army?"

"An army requires personnel," Monty said, looking toward the hangar. "Cecil and SuNaTran by default specialize in runically enhanced vehicles, not people."

"Somehow that doesn't make me feel better," I said, gazing at the plane. "That plane looks cutting-edge and dangerous. Why would he need something that sophisticated?"

"Judging from the craft in that hangar, this property seems like a justified purchase," Monty said, peering off into the distance where the futuristic plane sat. "I doubt most countries would feel comfortable with some kind of non-governmental experimental plane sitting in a hangar within their borders."

"And somehow *we're* okay with it?"

"Cecil has extraordinary influence due to his—and SuNaTran's—contributions during the war," Monty said, turning at the sound of footsteps. "Speak of the devil."

Cecil was approaching from the terminal building.

He wore a deep blue suit, with an off-white shirt and a silver-blue tie. With my newfound ability to see and read runes, he became a runic encyclopedia. Every rune I could decipher, which was only about half of them, warned me that engaging Cecil in any kind of combat would end badly—for me.

His short, gray hair looked freshly cut and his goatee was as I remembered, neatly trimmed. In other words, Cecil's hair embodied everything Monty's didn't. His dark eyes fixed on us and pierced Monty as he looked in our direction.

As he closed, his energy signature came off him in waves of subtle but very real power. I got the same impression from him as when we had first met; he carried a signature of immense power and barely controlled devastation.

He gave us a tight smile as he approached.

"Welcome to SuNaTran-Terminal X," Cecil said, looking

down and rubbing Peaches' massive head, while providing him with several sausage treats that my hellhound hungrily vacuumed into his bottomless belly. "He's getting big. Are you feeding him enough?"

"More than," I said, eyeballing my ever-voracious hellhound who acted as if he hadn't eaten in days. "Not too long ago, in fact."

"Huh," Cecil said with a short nod. "Then he must *still* be growing if he's eating like this."

"I'm wondering if he will *ever* stop growing."

"That's actually a good point," Cecil said, turning back to the terminal. "I'm no expert on hellhounds, but you may want to find out what his expected eating patterns will be as he matures." He paused and shot me a small smile. "If he continues this way, you'll need to start feeding him entire cows before long."

"Not even remotely funny."

"Slightly funny," he replied and waved us on to follow him. "If you would come this way, please."

He turned and led the way to the hangar where the plane waited for us.

"I know I'm not hallucinating," I said, pointing at the plane in the hangar. "That is not the Shrike."

"No, it's not," Cecil said with a smile that exuded pride. "This plane exists for those moments when a client needs to get into...*sensitive* airspace with minimal to no detection. This craft will do that and more."

"Sensitive? Do you mean *hostile*?"

"A hostile airspace *is* sensitive."

I nodded in understanding.

"It looks like a B-2 bomber."

He gave me an approving nod.

"You know your planes," he said. "This comes from the

same BWB family with some changes particular to SuNaTran."

"BWB?" I asked. "I thought they were just known as fixed-wing aircraft or flying wings?"

"They are," Cecil clarified. "The actual definition is: Blended Wing Body—it's what a plane design like the B-2 is known for. However, we've blended more than the fuselage and the wings. The cargo space is exceptional, easily rivaling that of the original Shrike among other features."

I gave the futuristic plane a once-over. There was no way it could rival the cargo space of the original Shrike. Where the Shrike appeared to be a shrunken C-130, this plane just seemed to be a much thicker B-2.

I had a hard time believing it had more cargo space than an oversized closet.

"Okay, it's not the Shrike," I said, stating the obvious. "What *exactly* is this plane, then?"

"That...is the reason we needed to purchase this land," Cecil answered, extending an arm around us. "That is the Shrike MKS. She's a stealth transport and cargo platform modeled after the B-21 Raider with some modifications, of course."

"B-21 Raider?" I asked, confused. "I thought they were still working on that? This plane looks like it should be classified."

"It *is* classified," he said. "Which is why we're standing in a mostly empty terminal, and the plane is resting in an empty hangar."

"How?" I said, glancing at the new Shrike. "Are you saying they let you look at the B-21 plans? How is that even possible?"

"Let's just say I have certain connections within the Defense Advanced Research Projects Agency," he said. "Connections which I'm not at liberty to discuss."

"Of course not," I said. "Monty mentioned something about another vehicle, since we're not taking the Dark Goat?"

"We'll get to that in a minute," Cecil said, glancing at Monty. "Are you certain you want to do this, Tristan?"

"I am," Monty said, pulling on his coat sleeve. "How goes the re-creation of the Duesenberg?"

"Nice try on the deflection," Cecil said, shaking his head. "How did you manage to make an enemy out of the Grand Council?"

"It was inevitable," Monty said. "Once my uncle Dexter relocated—"

"*Stole*," Cecil corrected. "He stole the Golden Circle. Did he really think they would let that act go unanswered?"

"No," Monty said, glancing at me. "He just didn't expect them to come after us."

"They're insane, but they are certainly not suicidal," Cecil said. "There is not a viable scenario where the Grand Council launches an attack on Dexter Montague and survives. They went after his weakness—you, it was the most logical and strategic thing to do."

"Indeed," Monty said, glancing at the Shrike MKS. "A question: is SuNaTran in the business of entering restricted and sensitive airspace these days?"

"We go where our clients need us to go," Cecil said. "We don't deal or interfere with normal affairs, but we both know the intrigues of the mage world are complex and global. SuNaTran facilitates travel anywhere in the world for the supernatural."

"For a fee," Monty added. "You *do* charge your clients?"

"SuNaTran is not a charity," Cecil said. "We have our standard fees, of course. I figured we needed a way to defray the costs of the odd Aventador or Duesenberg mishap incurred."

"Of course," Monty said. "That makes perfect sense. And

these clients request entry into what is considered *hostile* territory?"

Cecil nodded, a wary expression on his face.

"On occasion…that requires venturing into what may be considered inhospitable territory. Why do you ask?"

"Inhospitable?" Monty asked. "Like the Black Forest?"

"I'm not flying *into* the Black Forest," Cecil said. "No aircraft is allowed into the actual forest. Even with the runic modifications on the new Shrike, the interference would disable and cripple her after a few minutes. I'm not scrapping an experimental design just to get you closer to Shadowpeak. You have the new vehicle for that."

"Do you expect her to face any other complications?" Monty asked. "You did mention she is experimental."

"I'm flying you three," he said, "I expect complications to be part of the package."

"You're flying?" I asked, surprised. "You don't have a designated pilot?"

"Myself and one co-pilot, yes," Cecil said. "The MKS is a prototype x-craft. She's untested in long-range flight. In addition, her defenses haven't been fully pushed in an actual combat scenario. I couldn't in good conscience ask another pilot to risk his life flying her without doing the same."

"Excuse me?" I asked. "Did you say prototype x-craft? Are you saying this Shrike is untested?"

"Not entirely," Cecil added. "Yes, she's experimental, but she's solid where it matters. We'll be fine. Also, I'm an accomplished pilot. I just haven't flown in a bit, I might be a bit rusty."

"Rusty? Now my confidence is rock solid," I said, glancing at Monty. "Did he say combat scenario? Why would we be facing a combat scenario? This is supposed to be an uber-stealthy, non-detectable, low-observability cargo plane. Why would we get into a fight?"

"While that is true," Cecil said, "it's better to have the combat capability and not need it, than to need it and not have it. Don't you agree?"

"We're going to die," I said, shaking my head. "This is an untested prototype disaster waiting to happen."

"Not at all," Monty said. "Cecil would never fly an untested prototype. He's just using our trip as an excuse to get away from the office and having some fun at your expense."

"You are no fun," Cecil said with a smile before growing serious. "Seriously though—Shadowpeak—can't another Montague do this?"

"Who do you recommend?" Monty asked. "My uncle can't. Who else from the family do you suggest?"

"Has no one else stepped forward after the news of the Guardian Monks' deaths?" he asked. "Not one Montague?"

"The silence of their requests to secure Shadowpeak is deafening," Monty said. "They lend more credence to the rumors of the lethality of Shadowpeak, than to our responsibility as stewards of the estate."

"The rumors hold some validity," Cecil said. "Shadowpeak is especially deadly to your family."

"Only if they succumb to the call of the Gauntlet," Monty said. "Our responsibility lies in protecting others from the dangers Byron set loose in that place—no matter the personal risk. We are not running the Gauntlet."

"Easy to say when you are half-a-world away," Cecil answered. "What will you do when you are in Shadowpeak?"

"Resist, and not run the Gauntlet," Monty said. "Was I not clear?"

"I've heard the stories about Shadowpeak," Cecil said. "Are you saying they're unfounded?"

"I'm saying that they, like most rumors, are greatly exaggerated and based on fabrications and conjecture."

"And yet we both know that Shadowpeak is deadly," Cecil said. "That much is not conjecture or fabrication."

"Then you know why I *must* go," Monty said, his voice firm. "The danger a vulnerable Shadowpeak poses to the world is unacceptable."

Cecil turned to me.

"I know why *he* has to go," he said, glancing at Monty. "Why are *you* going? You're not a Montague."

"I'm going to make sure he remains a Montague."

Cecil nodded and continued heading to the hangar.

SEVEN

We crossed the tarmac in silence for a few minutes until we reached the exterior of the terminal building. I could tell Cecil was lost in his thoughts and Monty was giving off major 'I'm in no mood to discuss the matter further' vibes, as we walked.

The terminal building had plenty of space around it, but there was no clear path to any of the runways. Basically, SuNaTran Terminal X sat on a large corner of open tarmac where planes could park, but not take off.

I made a mental note to ask Cecil about that later.

From outside, the hangar seemed small, but once inside, I realized how large it really was. From where we stood in front of the terminal, we were only able to see one side of the interior.

After we entered, the size of the interior didn't compute for my brain. I took a moment at the entrance to step back and look at the exterior of the terminal building.

Then I stepped back inside.

My brain was having trouble processing the visual of the interior space with the actuality of the exterior dimensions.

The terminal was actually larger on the inside than the exterior made you believe.

"This building looks…" I started, doing a double-take. "It's…"

"The time and relative dimensions in space have been enhanced and expanded to increase our housing capacity," Cecil said. "We only have the Shrike MKS housed here now, but this will become a major hub of operations in the near future. We wanted to make sure that space would never be an issue—another reason for the privacy. It took forever to stretch the inside to the appropriate dimensions."

"Stretch the inside?" I asked. "You stretched the inside?"

"We nearly lost several brave SuNaTran engineers on this project," Cecil said, his voice serious. "Manipulating dimensional space at this scale is unheard of, not to mention a life and death risk."

Monty raised his eyebrow at Cecil.

"Life and death? Hardly," Monty said, glancing at me. "It's bigger on the inside than it is on the outside—I'm sure Aria and her Wordweavers lent him their expertise with the design."

Cecil frowned and threw a hand up.

"Really? You realize you are *quite* the killjoy?" Cecil said. "I seem to recall you using your elevated mage definitions for the simplest of casts, yet you deprive me of my humble moments of explanation?"

"Humble?" Monty asked. "When I explain a cast, I do it in the simplest terms possible."

"To *your* mind," Cecil answered. "Not everyone follows your elevated magical conversations, Mage Montague."

"Unlike some," Monty said, glancing at Cecil. "Some prefer an involved and complex explanation when a simple one will suffice."

"You are incorrigible," Cecil said with a smile. "In any

case, let's head into the Shrike, I need to show you your new vehicle for this trip."

"Before you do," I said, "how is the re-construction of the Midnight Simone going?"

"She's coming along," Cecil said, glancing at Monty again. "I won't say that one didn't hurt, because it did. I'm glad we're rebuilding her again."

"I'm glad to hear it as well," Monty said. "Maybe increase the defensive runes on the model this time around?"

"Did you just—?"

"I'm sure he's kidding," I said, quickly looking at Monty. "You're kidding, right?"

"I was only suggesting steps to prolong the vehicle's lifespan," Monty said. "A stronger defensive treatment would make it more resistant to extensive damage."

Cecil stared at Monty for a few seconds, then shook his head.

"I have a better plan," Cecil said after a moment of disbelief. "How about I make sure to never lend her to the two of you? That should radically increase her lifespan?"

"That may work, but—" Monty started.

"Excellent idea," I said, cutting Monty off before Cecil blew a gasket. The Midnight Simone was still a sore spot for him, but Monty, is his typical obtuse Monty way, wasn't quite seeing that. "We won't ever ask for it anyway. Right, Monty?"

He finally got the message and nodded.

"Correct," Monty said. "We will never need to borrow it ever again. I hope the rebuilding goes well. Do send us an invite when she's completed."

"I'll think about it," Cecil grumbled as we made our way to the rear of the Shrike MKS and pointed at the plane. "Right now, this is the pride of SNT-SEC."

"Right, SuNaTran Security," I said. "Is Elias still—?"

"Yes," Cecil said. "He sends his regards, but was called away on some urgent matters, overseas."

"Urgent matters?" Monty asked, raising an eyebrow. "Where exactly overseas?"

"Nowhere near the Black Forest," Cecil assured him. "No need to worry, Elias will be occupied elsewhere."

"Cecil…"

"You will be left to your own suicidal devices," Cecil said, raising a hand in surrender. "You know very well that neither Elias nor I will or *can* set foot in Shadowpeak without dire consequences, or did you forget?"

"What does that mean?" I said. "What dire consequences?"

"Anyone not of the Montague bloodline begins to suffer the walking death upon stepping onto the property," Cecil said. "It's a slow deterioration of the body caused by the runes inscribed on the estate. The longer you stay, the greater the chance you never leave…alive that is."

"Is that what Dex meant by 'Shadowpeak kills'?"

"I think he was being a little more literal," Monty said. "Shadowpeak has more immediate ways of deterring unwanted or uninvited guests."

"Wonderful," I said. "On top of the failsafes we have to deal with, the estate will be actively trying to kill us?"

"More like passively, but yes," Monty said. "We won't be there long enough for it to become an issue."

"You say that now," Cecil said. "But you haven't heard the call of the Gauntlet—yet. What will you do then when that happens?"

"Ignore it," Monty said. "My purpose for this visit is clear: secure Shadowpeak and investigate what killed the monks. Nothing more, nothing less."

"You're not going there to attempt a run at the Gauntlet?"

"No," Monty said. "My uncle advised against it, and

contrary to popular thought, I am not an angry mage bent on self-destruction. I am quite fond of living."

"Just asking," Cecil said, raising a hand in surrender again. "Nothing good comes from running the Gauntlet, or so I hear."

"I'm aware of the stories," Monty said. "Did you want to show us the new vehicle, or are we going to discuss how I'm rushing to my imminent destruction?"

I could tell Monty was upset, but Cecil had said what I was thinking. A part of me couldn't shake that Monty was taking on this whole 'secure Shadowpeak' mission to access the power of the estate.

I really hoped I was wrong.

"We can do both," Cecil said as he led us to the rear of the plane. "Your reluctance to address this issue concerns me."

He raised a hand and gestured. Silver symbols floated in the air, gently landing on the Shrike MKS.

A ramp descended, exposing the interior of the Shrike MKS.

"Does the Shrike MKS have a casting lab?" Monty asked. "I have a weapon I need to modify."

"Yes," Cecil said as he walked up the ramp. "It's not very large, but it should be potent enough for your needs."

"Excellent," Monty said, following Cecil up the ramp. "Is it shielded?"

Cecil shot Monty a look.

"What exactly are you going to work on?" Cecil asked. "Do you intend to work on your Sorrows? If so, I have to advise against it; I still recall the last time you were modifying the runes on those. I'd rather not have you explode the lab while at high altitudes. That would be catastrophic."

"I'm not working on the Sorrows," Monty replied. "I'm modifying Simon's weapon to utilize enhanced rounds."

"Oh, in that case it should be fine," Cecil said relieved. "That's a much smaller scale than your blades."

Monty nodded as we stepped into the cargo bay.

This time I was prepared for the whole, 'bigger on the inside than on the outside' visual effect.

"Excellent use of the dimensional space allocation," Monty said, looking around. "What is the ratio? Three to one?"

"Five interior meters for every external meter," Cecil answered proudly. "We pushed it to the maximum. I have to say it turned out well."

Monty nodded as Cecil gestured again, causing the ramp to rise and close behind us. The space around us made me feel like we were standing in the original Shrike. Off to one side, under a tarp sat some kind of wheeled vehicle.

I looked around the immense interior in wonder and awe.

"Doesn't this cause a strain on the plane?" I asked as I took in the interior of the large cargo space. "The amount of energy it must take to create a space like this and not only create it, but to fly around with part of the plane in adjacent space must be enormous. How do you manage to power the energy differential?"

Cecil looked at me, his expression stunned for a few seconds.

Monty simply nodded his approval.

"How did you—?" Cecil asked. "How did you know to ask that question?"

"What?" I asked. "I've been paying attention."

"That's not a question regarding observation," Cecil said, still surprised. "That question is beyond most mages, even."

"I'm not a mage," I said with a smile. "I figured it was obvious. If you made the Shrike bigger on the inside, it would require powerful runes to design the dimensional space. That won't be cheap in terms of power. Also, the Shrike would need to move in various planes simultaneously—another power-heavy function."

Cecil stared at me and just shook his head before looking at Monty and pointing at me.

"Did you—?" Cecil started.

"No," Monty said. "He may not be a mage, but he has been around enough of us to gather an understanding of how certain runic properties function. It could be he just lacked the understanding to express himself this eloquently."

"That was eloquent, wasn't it?" I said. "Pretty soon, my entire lexicon will be entirely mageified."

"Mageified is not an actual term," Monty said. "At least not one recognized by any mage, anywhere—ever."

Cecil recovered quickly and cleared his throat.

"The short version—"

"Yes, please, and light on the mage concepts, really," I said. "I may sound like I have a grasp on these ideas, but it's a slippery one at best."

Cecil nodded.

"The Shrike MKS is designed to plane-shift as it travels," Cecil explained. "By harnessing intraplanar dimensionality, we can create more space inside than outside. Did that make sense?"

"You lost me when you started harnessing intraplanar dimensions," I said. "But I get the general idea. It's bigger on the inside than it is on the outside. I'm sensing a theme here."

"Yes," Cecil said, becoming excited. "By harnessing intraplanar dimensionality, we can push the limits of velocity, observability, radar signature, even cloaking options. Radar can't detect what isn't even there. Do you see?"

I nodded and figured it was very similar to what Peaches did when he blinked in and out, except that this Shrike managed to somehow travel both in our plane and in-between.

"I think so," I said. "Don't you worry about getting stuck on the other side of the intraplanar equation?"

"You *do* understand."

"Just a little," I said. "My hellhound has been known to take short intraplanar trips."

"Hmm," Cecil said, looking at Peaches. "Perhaps when we have more time, we could examine your hellhound's abilities and record them?"

"I'm sure he would be onboard, as long as you had enough sausages," I said. "Can you even record something like that?"

"We can," Cecil said. "We have the technology."

"Amazing," I said. "I would be interested in knowing more about how he does it too."

"Excellent," Cecil said, heading over to the vehicle under the tarp. "Here we are. I'm sure you're anxious to see the newest vehicle in the Strongmonte family."

"Cecil," I said, my voice a warning. "I know you're still a little bent about the Aventador and more than a little bent about the Duesenberg, but this better not be a Hybrid-Yugo, or something close to that."

Cecil laughed.

"Not at all," Cecil said once he stopped laughing. "I'm certain you will approve."

He removed the tarp.

EIGHT

Underneath the tarp sat a vehicle my brain had trouble processing. It appeared to be a luxury vehicle and yet at the same time it was an off-road beast.

"What...what is that?" I managed after a pause. "It looks amazing and impossible."

I was looking at what looked like a Lamborghini, except that wasn't exactly a Lambo. This was a cross between a Lambo and an off-road Jeep. Somehow Cecil had smashed these two vehicles together, keeping the sleek styling lines of the Lambo, while showcasing the off-road ruggedness of the Jeep to create this hybrid feat of automotive artistry.

The pale matte black color barely reflected the light of the cargo hold, making the car resemble a shadow. The rugged tires raised the entire vehicle off the floor much higher than any other Lambo.

Where the Dark Goat just terrorized everyone who even stepped close to it, part of me felt that whatever runes Cecil had used on the Dark Goat made it semi-sentient and menacing on some deep level. This vehicle was different; it held an undercurrent of anger and defiance, without the feeling of mind-numbing terror.

"I know," Cecil said, the pride evident in his voice as he brought me out of my thoughts. "You need to get through the Black Forest—intact. I needed to design something durable and fast that could serve this purpose. I think this meets those qualifications."

"Discretion is the better part of valor," Monty said. "This vehicle provides ample amounts of discretion."

"Why does that sound like running away?"

"We don't know everything that inhabits the Black Forest," Monty explained. "Shadowpeak has had some… collateral effects on the land around it. Unexpected effects."

"Which this vehicle should be able to evade," Cecil added. "Or at the very least, withstand."

I looked over at the vehicle again.

"Is it an actual Lamborghini?"

"Yes," Cecil said, glancing at Monty. "Tristan said you were partial to Lamborghinis."

"I am."

"I informed him that you were partial to *disintegrating* Lamborghinis," Cecil replied, raising a hand to stop me from protesting. "I know *you* didn't explode the Aventador, but I did lend it to *you*, which means—"

"I *was* responsible for it."

"Exactly," he continued. "In any case, since we weren't going with the normal preference of an American muscle car base, we opted for a Lamborghini base with a twist. This vehicle is based on the Lamborghini Huracan Sterrato."

"It's incredible," I said in a mild daze as I continued admiring the vehicle that sat in front of me. "It's made for off-road? A Lambo for off-roads?"

"Well, we *started* there," Cecil said with a nod. "Then my engineers found out it was to be part of the new Strongmonte family of SuNaTran vehicles and requested complete latitude in the runic design."

"Complete latitude?" I asked warily. "What exactly does that mean?"

"It means they took every precaution possible to keep you alive," Cecil said. "They even added some things I felt were unneeded."

"Exactly how much latitude did you give them?"

"All the latitude they wanted, short of the life-draining runes that were used on the Beast and the Dark Goat," Cecil said. "Those runes are too dangerous to place on any car."

"I can understand that," I said, approaching the vehicle. "I'd rather not have a vehicle trying to kill me as I drive it, thank you."

Cecil nodded.

"She has a name," Cecil said.

"Is it Shad—?"

"It has nothing to do with shadows," Cecil said, cutting me off. "The engineers felt that would be too…ordinary."

"Ordinary?" I asked, surprised. "This vehicle is anything but ordinary."

"I agree, however Shadow anything was shot down immediately," Cecil clarified. "I also asked them to let you name her. They weren't exactly keen on that idea. Something about disliking the Dark Goat title."

"It's a GTO," I protested. "And it's dark purple. What did you want me to call it, the Grape?"

"This is why they denied the request to let you name her."

"What did they call it, then?"

"Edith, the chief SuNaTran engineer dubbed her the Strongmonte Sandhog," Cecil said. "She is nearly as indestructible as the Dark Goat and designed to excel in the dirt roads you will find in the Black Forest. I think the name fits."

"The Sandhog," I said with a short nod. "I like it. We can dub her Sandy for short."

Cecil nodded.

"What are the vehicle's defensive capabilities?" Monty asked, glancing at the Sandhog. "Did you give it the complete Strongmonte runic defensive platform?"

"Yes, I insisted she be on par with the new Strongmonte standard defensive platforms," Cecil answered. "She won't let you down, no matter what you face in the Forest."

"What exactly are we going to face in the Forest?" I asked, wary. "It's just a forest, right?"

"Not exactly," Cecil said. "I'll leave that to Tristan to explain. Both of you can drive the Sandhog; just make sure to bond with it by placing your hand on the identification panel on the dash. She can have a limit of three drivers, choose your third wisely."

"And she's ours?" I asked. "I mean really ours? Or is this another expensive loan?"

"She's yours," Cecil said. "That doesn't mean disintegrate it though."

"We can take her back with us?"

"Yes, if she survives your trip to Shadowpeak and through the Black Forest," Cecil said, looking from Monty, to me and finally at Peaches. "Her purpose is to keep you all alive. I'd rather sacrifice a vehicle than any of you."

"We're not going to drive her through Shadowpeak," I said, confused. "Why would that be a danger?"

"One second," Cecil said, looking at his watch before heading over to an intercom. "Daniel, begin pre-flight. We take off at nightfall."

"Roger that," a deep bass voice answered through the speaker. "Pre-flight check will be completed in T-minus twenty, give or take."

"Understood," Cecil said. "I'll be topside for take-off."

"Daniel?" I said. "Is that—?"

"Yes, the same pilot that flew the Shrike and you in England. He is rated Level Black, like Robert, which means he's cleared to fly the MKS and you to the Black Forest."

"About that," I said, tearing my gaze away from Sandy the Sandhog. "On our way to the terminal, I didn't actually notice a runway connecting to the terminal. Something this size would need substantial room for take-off."

"Astute," Cecil said. "I'll get to that in a moment." He walked past Sandy and pointed to a reinforced door, opening it. Beyond the door, I saw a short corridor. In the corridor, Cecil pointed to some doors. "Bathroom, kitchen, casting lab, and your quarters. Everything clear?"

Monty and I both nodded.

"Good," Cecil said. "Pilot's quarters are upstairs. If you need me, that's where I'll be. In regards to our take-off, we don't need a runway."

"No way," I said. "This plane is VTOL?"

Cecil nodded approvingly.

"Very good," he said. "It's actually a re-VTOL—runically enhanced-Vertical Take Off and Landing craft. Which means that we—"

"Don't need a runway," I finished. "How can a plane this large use VTOL engines? Not to mention stay stealthy? VTOLs are the opposite of stealthy."

"Don't forget the 're' part of the classification," Cecil said. "This entire plane is runically enhanced, and she is so cutting edge, that standing next to her will make you bleed. The VTOLs are orders of magnitude more powerful than conventional engines and have the capability to run in whisper mode."

"I've always wanted to ask you," I said. "Who handles the runing of all your vehicles? I mean who *actually* does it?"

"SuNaTran has a team of master runers," Cecil said. "They

are overseen by a Grandmaster runer who makes sure there are no errors in the runing."

"Is that you?" I asked. "Are you the Grandmaster runer?"

"No," Cecil said, covering the Sandhog with the tarp again. "I'm the one that makes sure the Grandmaster doesn't make a mistake. If that's all, I need to head up to prep for take-off."

"That's all," Monty said with a short nod. "Thank you for this."

"Don't thank me," Cecil said. "Taking you to Shadowpeak feels like throwing you to the wolves with large pieces of steak attached to your necks, and I'm not happy about it one bit."

"Then why?" I asked. "Why are you doing it?"

He paused and stared at me as he began to head to the short ladder that led up to the cockpit. For a moment, I looked into his eyes and saw a mix of emotions in them.

"Why are you?" he asked in response. "Why are you volunteering to go into a place that is a known deathtrap?"

"It wouldn't be the first time," I said, giving the question thought. "There's no way I can let Monty go in alone."

"Take that feeling, multiply it by one million, and you'll have your answer as to why I'm doing it," he said. "I'm not going to go in with you." He glanced at Monty. "But I'll be damned if I let anyone else take you there and bring you back."

"You're bringing us back?"

"Provided you escape Shadowpeak, yes," Cecil said. "Did you think you were driving the Sandhog back to the States?"

"Well, it is a long trip—"

"Longer than the Sandhog can handle," Cecil said, shaking his head. "Provided you all make it out in one piece, you'll go back the way you came. On the Shrike."

"Thank you, Cecil," I said. "I really—"

"We haven't even taken off yet," he said, cutting me off. "Thank me by making sure you all survive Shadowpeak."

I nodded.

"Now, if you'll excuse me," he continued, "I need to assist Daniel. Why don't you two get settled in? We have a long flight ahead of us, even at the speeds the Shrike can reach, we're still looking at about five hours of flight time. Use the time to get some rest, do your casting, and plan on how to approach Shadowpeak so that you survive the encounter."

"Understood," Monty said. "Thank you again, Cecil."

Cecil waved Monty's words away as he headed up to the cockpit. I followed him with my gaze but the interior of the Shrike made no sense to me. The proportions and scale of the inside were beginning to give me a headache.

"Are you sure this plane wasn't designed by Escher Aeronautics?" I asked. "Because all of the interior dimensions feel off and I'm seeing staircases and ladders that lead nowhere or double back on themselves."

"It *is* slightly disconcerting," Monty said, glancing around the interior. "It's best if you don't give it too much thought. Besides, we have other matters to focus on. We need to approach the Shadowpeak estate without being spotted."

"Does the Sandhog have stealth capability?"

"I don't know, but knowing Cecil I expect it does," Monty said. "The Strongmonte platform requires stealth to be part of the specifications."

"Then we use Sandy to sneak in close," I said. "Park nearby and sneak in. Should be easy."

"When has anything we ever attempted gone *that* easily?"

"I would say…never," I answered. "How bad is this approach?"

"The estate exudes a potent area of effect nullifying field," Monty said as we headed to the casting lab. "It's roughly a three-mile radius of effect."

"A three-mile radius?" I said. "Can we drive through this field?"

"Not likely," Monty answered after giving it some thought. He led the way to the casting lab. He stopped at a large, flat, filing cabinet that was located just inside the lab room and opened a few of the drawers as if looking for something. "I know I asked him for the actual hard copies." He tugged on a tube of paper and walked over to one of the three long tables, rolling it out.

It was a map.

He flattened out the map and gestured. The map straightened out and remained perfectly flat on the lab table as I took in the space.

In addition to the map that was on one of the tables, Monty stepped over to a large screen that rested on one of the walls. With a few taps, he pulled up a map of the Black Forest and the surrounding area.

"Why do we need a map if we have that?" I asked, pointing at the screen. "We only need the digital copy, don't we?"

"No," Monty said. "The digital copy displays the routes we can use as options, but this map"—he pointed at the map on the table—"this map contains potential threats which have been mapped out over time by visitors to Shadowpeak."

"A victims map?" I asked, looking at the map. "Is that what this is?"

"Not exactly," Monty said, glancing down at the map. "The victims never had a chance to contribute to this map. This is a survivor's map if we're being technical."

"How accurate is it?"

"From my understanding, it details the major dangers of the area we will be traversing on foot"—he pointed to the series of concentric circles around what I assumed was Shadowpeak—"within reason, of course."

"Of course," I said looking at the map on the table. "I'm sure some of this has changed."

The casting lab was covered in various runes situated at the door and what I assumed were strategic points in the room, floor, ceiling, and walls. It was about ten foot square, which I felt was large for a room inside of a plane, until I realized that this room probably operated under the same rules as the hangar.

Bigger on the inside than on the outside.

I leaned over the table and looked down at the map. Monty pointed to a large red cross which I assumed was Shadowpeak. Around the red cross, I saw a large orange circle.

"Area of effect?" I asked, pointing at the circle. "I'm not seeing any roads to and from Shadowpeak."

"Because there aren't any," he said, gazing down at the map. "The Sandhog will get us to within two miles of Shadowpeak. We will have to traverse the rest of the way on foot."

"On foot, through two miles of enchanted forest?" I asked concerned. "Why does that sound like a bad idea?"

"Granted, it's not one of the best," Monty said. "But it's the safest for us."

"How is walking two miles through this area of effect *safe*?"

"If we take the Sandhog, with its unique energy signature, what do you think will happen?"

"We get through there faster?"

"The trees are too thick," Monty said. "You do realize that the name Black Forest derives from the darkness of the forest due to the sheer amount of trees it contains."

"I thought it was because Shadowpeak added to the actual darkness of the place," I said. "So us hiking two miles is safer because Sandy will attract too much attention?"

"The *wrong* kind of attention," Monty said, tracing a

finger on the map. "We can take this road. I should be able to mask us three; masking the Sandhog and us would pose a problem."

I looked at the line he followed with his finger.

"When you say road," I said, leaning even closer to the map and squinting, "do you mean an actual road or some barely existent dirt path? I ask because I'm not getting road vibes from this trail you're pointing at here."

"Trail is probably more accurate," Monty said with a nod. "The Sandhog should provide us enough cover to get close. Once we exit the vehicle, however, we will be assaulted by the defenses of Shadowpeak."

"These defenses," I said. "What exactly are we talking about here? Failsafes? Sirens? Traps? What exactly are these defenses?"

"Nothing so passive," Monty said, still looking down at the map. "Byron, from my studies, was a firm believer in active deterrence."

"Active deterrence sounds painful," I said. "Can you be more specific? Exploding traps?"

"Think more along the lines of ogres and other assorted creatures," Monty answered. "Byron didn't want anyone wandering into Shadowpeak accidentally, so he populated the Forest with all manner of creatures to act as the first line of defense."

"He *populated*?" I asked, surprised. "What exactly does that mean, he populated? He invited these creatures into the forest?"

"According to the Shadowpeak archives, Byron summoned and in some cases, created, the creatures that inhabit the forest around Shadowpeak."

"Wonderful, he was some kind of Archmage Frankenstein?"

"Of sorts," Monty said. "He was unimaginably powerful. I

can only assume that creating these beings was child's play for someone of his level. That being said, I only have the records to go from. I've never met any of these creations."

"So it could all be rumor?" I asked. "A PR story to keep people away?"

"I suppose there's always that possibility," Monty said, "but I doubt it."

"This Byron was truly twisted," I said. "How did he even justify doing all of this? All he did was create a menace to the world."

"He justified it the same way all dangerous weapons are justified," Monty said, clearing off one of the other lab tables. "The power inside Shadowpeak is neither good nor evil. It all depends on how it's used and by whom."

"I call BS," I said, feeling the anger rise inside of me. "Some power…some power should never be unleashed on the world—ever."

"This is one time I find myself agreeing with you," Monty said. "The purpose of our trip is to make sure that the power that lies currently dormant within Shadowpeak is never released into the world or never falls into the wrong hands."

"Do you think we can do that?"

"Absolutely," he said and outstretched his hand. "Now, hand me your gun. Let's prep the table to modify it, before we take off."

I handed him Grim Whisper.

NINE

"You want to do this now?" I asked. "Wouldn't it be better to get some sleep and prepare for Shadowpeak?"

Monty took Grim Whisper and touched sections of the table. A specially designed stand rose from the center of the table onto which he placed my gun. The stand locked around the barrel, extended a section around the trigger to prevent an accidental discharge, and secured the grip.

"There," he said once Grim Whisper was secured. "That will hold it in place and allow me to inscribe it."

"Is this safe?" I asked. "Not the stand holding Grim Whisper, I mean the whole inscribing it, *inside* a plane. The last time I cast an orb inside a plane we ended up punching a hole in the Strix."

"*We* didn't punch a hole in the plane, *you* did," he said with a raised eyebrow. "However, to be fair, it was my uncle's suggestion that precipitated that rough landing."

"Rough landing?" I said, incredulous. "I seem to remember pieces of the Strix all over that island. René was not pleased. I'd like to not repeat *that* experience."

"We won't and we replaced the Strix with a better model,"

Monty said. "I think your abilities, while considerably more dangerous, are also under a greater degree of control now. Still, let's not follow my uncle's advice on in-flight orb practice while I'm inscribing a volatile weapon."

"For the record, he was the one that suggested I form a magic missile inside a plane," I added, "when I had little to no experience. Just making sure we're clear on that point."

"I recall," he said. "To clarify, *we* are not casting anything. *I* am going to inscribe some runes on your weapon. You will do *some* assisting while I inscribe, but the dangerous part will happen after we land."

"The dangerous part?" I asked, concerned. "What dangerous part?"

"We will get to that later. Right now, it seems like we're departing," Monty said, moving over to one side of the room, where I noticed a row of seats against the wall. "It would be wise to strap in for take-off."

I nodded as we made our way over to the seats.

The seats were oversized and instead of a belt across the waist with another across our torso, these seats were equipped with a modified five-point harness, making sure we were secured into our seats.

Peaches rumbled and plopped down on the floor next to my feet. I wasn't too concerned about my hellhound; I figured he could withstand the turbulence of the Shrike's take-off without needing to be strapped down.

"This is Daniel, your captain, speaking," Daniel said in his silky smooth voice over the plane's speakers. "We are currently preparing for take-off."

"If he ever needs another gig, he has the perfect voice for vocally-induced anesthesiology," I commented, securing my straps and tightening them. "He can put anyone to sleep with that voice. In fact, I think I'm feeling groggy already."

"We are currently sitting in SuNaTran Terminal X and will

be taxiing out to our designated lift-off pad," Daniel continued. "Please be seated and strap in. Our flight will take approximately four hours and twenty-five minutes, give or take a few minutes."

"Under five hours to Germany?" I asked. "Is this thing supersonic?"

"I assume Cecil improved on the design of the previous Shrike," Monty said, adjusting his straps. "It still seems a little slow for this radical design."

"That seems slow, really?" I asked. "You want us to break the speed of light— would that be fast enough for you?"

"Don't be ridiculous, the design would need to be radically altered to achieve those kinds of speeds," Monty said. "Not to mention we would need to be out of Earth's atmosphere to make sure it was safe."

I stared at him as he answered with a straight face.

"Faster-than-light travel is impossible," I answered. "You know this, I know this, everyone knows this. Just ask Einstein."

"This, from the person who has been cursed alive, is currently bonded to a hellhound, while wielding darkflame, and manages to hold a necrotic, seraphic siphon weapon *within* his body, which he can summon at will," he said. "All of which would be considered patently impossible by most normal individuals."

I opened my mouth to answer, but Daniel interrupted me as his voice came over the speakers again.

"We will be reaching our cruising altitude of eighty thousand feet shortly after take-off," he informed us. "Please remain in your seats until indicated to prevent any unwanted injuries."

"Eighty thousand feet?" I asked. "Is Cecil thinking of visiting other planets?"

"Hardly," Monty said, laying his head back. "The Karman

line rests at sixty two miles above sea level. Eighty thousand feet is just over a quarter of that. Not to mention, the thrust required to escape Earth's gravity exceeds the capacity of this Shrike's engines, even as an experimental prototype."

I stared at him.

"You know entirely too much about this," I said. "How is *that* information helpful in your mage life? Do you need to calculate the thrust of an orb in relation to its mass as it speeds across the curvature of the earth to counter the Coriolis Effect before smacking into a designated target?"

He gazed at me for a few seconds, a faint smile across his lips.

"Depends."

"Depends?" I asked. "Depends on what?"

"I think the real question is: what made you frame your question in that manner?" he said. "You almost sounded like a mage there for a second."

"Never in a million years," I said, shaking my head. "My brain isn't filled with centuries of information, like someone I know."

"True, you would be surprised at the amount of information a mage is required to know," he said, closing his eyes. "You should take this moment to rest. We have about thirty minutes to an hour before we hit cruising altitude. Then we need to work on your weapon."

"I'm not exactly feeling confident about inscribing Grim Whisper in a contained space—on a plane," I said. "Why don't we do the whole process after we land?"

"Two reasons," Monty said. "First, *we* are not inscribing, *I* am and I need time to etch the runes into your weapon, time we won't have after we land. Second, the risk is minimal on the Shrike, this is a contained space designed for casting. If something does go wrong, this entire room can be jettisoned from the Shrike, in the case of a catastrophic mishap."

"Jettisoned?" I asked, glancing around warily. "You do realize we are in the 'contained space' that would be jettisoned in the case of a mishap?"

"Then we best make certain no mishap occurs."

"We will be landing at FKB-Karlsruhe/Baden-Baden Airport, located on the western edge of the Black Forest," Daniel continued. "Once we land, you will continue the next leg of your journey by Sandhog. As always, it is my pleasure to be able to fly with you again, and I wish you a safe trip."

"Will the Shrike wait for us while we secure Shadowpeak?"

"Cecil will give us ninety-six hours before attempting an exfiltration," Monty said. "That should be plenty of time to uncover what happened to the monks and secure Shadowpeak."

"Four days?" I asked. "Are you sure that's enough time?"

"Yes, considering that the entire concept of linear time is not exactly fixed in Shadowpeak," Monty answered. "We will use that to our advantage."

"What could possibly go wrong with a location where time is a loose concept?" I said, giving him a look. "Four days to uncover what iced the monks and to secure a murderous estate—totally doable."

"I'm glad you understand the scope of our mission."

I stared at him and kept silent. It made no sense to point out that this whole plan seemed like we were stepping into a death trap.

He was determined to go in.

Which meant I was going in with him.

My only concern—well two concerns—were preventing whatever killed the monks from killing us, and making sure Monty didn't suddenly decide he needed to run the deadly Gauntlet.

TEN

"Do you have the route from the airport to Shadowpeak?" I asked. "And is that route going to be available to us when we need to get *back* to the Shrike?"

"I do and I would assume so," Monty said. "Provided the Sandhog remains where we leave it, I would say it should be an uneventful trip back to the airport."

I narrowed my eyes at him in disbelief.

"Only in your imagination," I said. "The odds of us and the term *uneventful* occupying the same place are nearly impossible."

"But there is a chance, slim as it may be," he said as the Shrike lurched forward. "I'm more concerned with uncovering what killed the Guardian Monks. That is one of our main priorities on this trip."

"With the other being *securing* Shadowpeak, right?" I asked. "Not running the Gauntlet, just securing."

"We investigate the monks first," Monty said with a small nod. "Then we secure Shadowpeak. If we can do both simultaneously, it would be more efficient."

"I have a feeling that whatever eliminated the monks will be tied to Shadowpeak somehow," I said. "Do we have any idea what could have taken them out?"

Monty shook his head, keeping his eyes closed.

"Unfortunately, no," Monty answered after a pause. "Uncle Dex provided us with a file, but it's sparse. It seems that even those who found the bodies, didn't do much investigating."

"Maybe it had something to do with being inside a creepy estate killing people?" I asked. "Just a guess, but that may have something to do with the lack of a thorough report?"

Monty was about to answer when the Shrike came to a stop. A sudden roar, muffled but powerful, filled the plane, as we were pressed back and down into our seats.

For about a minute, it felt like an elephant had decided that my chest was the perfect place to rest on as I was crushed into my seat.

I looked down and saw my hellhound sprawling comfortably on the floor beside me. He was completely unaffected. After about a minute, the pressure on my chest disappeared. I barely felt the Shrike change angle as it headed upward.

It made me think.

"Has Cecil ever created his amazing vehicles for governments?" I asked. "I mean, why isn't he the head of some top secret organization providing these prototypes for nations?"

"The existence of SuNaTran isn't exactly public knowledge," Monty replied. "His organization *is* secret."

"You know what I mean," I said. "SuNaTran could be a massive shadow company supplying the world with cutting-edge tech and vehicles."

Monty shook his head

"Cecil was in the Supernatural War," Monty said. "He helped create all manner of vehicles during that time."

"For the government?"

"No government fought directly in the war," Monty said, his expression darkening briefly. "It was a *supernatural* war and Cecil supported the mages who wanted to preserve a peaceful coexistence with humanity, not subjugate it."

"What happened after the war?" I asked. "What did he do?"

"He created SuNaTran, which had been conceived during the war," Monty said. "Through SuNaTran, he created a transportation conglomerate serving the supernatural community all over the world. He stepped away from creating enhanced weapons once the war was over. Considering his potential, I much prefer him creating vehicles, not weapons."

"You could argue that this plane could easily be converted into a weapon," I said. "I mean, it's only a few steps away from a B-21 stealth bomber."

"Not while Cecil is breathing," Monty said. "He vowed never to create weapons of mass destruction after the war ended. He saw what was possible, and chose to never be responsible for the deaths of others through his creations…again."

"Well, his runes have *saved* us a few times," I said, giving it thought. "I'm glad he's on our side."

"Cecil isn't on *any* side," Monty said. "Some of his clients would seem questionable to us, yet he provides a transportation service to them. I do know he has refused some requests, but he has never explained his criteria, nor have I asked him to. He has earned the right to make his choices, whether I agree with them or not. I'm sure he takes issue with my trip to Shadowpeak."

"Yet, he hasn't tried to stop you," I said. "Why not? In fact, he's *flying* us there."

"Because deep in his core, he knows I'm right," Monty said, glancing down at the Radiant Star bracelet his uncle gave him. "Just like my uncle knew I had to go. Cecil knows I *have* to do this."

"That Radiant Star, thing," I said, looking at the bracelet. "What does it do, exactly?"

"It allows for a mental restart."

"A mental restart?"

"If I ever find myself in a mental construct not of my making, it provides a way out," he said. "It's a type of emergency exit. I hope I don't need it, but I feel better having it."

"Are you saying it will help you if you lose your mind?"

"That's a somewhat literal interpretation," he said. "It doesn't impact my mental faculties."

"Oh," I said. "Because if that was the case, you needed that Radiant Star long before today. Your mind has been lost for a while now."

"Ah, yes, Aspis humor," he said, shaking his head. "I had almost forgotten how unentertaining it is, thank you for the reminder."

"Are we planning on walking into mental constructs not of your making?"

"In Shadowpeak, anything is possible."

"I'd still feel better if I knew Dex was with us," I said. "It can't hurt to have all that extra mage firepower backing you up."

"Actually, in Shadowpeak, it can," Monty said. "The stronger the mage that enters the property, the stronger the response of the failsafes. Consider the ramifications if my uncle joined us."

I gave that scenario some thought.

If Dex came with us, it would mean that the failsafes that would be activated would be on par with Dex's power level. That meant that Monty and I would get blasted to memories in seconds, maybe a little longer, but not by much. My hellhound would probably survive, not that I wanted to find out.

"It would mean that Shadowpeak would be even deadlier than it currently is," I said. "All of the defenses would ramp up to meet the threat Dex posed. That means we wouldn't be able to deal with those defenses, not even on our best day."

He nodded.

"Which, I think, is the real reason he didn't join us," Monty said. "By refusing to accompany us, he's actually looking out for our safety."

I gave Monty a glare of disbelief.

"That makes *perfect* sense," I said, shaking my head. "By not coming with us and letting us face this deadly house on our own, he's actually looking out for us. Of course, how did I miss that amazing mage logic?"

"I'm glad you understand," Monty said. "I'm sure he wanted to be here, but the circumstances are…complicated."

"If I end up facing some creature trying to remove my head from the rest of me, I'm going to explain that it shouldn't, because, you know—the circumstances are *complicated*," I said. "I'm sure that will work. In fact, I'm going to file that tactic right up there, next to using tact and diplomacy."

I felt the Shrike level out as notification lights came on, letting us know it was safe to leave our seats.

Monty unstrapped his harness and made his way to the lab table that held Grim Whisper. The stand Monty had placed it in rotated ninety degrees as he approached, holding the gun in place and at the ideal angle for inscribing.

He called me over to the table.

I nudged my hellhound away from my feet, succeeding in moving him about an inch. As I made room to step around the mass of mountainous snoring, he resprawled, nearly knocking me down as he got tangled up in my legs.

After performing some spontaneous gymnastics, I headed over to the casting table where Monty stood. When I reached the table, Monty was examining Grim Whisper with what appeared to be a magnifying glass, except this was different from most magnifying glasses I had ever seen.

This device had three lenses attached to an arm, allowing for each lens to fall into place, forming a concentric configuration which allowed, I guess, for closer examination of whatever Monty was viewing.

"What exactly is that?" I asked, pointing at the triple magnifying glass. "How much magnification do you need for this inscribing?"

"It's not exactly a magnification glass," Monty explained. "This is a trinary runic glass."

"Oh, a trinary runic glass," I said, shooting him a look. "That explains it perfectly. How about you tell me what it does, in plain non-mage English?"

"It assists in the inscription of runes on magical artifacts," Monty said. "Your weapon qualifies as a magical artifact, hence my use of this device."

"That much I understand," I said. "How does it do that?"

"It allows me to view your weapon in several states at once," he said as if that made sense. He looked at me and saw I still didn't understand him. "It allows me to inscribe without making an error."

"An error would be bad."

"Catastrophic even," he said. "This device allows for accuracy, by enhancing my vision as I work."

"Basically uber mage glasses?" I said, gazing at Grim Whisper as he started to gesture. "And this trinary glass allows for what, a better view as you inscribe?"

"Not exactly," Monty said. "It allows for layers of runes to be placed on the same artifact without runic overlap or conflict."

"You know sometimes I pretend you're speaking English," I said, shaking my head. "Then you say things like *without runic overlap or conflict* and I realize we speak two different languages most of the time."

"You feel your weapon is inadequate to meet the threats you face, correct?" he asked, pointing at Grim Whisper. "It's not powerful enough."

"That's not a feeling, that's a fact," I said. "Drawing Grim Whisper against the enemies we face now is about as effective as pulling out a straw and shooting spitballs."

"Crass but accurate," he said, still focused on Grim Whisper. "You certainly are attracting a different level of adversary these days."

"Not because I want to," I said. "I may as well try aggressive tickling than persuader rounds. All entropy rounds do is piss off the creatures I'm firing at. We are facing threats that laugh at my drawing Grim Whisper these days."

Monty nodded.

"Indeed," he said, rubbing his chin. "The caliber of enemy we are facing is considerably more potent."

"What gave it away?" I asked. "Was it the fact that the Emissaries that came after us recently were one-person armies? Or that it took an entire mountain of monks to hold off Emissary Salya?"

"There is that," he said, still lost in thought. "In addition, we need to be proactive and forward thinking. In the not too distant future, we may have to face that Fifth Pillar."

"The one you're related to?" I asked. "He did say he was a Treadwell."

"I'll have to inquire further about him," Monty said. "I'm certain my uncle will have some information about him."

"What about the other four pillars?"

"Them too," Monty said. "The Grand Council has paused in their attack, but I can guarantee you, they won't stop—until we stop them."

"You don't think a strongly worded letter will get them to

change their minds?" I asked. "Something on official Montague letterhead?"

"The only language they understand involves blood and death."

"I had a feeling you were going to say something like that."

"Because it's the truth."

I looked down at Grim Whisper and shook my head.

"I don't think this one weapon is going to make much of a difference," I said. "The stronger they are, the more immune to bullets they seem. If this was an arms race between us and our enemies, they hold the strongest hands and I'm walking around disarmed."

"You still have your abilities and Ebonsoul," Monty pointed out. "You're not exactly defenseless."

"True," I said. "Grim Whisper, when it was a threat, was a useful deterrent. My abilities, I'm still learning about those, and Ebonsoul, most of the time requires I get up close and personal. Not exactly ideal when someone wants to squeeze my head flat, or rip my heart from my chest. Both unfun options by the way."

"Understood," he said. "This alteration requires an extensive upgrade in the power output of this weapon."

"If you could make it fire mini-nukes, I think that would be perfect," I said with a nod. "Taking down an ogre in one shot works for me."

"Except that the recoil a weapon of that magnitude would produce, after firing a mini-nuke, if such a thing were even possible, would rip your arm off at the shoulder," Monty said. "I don't think that's the desired outcome."

"Not desired at all, I'm pretty attached to my arms."

"I have an idea," Monty said, glancing at me. "However, it may require some pain."

I narrowed my eyes at him.

"Of course it requires pain," I said. "Why would I ever think this would be easy or painless? What is it and how much pain?"

"We transform your weapon to use darkflame rounds," he said. "The pain, to be honest, should be mostly minimal."

Famous last words.

ELEVEN

"Darkflame rounds?" I asked, confused. "How exactly is that supposed to work? I've never even heard of darkflame rounds."

"That's because in the realm of banned ordnance, something like darkflame rounds would be met with severe consequences."

"Severe consequences?" I asked. "What kind of severe consequences?"

"You are perfectly within your right to refuse this upgrade," he said, glancing at me before looking down at Grim Whisper again. "Every Council, once they hear you possess a weapon that fires darkflame rounds, will attempt to sanction you."

"Why?"

"Darkflame rounds would operate under a different principle than your use of darkflame in an orb or as a beam," Monty said. "These rounds, with the runes I shall inscribe on your weapon, would be akin to wielding a gun that behaves as a *kamikira*."

"You're turning Grim Whisper into a god-killer?" I asked, surprised. "Wouldn't that bring you some heat as well?"

"Yes, providing these runes would label me as a dark mage," he said. "Nothing I haven't heard in the past."

"Dark mage?" I asked. "But you're not a dark mage. I mean you're not, right?"

"I'm not, nor do I have any intention of ever becoming a dark mage," he said, his voice hard. "That doesn't stop the fear and misconceptions from arising, especially among those who don't understand."

"The runes you're going to inscribe on Grim Whisper, are they dark runes?" I asked, trying to make sure Monty wasn't stepping into some dark aspect of his casting. "You aren't using blood or darkness to create these runes, are you?"

He looked at me and smiled.

"Who is it among us here who uses darkflame?"

"I do," I said. "But I'm not a dark anything."

"Who has recently been given the name Deathless?"

"Again me, but that was not my idea."

"And recently," he said, tapping his chin, "who has managed to communicate and direct the dead to act according to his will?"

"Shit, fine, that was me, too," I said. "But I'm not dark."

"*You* know that, and *I* know that," he said, raising a hand to stop me from protesting. "To anyone who doesn't know you, but learns that you are the Marked of Kali, cursed alive, wield a necrotic blade, and can summon darkflame, what do you think is their *initial* impression?"

"They would think I was some sort of dark mage creature," I said, realizing the truth. "Even though that's the furthest thing from the truth."

"You're also bonded to a hellhound," he added. "If that doesn't say friendly wielder of light and goodness, I don't know what does. How could anyone misinterpret your motives?"

I stared at him for a few seconds.

"You made your point," I said. "You'll never hear me ask you about being dark again. I apologize."

"Apology accepted," he said with a nod. "If there is anyone walking this earth who knows if I'm a dark mage, it would be you. That is why I tasked you with my neutralization, as my Aspis."

"But you're saying that if you do this upgrade to Grim Whisper, I'm going to be seen as a—what exactly am I going to be seen as?"

"Well, with the makeover to your name, the fact that you can command the dead, or at the very least communicate with them, and are bonded to a hellhound," he said with a small smile, clearly enjoying himself as he counted off the reasons on his fingers, "I would imagine you would be perceived as some kind of newly formed undying necromancer."

"What? Are you serious?"

"Perhaps even a necromantic lord of some kind," he continued, giving it some thought. "An Eternal Necromantic Lord. That does have a certain ring to it. Deathless—the Eternal Necromantic Lord. It works, don't you agree?"

"No, I do *not* agree," I snapped. "What is wrong with you? I sound like some creature from a bad horror movie."

"If I inscribe this weapon for you," he said, growing serious, "it will be one more thing that will convince the so-called authorities in the magical community as to your alleged corruption and darkness."

"Which is bullshit," I said, getting angry. "That's just an excuse to come after me, after us."

He nodded.

"Remember the justification Salya expressed for your

extermination," he said. "When you undid the magistrate on Naxos?"

"I do," I said, remembering her words. "She called me a monster."

"In addition to calling you a monster, she said you would begin to kill indiscriminately," he said. "No one would be safe from you or your blade. I recall something about the blade controlling you."

"I remember. Your point?"

"Those ideas didn't start with the Emissary," Monty said. "They were propagated by the Grand Council. The easiest way to confront and stop you is to convert you into—"

"A common enemy," I said. "Get everyone to hate and fear me and it almost becomes self-fulfilling. They will attack me based on fear alone."

He nodded.

"This pause they are taking is no real pause," he said. "You can rest assured they are working behind the scenes to tear us down."

"That means we need to be prepared for what's coming," I said. "If they want to play dirty, I can get my hands dirty. If that means dealing with being blacklisted by everyone, I can live with that."

"Are you certain?"

"Do I have much of a choice?"

"No, they will resume their attack when you least expect it, or when they feel you are vulnerable and weakened."

"Which means I should have every tool possible at my disposal, right?" I asked. "I should be armed to the best of my ability."

"Yes," he said. "That would be the most prudent course of action."

"That means having a gun that can kill gods would even

the playing field, since I would be facing mages much stronger than I am, right?"

"Yes, even an Archmage would be wary of the final iteration of your weapon," he said. "It would also motivate them to end your life with haste."

I smiled at that.

"They may have a little trouble with that last part."

"True, but it won't stop them from attempting your extermination," he said. "They may not know about your cursed status, but they will."

"Do it," I said. "Make Grim Whisper a kamikira. I will deal with the fallout. You said it involves pain...how much pain?"

"Nothing you haven't experienced in the past," he answered. "As I said, mostly minimal."

"Monty...you realize I have gone through some major pain," I said, my voice low. "How much pain...exactly? 'Mostly minimal' sounds vague in a bad way. The same way a root canal is a small pinch."

"You will have to imbue the weapon with lifeforce and darkflame," he said. "It's the equivalent of a runic transfusion, using your own life. In plain English, the process will rip a part of your lifeforce away, infuse it into your gun, and mix it with darkflame to increase its potency and ensure that only you will be able to wield your weapon."

"That sounds like the opposite of minimal."

"It will be uncomfortable," he said. "However, you have quite the pain tolerance. I think you will weather the process well, for the most part."

"Your level of confidence building is staggering," I said, shaking my head. "Almost on par with the non-existent mage morale-building program."

His expression darkened for a few seconds.

"The pain will be excruciating," he said, his voice serious. "Are you certain you want to do this?"

I took a few moments to consider my options.

I could keep practicing and get better with the casts I was new at and learning. There was still so much about the Hidden Hand I didn't know, but I was learning about probability casts. I also had Monty and Peaches to back me up if everything went sideways, not to mention the other casts I knew, and Ebonsoul.

If I refused, I wasn't exactly defenseless, but I was the Aspis. It was *my* job to protect those my life touched, not the other way around.

What was the point of having this power if I couldn't do what I was meant to do? What would happen if something incapacitated Monty and Peaches? I would have to face whatever it was. Alone—with no help.

Could I—or would I—fail, and lose everyone who mattered to me?

I knew the answer.

"Do it," I said. "With one adjustment. I want to stow Grim Whisper the same way I stow Ebonsoul."

He narrowed his eyes at me.

"That will increase the difficulty somewhat."

"Can you do it?"

"I can," he said. "It will also take the pain from mostly minimal to beyond excruciating in ways you have never experienced. You are asking for a specific bonding to your weapon, one similar to the bond you have with Ebonsoul."

"Yes," I said. "If this weapon is going to be so dangerous, I'm not running the risk of losing it or having it taken from me. If I can convert it to mist, then I can always keep it safe."

"Did I mention this was going to be in the upper echelons of excruciating?"

I nodded slowly.

"Excruciating is just another Tuesday."

"Understood," he said and began gesturing at the door. "Lock the door. We can't have anyone trying to interrupt the process once we start."

"Will it be enough?" I said, moving to the door. "Cecil could probably undo this lock."

"Probably," Monty said and gestured, sending more symbols which formed a deep orange lattice, securing the entire door. "He can't undo *that*, though."

I moved back to the table.

"Let's do this," I said. "I'm ready."

TWELVE

There was no way I could ever have been ready for what happened next.

"Create your darkflame," Monty said. "Cover the weapon with it,"—he pointed—"here and here. Make sure all of these parts of the weapon are immersed in the flame."

I focused.

"*Mors Ignis,*" I whispered, filling my hands with darkflame.

I extended my hands and wrapped my fingers around the sections of Grim Whisper he indicated. The darkflame felt cool to my touch.

Monty gestured again and motioned for me to move my hands. I moved my hands back and saw that the darkflame remained on Grim Whisper.

Monty grabbed the flame with his fingers and began tracing symbols into Grim Whisper, using the darkflame as a writing tool. The darkflame blazed with energy as the symbols seared into the gun. Sweat broke out on his brow as he worked.

With one hand, he etched the symbols; with the other, he

angled the runic trinary glass to make sure he was doing the work accurately.

He motioned for me again to step close.

"Brace yourself," he said, looking at me. "This is going to hurt."

I nodded and grabbed the sides of the table.

Monty gestured with one hand, the other hand still resting on Grim Whisper. Silver symbols formed in the air in front of me. Monty shoved his hand through the symbols and into my chest with a sudden strike.

The force of the impact shocked me to my core, but rooted me in place. Monty removed his hand from my chest and I saw the trail of silver energy flow from my chest to his fingers.

My lifeforce.

He moved that hand to join his other, holding Grim Whisper. Together, the darkflame symbols and silver threads of my lifeforce merged.

It was amazing to watch—but there was little pain, just some discomfort. I was about to mention this to Monty, when the pain train crashed into my chest.

What felt like a blade plunging into my chest stole my breath from my lungs as the pain traveled across my chest and settled in the center of my torso, nestled in my solar plexus and slowly melted me inside.

From there, the pain radiated outward as the darkflame and silver threads erupted from Grim Whisper and punched into me, nearly doubling me over in agony.

Somewhere in the distant recesses of my mind, I heard my hellhound whine as he approached. The pain was so overwhelming, I couldn't turn to look at him. It was all I could do to remain standing. The force of this process was the only thing that kept me upright next to the table.

I felt my eyes water as the pain ratcheted up a few more

notches. When I blinked to clear my eyes—since raising my arms to wipe them was out of the question due to the pain—I realized I was crying tears of blood.

"Blo...blood?" I managed through the mind-numbing agony. "I'm crying blood."

Monty nodded, but remained silent.

I tried to take a few deep breaths to ride the waves of pain, but it was pointless. These waves were a tsunami of destructive force and I was drowning in them.

The pain washed over me and I think I screamed then, but I wasn't sure due to the roar of sound that filled my ears. A blast of power reached me from Grim Whisper as my body answered with a spasm of muscle contractions that locked me in place, gripping the sides of the table.

Monty gestured one more time as he traced something else on Grim Whisper. A cloud of silver mixed with darkflame wafted up from the table and surrounded me.

In moments, it changed shape from a harmless cloud to something resembling a group of spikes. The spikes hovered near me, but remained clear of my body.

I knew that wouldn't last long.

With another gesture from Monty, all of the spikes punched into me and my world was pain—unending, mind-destroying agony that threatened to undo me.

I wanted to tell him to stop, that it was too much, but I couldn't form the words. I saw Monty trace something else on Grim Whisper and follow that with a symbol on my chest.

A thin beam of violet energy formed between me and Grim Whisper.

"One more thing," Monty said, clenching his teeth as I barely noticed him fighting some force of energy as he did this. He gestured and formed a lattice of golden energy around me. "You may not be able to withstand this part, but try. Ready?"

All I could do was nod.

He moved his hand in an intricate manner near me, while saying something under his breath. My vision compressed to Grim Whisper and the silver darkness around me. Everything else vanished from sight as the pain became white-hot and burned me to ash.

I saw the runes on Grim Whisper begin to glow as the threads around my body matched their intensity. In seconds, all I could see was the silver energy all around me.

Then everything became black.

I was in my quarters when I opened my eyes again.

My hellhound was by my side and proceeded to slap my face with his tongue in affection and concern as I came to.

<Ow! You can stop trying to drown me now.>

<My saliva will heal you.>

<Your saliva will drown me. Really, you can stop now, boy. Where's Monty?>

<He is in the other room. He told me to bring him when you woke up. I will be back.>

He blinked out and a few seconds later, he blinked back in.

<Where did you go?>

<To let the angry man know you were awake. He promised me meat if I did it as soon as you opened your eyes.>

<You blinked out and back in while we're on a supersonic moving plane?>

<Yes. I am a mighty hellhound. Blinking while I move is not difficult. Maybe one day, if you eat enough meat you will be able to blink like me.>

I shook my head and smiled.

<I don't think I will ever be that mighty, but thanks for the vote of confidence.>

<You are my bondmate. If I can do it, you can do it.>

<I don't think that's how it works. We may be bondmates, but you're also a hellhound, while...I'm not.>

<I will help you to reach your mighty level.>

<I don't think there's any amount of meat that can help me reach a hellhound level of mighty. I'll settle for minor mightiness.>

The door to the room opened and Monty walked in.

"How do you feel?" Monty asked, narrowing his eyes at me. "You've been unconscious for two hours."

"Two hours?" I said, trying to sit up and failing as the bed shifted under me, with the room following a few seconds later. "Okay, sitting up may not be the best idea right now."

"Were you successful?" I asked, trying to get my bearings as the room settled down around me. It stopped spinning and slowed to a stop as I remained still. "Did it work?"

"You tell me," Monty said, gesturing and creating a large sausage he proceeded to feed to my hellhound. My hellhound took the sausage gently, graciously leaving all of Monty's fingers attached, and moved to a corner of the room to inhale his meal.

I closed my eyes, which helped in settling the room, and focused. Inside, I felt my power, which pulsed with every second that passed.

I felt Ebonsoul, which I had grown used to, Beside that, I felt the power of the darkflame coursing through me, ready to erupt at any second. I sensed the bonds I held, thrumming powerfully within me, each one distinct and clear.

Beneath it all I felt something else, something new, deep and dark. It felt subtle and quiet, almost non-existent, but it was there.

A new bond.

I focused on this energy, this bond, and drew on it, pulling it to the surface.

"Slowly," Monty said. "You're still recovering from the process. You may be a special individual, but even your body has to deal with the aftereffects of a weapon bonding and inscription."

I slowed down and focused on the bond.

In moments, a violet mist formed around my hand. It slowly solidified into Grim Whisper, surprising me.

It looked the same, except for the black smoke wafting from its length. I checked to see if it held ammunition but it was empty. The weight of the gun told a different story—it weighed as if it were fully loaded.

"It feels heavy," I said. "But it's empty."

"I don't suggest firing any practice rounds inside the Shrike," Monty said, shaking his head. "Aside from the damage, Cecil would be livid if you contributed to the death of his prototype. I suggest waiting until we are in the Black Forest before firing your new weapon."

I noticed he looked worn out.

"Are you okay?" I asked. "It was bad for me, I know, but it looks like it took something out of you too."

"I'll be fine," he said, waving my words away. "Nothing a good cuppa can't fix."

"Was this a good idea?" I asked. "Right before we go to Shadowpeak? My body feels mangled."

"I'm certain your body will recover soon enough," he said. "In fact you were recovering even before you were moved in here."

"Speaking of moving, my hellhound blinked out, got you and blinked back on a moving plane," I said. "How did he manage that?"

"He's *your* hellhound," he said. "I suggest you ask him, or refer to the only bondmate of a hellhound you know."

I rubbed my eyes.

"We really do have to go visit Hades soon," I said. "I find it incredible Peaches was able to do all that while we are in flight."

"As do I," Monty said, glancing at my ever-voracious hellhound. "However there is much we still don't know about your creature or your newly acquired battleform. We should strive to learn as much as possible."

"Right after Shadowpeak," I said. "I think I need to close my eyes for a few minutes or years."

"You should," he said. "I'll be back when we're close to landing. We can discuss the particulars of your weapon then."

"Good plan," I said as the heat rushed through my body repairing any damage. "I just need to rest my eyes for a bit."

I laid my head back and drifted off into a world of silver threads, laced with violet and black.

THIRTEEN

"It's time, Simon," Monty said, entering the room. "We're almost there."

If I focused, I could feel the Shrike descending.

"How long was I out?" I asked, getting to my feet. "Where are we exactly?"

"Total? Nearly three hours," Monty said, moving to the central area near the Sandhog. "We are over Karlsruhe/Baden-Baden Airport."

"They're letting *this* plane land there?"

"Apparently, Cecil has clearance to land pretty much anywhere he wants," Monty said with a short nod. "We are landing in a private section near the furthest edge, away from the passenger terminal."

"That makes sense," I said. "Last thing we need is curious passengers trying to figure out what kind of plane this is and where it's from."

"Indeed," Monty said, sitting in one of the large chairs, similar to the one in the casting lab. "You may want to sit for this part."

He motioned to the nearby chair.

I sat in the chair and strapped in.

"Four days," I said mostly to myself. "Does that timer start the moment we leave the Shrike or the moment we cross into Shadowpeak territory?"

"Neither. The moment we leave the Sandhog, I will alert Cecil," Monty said. "The timer will begin then."

"Not that I'm doubting Cecil's resourcefulness," I said, "how exactly does he intend on locating us if we are in the middle of Shadowpeak four days from now?"

"Cecil has our energy signatures, in addition to the signatures of Ebonsoul and my Sorrows," he answered. "In addition, he also has your creature's singular signature, seeing as how there aren't many hellhounds traipsing through the Black Forest."

"He can literally find us anywhere, can't he?"

"Anywhere on this planet, yes," Monty said. "If we choose to leave this plane of existence, I daresay his options are significantly narrowed."

"How?" I asked. "Does Cecil have some SuNaTran energy signature finder on board?"

"In a manner of speaking, yes," Monty said. "Cecil is a highly skilled tracker. He is the energy signature finder. A skill which has served him well in the past."

"Cecil has quite a diverse past," I said. "Served in the war, created SuNaTran, is a master runic armorer, and now you're telling me he's a tracker too?"

"Don't forget an accomplished pilot," Monty said. "Cecil has many skills he keeps away from the magical community. For good reason. He prefers his privacy."

"So I'm noticing," I said as the engines roared, slowing our descent. "Next thing you'll tell me he was some kind of spy during the war."

Monty paused until the engines died down.

"I can neither confirm nor deny Cecil's official status as an operative during the war," he said, unstrapping the harness that kept him in place. "I will say…I'm glad he was on our side."

I stared at him for a few seconds before unstrapping.

I saw a hatch open above us. A few seconds later, Cecil climbed down a ladder.

"How was your flight?"

"We had a moment there, earlier," Monty said. "Thank you for the assist."

"A little warning next time would've been nice," Cecil replied, heading over to the Sandhog. "I nearly ejected the entire casting lab, thinking it was a system failure jeopardizing the Shrike."

"Assist?" I asked, confused. "What assist?"

"Cecil sensed the spike in energy during the inscription of your weapon," Monty explained. "It must have appeared as a cast gone wrong."

"You could say that," Cecil added, placing two fingers close together. "I was this close to dumping the lab over the ocean."

"We were *in* the lab."

"If the lab is compromised and happens to explode—you don't want that to happen over a populated area," he said, shaking his head. "In fact you don't want that to happen at all."

"You would have gotten rid of it while we were inside?"

"As a last resort—yes," Cecil said. "When I tried to enter, the door was sealed beyond my ability to open."

"That was my doing," Monty said. "If you had opened the door, it would have shifted the integrity of the space. The cast I was executing depended on maintaining a runic homeostasis."

"Which is why I engaged the runic dampeners. Whatever

you were doing dropped to acceptable levels and here we are, near the Black Forest."

"How close were we to you dumping us?" I asked. "Really?"

"Closer than I would have wanted," Cecil said, removing the tarp from the Sandhog. "The GPS has been pre-programmed for Herrenwies, a small village on the edge of Neuhaus, just off the L86."

"How close is that to Shadowpeak?" Monty asked.

"You have about a four mile hike," Cecil said. "The beacon on the Sandhog will let me know when you reach Herrenwies. My person on-site will garage the car and provide you with hiking packs."

"We can't drive any closer?" I asked. "I mean four miles isn't much of a walk, but I hear the defenses—"

"Will pay less attention to you on foot—I hope," Cecil said. "It's not like you three don't attract attention."

"You hope so?" I asked, concerned. "What do you mean... you *hope* so?"

He turned to look at me, crossing his arms across his chest.

He glanced from Monty to me, then to Peaches, before turning back to me.

"Tristan," he said, pointing at Monty, "is a mage. In case you haven't noticed."

"I've noticed."

"Oh good, guess who else will notice once you leave the Sandhog and enter the insanely thick forest with no roads or trails for this vehicle?"

"But it's an off-road vehicle," I said, looking at Sandy. "It's *meant* for this kind of terrain. That's kind of the whole point of it being an off-road—it drives on dirt trails?"

"Normally, I would agree with you, but the particular trails around Shadowpeak—for about a three mile radius—are too dense with trees for the Sandhog," Cecil explained. "Not to mention they are populated with...creatures—creatures which would pick up on the vehicle's unique energy signature."

"You just said *we* will attract too much attention."

"I said you *will* attract attention, like a flashlight in a dark forest, subtle and small," Cecil said. "If you tried to take the Sandhog into the forest, it would be like setting off the sun in the middle of the forest at night."

"Not subtle or small."

"Neither, in fact," Cecil continued. He pressed a button on the wall and the ramp on the rear of the Shrike dropped down, showing us a road leading off the runway. "Tristan is a mage, you are...I don't really know what you are these days, but it's neither small nor subtle. Your hellhound, even though he is a good boy, may as well be wearing a hellhound beacon pointing to where you are."

"Oh," I said. "I didn't realize we would be *that* noticeable. Then I don't understand...why did you give it to us? We can hide in the Sandhog, right?"

"Contingency plans," Monty said. "Cecil is all about contingency plans. The Sandhog isn't for infiltration in this case."

"No, it's for your exfiltration," Cecil said. "No need for subtlety if you're fleeing for your lives."

"You think we're going to be pursued out of Shadowpeak, don't you?" Monty asked, glancing at the Sandhog. "This is our mode of escape."

"You can mask yourselves on your way in," Cecil explained. "You're skilled enough for that. You can't mask the Sandhog, at least not yet."

"If someone or something is pursuing us out of Shadowpeak, a mask would be—"

"Pointless," Cecil finished. "My research of the place leads me to believe there's a strong chance of pursuit," Cecil admitted. "You just have to make it back to Herrenwies and the Sandhog."

"Then we're on the highway or freeway and out of there," I said.

"You won't be able to use the regular roads if you're being pursued," Cecil said. "Forget highways or freeways."

"Why not?" I asked. "Wouldn't that be faster?"

"No, it would be populated and slow you down," Cecil said. "If you're being chased, not only are you in danger—"

"We would be putting innocents in danger," Monty said. "I doubt anyone or anything giving pursuit would be considerate enough to avoid harming other drivers."

"Something to consider," Cecil said, glancing at me. "That means your fastest route would be—"

"Through the forest," I finished. "*That's* why you gave us the Sandhog."

"Precisely," Cecil said. "I hope you don't need it, but I've dealt with you three long enough to know not to take chances. If I'm proven wrong, I'll be happy to admit I was wrong—hasn't happened yet with you three, but there's always a first time."

"Who's our contact at Herrenwies?" Monty asked. "Anyone I know?"

"You'll know when you get there," Cecil said. "They will be expecting the Sandhog. You take that road"—he pointed down the ramp to the end of the runway—"that will lead you to 500 South. You take 500 to L86 East which will lead you to Herrenwies."

"How big is this small village?" I asked. "I mean we're just supposed to drive into a town and they will know to expect us?"

"This is a small village in the middle of the forest in

Germany," Cecil said. "How many Lamborghinis do you think drive through this village on a daily basis?"

"None?"

"Exactly," Cecil said, looking outside at the setting sun. "If you leave now, you can get there by nightfall."

"You're suggesting we cross the forest at night?" I asked. "Seriously?"

"Yes, seriously," Cecil said with a nod. "The night will hide you better than the day. Give that some thought when you consider how dangerous this place is, and move accordingly." He pointed to the Sandhog. "Get in."

FOURTEEN

This Sandhog must've been the Hellhound Edition, because the entire rear of the vehicle was one enormous cavern that fit my hellhound perfectly.

Peaches laid out and sprawled, taking up all of the space.

"He's serious," I said as Monty strapped in. "The night is safer than the day?"

"He is," Monty said as I strapped in. "The creatures of the Black Forest are the stuff of legend, except that the legends in this case are deadlier and stronger. They will rend us to pieces in the day just as they would at night, except at night it may be slightly harder to find us."

"Slightly harder?"

"That small advantage can spell the difference between making it to Shadowpeak intact or as a memory," Monty said.

"I'll take whatever advantage we can get."

"That's getting in," I said. "What about getting out?"

"We'll burn that bridge when we get to it," Monty said, echoing one of Dexter's better known sayings of impending doom. "Let's get there, and do what we came here to do."

Cecil moved over to the driver's side and motioned for me to lower the window. I turned on the engine, and the Sandhog refused to start.

"What's going on?" I asked as I lowered the window and Cecil drew close. "It won't start."

"Not yet it won't," Cecil said. "You have to be recognized as an assigned driver. Before we get to that, review your driver's panel. Every feature is intuitively marked for easy understanding."

Cecil pointed at the array of switches near the steering wheel on the front dash. Next to the switches was a small recessed panel.

"What's that for?" I asked, pointing at the panel. "To take notes?"

"Do you really think you'll have time to take notes about *anything* while driving the Sandhog?" Cecil asked. "No, it's not for notes, Strong."

"Place your hand on that panel." He indicated the panel. "You first, Strong, then you Tristan."

We did as instructed.

A blue beam of light raced up and down the panel, reading my handprint for a few seconds before it turned golden. A few seconds later, it became blue again and Monty placed his hand on the panel.

"It's a biometric reader?" I asked. "That's sophisticated."

"It's part of the Strongmonte package," Cecil said. "Give it a second, the results should appear."

A moment later, the panel lit up with runic text I could barely read.

"What does it say?" I asked, trying to decipher the text. "I can make out some of the words like 'energy signature', but that's about it."

"Those are your runic biometrics," Cecil explained. "The

Sandhog recognizes you both as its driver, among other things."

"Other things?"

"I'll let Tristan explain those to you," Cecil answered. "For now, press the start button."

I pressed the button and the engine roared to life. Monty motioned to a switch marked stealth, and I flipped it.

A few seconds later, the engine was barely noticeable. It was so quiet I had to check it was still running.

"Use that function for your exit, it should help," Cecil said. "You don't need a silent approach going in, but it should help you getting out. When you get to Herrenwies, find the church—there's only one. Next to the church is a hostel; there is a garage for the Sandhog there."

"The person we're supposed to meet will be at the hostel?"

"Yes," Cecil said. "He will see you before you see him, trust me."

"Thank you for this, Cecil," Monty said. "I truly appreciate it."

"Don't thank me," Cecil said with a curt nod. "You have four days from the moment the beacon activates in Herrenwies. If I don't hear from you before then, it will trigger the exfiltration phase of this plan."

"I intend to be out of Shadowpeak before then," Monty said.

"I hope you are," Cecil said. "I'm not looking forward to venturing into Shadowpeak after you, but I will, and I will take a decidedly explosive route to get in there."

"You do realize that if you have to exfil, we will probably be inside Shadowpeak?" I said. "Taking an explosive route puts us in danger too."

"If that place has you, I'm going to make sure it gives you

up," Cecil answered, his voice hard. "Even if that means I have to reduce the entire estate to rubble to do it."

He pushed away from the Sandhog and nodded.

I started driving down the ramp and glanced back once at Cecil.

"He means it, doesn't he?" I asked. "He would blow up the entire place to find you?"

"Us," Monty corrected, "and I'm afraid he is deadly serious. I'm certain this plane carries armaments somewhere that he could drop on Shadowpeak from a safe distance."

"How much damage would it do?"

"Shadowpeak cannot be destroyed by conventional means," Monty said. "Not that Cecil won't try. Eventually he would realize whatever explosives he used didn't work and he would attempt a more hands-on approach."

"Could he destroy Shadowpeak?"

"I find it unlikely, but Cecil can be quite creative when he puts his mind to something," Monty said. "If we do what we have to in the time allotted to us, we won't have to find out."

I nodded.

"Sounds like a plan."

I stepped on the gas gently and the Sandhog crept down the ramp further. Once we were on the tarmac, Cecil raised the ramp and we sat on the open runway as the sun began to set.

Monty set the GPS and it pointed us to 500 South. The entrance to the highway near the end of the runway, currently out of sight.

I had an open runway and a rocket for a car under me.

I pressed down on the gas and the Sandhog leapt forward as it hunkered down, going faster. The road flew by us as we raced down the runway.

"Now this is what I call driving…in style," I said as the engine purred. "I wonder how fast Sandy can go?"

"You won't have much time to find out," Monty said, pointing ahead. "I believe that is the entrance to 500 South coming up."

I saw the curving road and realized that unless Sandy could fly, I was going to need to slow down in a hurry. I let off the gas and slowed down to merge onto the highway.

Night had fallen a few minutes earlier.

The rain arrived ten seconds later.

I fishtailed onto 500 South. For all the traction the Sandhog had, she had a fat ass and swerved all over the slick road as I corrected the merge onto the highway.

"Rain, really?" I asked as we sped down the highway. "Can you do something about this?"

"About what, precisely?" Monty asked, glancing at me as he adjusted the GPS. "The highway? You want me to fix the highway?"

"Not the highway," I said, shooting him a quick glare. "The rain."

"You want me to fix the *rain*?"

"Not fix, stop," I said. "Can you stop the rain?"

"I'm flattered you consider me powerful enough to affect the natural expressions of weather," Monty said. "I'm afraid the answer is no, I cannot stop the rain, nor would I want to, even if I could."

"We share a storm blood," I said, maneuvering around the light traffic. "Doesn't that give you some sort of advantage?"

"Two things," he said without looking up from the screen on the dash, "we *share* a storm blood. I do not wield it alone or exclusively. Secondly, did you forget what Josephine did when she unleashed her power on the countryside?"

"No, I didn't forget."

"Which would you prefer?" he asked, glancing at me. "Driving through this light rain, or driving through an apocalyptic, torrential storm of epic proportions?"

"Does that mean no? You can't stop the rain?"

"It means no, I will make no attempt to stop or influence the rain in any way whatsoever," he said. "We may be in Germany, but if I were to attempt something like that, a visit from Josephine would not be out of the realm of possibility."

"You think she could sense it from where she is?" I asked. "We're several hundred miles away."

"London to Shadowpeak is a ten hour drive, conventionally," he said, returning his attention to the screen. "On average about a five hundred and thirty mile trip."

"See?" I said, making my point. "Hundreds of miles."

"Simon, distance is not a factor when dealing with magic users at Josephine's level."

"Hmm, is it similar to the way Obi Wan felt the destruction of Alderaan?" I asked. "He was nowhere near it when it was destroyed, but he felt a great disturbance. Are you saying Josephine would feel a great disturbance?"

Monty sighed and I smiled because I managed to use a Star Wars reference in a way that was technically correct, but it was a Star Wars reference, so it irked him.

"The only ones feeling a great disturbance would be us as she blasted us for misusing such a power for something as trivial as light rain," he said. "She would disturb us into oblivion just for making her have to pay us a visit. I think we have other concerns at the moment, don't you?"

"Agreed," I said with a sharp nod. "Let's not have the powerful witch come pay us an unscheduled visit. Although..."

"No," Monty snapped. "We will not use subterfuge to then enlist her help with Shadowpeak—that would be worse than trying to stop the rain. She would blast us for sure, after berating us for acting dishonorably."

"It was just a thought," I said. "Can't hurt to try."

"Actually it can and will," he said, looking out of the

window. "Do not forget she is part of the Ten. When do we employ their assistance?"

"When there's no one else to call," I said. "But we've had their help when it wasn't the end of the world."

"Only because my uncle has been able to enlist their aid," he said. "Consider how dangerous the situations were. Without their assistance, the odds of our making it out unscathed would have been greatly reduced."

"We barely escaped most of those situations *with* their help."

"Precisely," he said. "You don't use a sledgehammer to deal with a fly."

"I don't know," I said. "I wouldn't mind a sledgehammer for this situation. I don't think a flyswatter is going to help us in Shadowpeak."

"A flyswatter will have to do," he said. "If we bring in stronger assistance, we risk attracting too much attention. Besides, you have a battleform now." He glanced to the rear of the Sandhog where my hellhound snored. "Between my abilities and your battleform, we should be able to face anything Shadowpeak throws at us."

"We've never faced a sentient haunted castle," I said, glancing at the GPS. The turn off for L86 East was coming up. "We don't know what Shadowpeak is going to throw at us."

"I have every confidence in our ability to adapt."

"That's exactly what has me concerned," I said as we turned off 500 South to L86. "What if we can't adapt?"

"I don't think we have much of a choice," Monty said. "We either adapt or the odds of us leaving Shadowpeak are slim."

"That's your answer?" I asked. "Adapt or die?"

"Do you want a pretty lie or the honest truth?"

"Truth, always."

"We adapt or we die," he said. "I for one have no intention of meeting my demise in Shadowpeak, do you?"

"No."

"Excellent, we are in alignment, then," he said, pointing. "The road to Herrenwies, L86 is coming up fast on your right. Try not to miss it."

I moved to the far right lane.

FIFTEEN

I made the switch to L86 East easily.

This road was more of a challenge than 500 South, which was a four lane highway. L86 was a much narrower two lane road that was still flooded in parts. The rain had let up for a few minutes, but the road was still slick with water, which forced me to reduce our speed.

"This should help," Monty said, flipping a switch. "That should make navigating this road better."

The Sandhog immediately experienced greater traction on the wet road, allowing for better steering and driving.

"What did you do?" I asked. "That makes it much better."

"I merely engaged the slick surface feature," Monty said, pointing to the switch. "I imagine it feels much better driving on this wet surface now."

I glanced at him.

"I could've used that function on 500 South, you know."

"That would have been ill-advised," he said with a head shake. "You would have felt more confident in your driving and increased our speed."

"Not necessarily."

"Considering this is your first time driving the Sandhog, that would have been an unwise decision," he continued. "The risks of crashing would have increased exponentially."

"Thanks for that vote of confidence," I said. "Are you saying I would have lost control of Sandy?"

"I'm saying that given the current conditions and the fact that you swerved several times on 500 South trying to avoid traffic, yes, I did notice," he said, "the odds of a mishap occurring on the wider road at an increased velocity were greater."

"You could just say you thought we would've crashed."

"I thought I just did?" he said. "I have complete confidence in your driving skills. However, the Sandhog is a Strongmonte prototype. It's untested and unproven. I'd rather not discover its limitations in an automotive pyre of flaming destruction, if you don't mind."

"And you tell me I watch too many movies?"

"You do," he said. "The turn off for Herrenwies is a few miles ahead on your left. It seems obscured, be watchful. We will be arriving in the middle of the night. That is bound to attract some attention."

"You think?" I asked. "They don't get Lambos driving around this tiny village in the middle of the night? I'm shocked."

"I'll engage the whisper mode once we turn off and enter Herrenwies," he said. "No need to wake everyone up."

I nodded.

"Good plan," I said. "Maybe we can sneak up to this hostel and park Sandy without anyone noticing?"

"Unlikely," he said. "But it's worth an attempt. The turn off is there."

I saw the small sign that indicated Herrenwies. I would've driven past it if Monty hadn't pointed it out. He engaged the whisper mode and the Sandhog went silent.

The only sound I heard was the sound of the tires on the dirt road. Monty pointed ahead and I saw the church. Next to the church was a squat and wide building I guessed was the hostel.

This was a tiny village.

There was only one road in and out of the village. It was paved mostly, but it had branches that were more dirt trail than paved road. We pulled up to the hostel and coasted to the rear of the property where I saw the large door I imagined led to the garage.

We stepped out of the Sandhog and looked around.

Peaches bounded out and stretched. He sniffed the air and shifted into a protective shred mode almost instantly.

<*What is it, boy?*>
<*Someone is here. Can you smell him?*>
<*I don't have your nose. I don't smell things like you do.*>
<*You are my bondmate. You can smell, if you try.*>
<*I'll stick to my innersight, thanks.*>

I focused and felt the presence near the rear of the hostel.

"Someone's close," I said. "I can sense them and Peaches smells them."

"I would imagine it's our host," Monty said. "This is Cecil's idea of being careful."

"What are you talking about?" I said. "Why aren't you on higher alert? Maybe you should finger-wiggle an orb or two, just in case?"

"No need," he said, walking to the large door to the garage. "I know who's waiting for us." He turned to face the large door. "Isn't that right, Pirn?"

Elias Pirn materialized before my eyes.

He was wearing black combat gear which was covered by a black overcoat. He was keeping his energy signature masked, but I could feel the power of the sorcerer from where I stood.

He nodded in our direction.

"Evening, Mr. Montague," Elias said. "Hello, Strong. Seems like there's room for improvement in my masking ability. How did you notice me?"

I pointed to Peaches.

"You can't hide from that nose," I said. "He smelled you way before I sensed you. Hellhounds are amazing that way. I can't speak for Monty, he probably unleashed some mage skill to locate you."

"Nothing so esoteric," Monty said. "After my brief hiatus at Haven, it would be difficult to hide your energy signature from me, Elias. It is good to see you."

"And you, sir," Elias answered and looked down at my hellhound. "How is the scariest hellhound I know?"

Peaches chuffed in his direction.

"He's doing great," I said, extending a hand which Elias took. "What are you doing here? I thought you were supposed to be overseas?"

"Strong, we're in Germany," Elias said with a thin smile. "This *is* overseas from our home base."

"Cecil said you would be elsewhere from here," I said. "Know what mean?"

"I do," he said, rubbing Peaches' massive head. "SNT-SEC has been stationed here to deal with any fallout from your visit to Shadowpeak."

"You weren't supposed to be anywhere near the Black Forest," Monty said, pinching the bridge of his nose. "What fallout are you referring to, exactly?"

"We have reason to believe the creatures populating the Black Forest will not take kindly to your incursion of Shadowpeak," Elias said. "They seem to be connected to the place itself."

"Connected how exactly?"

"We tried to run a scouting op to discern what happened

to the monks," Elias said. "Let's just say it didn't go well. We managed to get two miles out from the target, before we had to pull out."

"What stopped you?" Monty asked. "What did you encounter?"

"To start, ogres, those were followed by an assortment of other nastiness," Elias said. "It was a menagerie of monstrosity. The closer we got to Shadowpeak, the worse it got. I was in danger of losing my team when I made the call to retreat."

"And you're still here, because?" I asked. "Don't tell me you stayed here just to park the Sandhog. Anyone can do that."

"I'm here just in case those creatures try to physically deter your egress from the Black Forest," he said. "They may present an obstacle to your getting back to Baden-Baden Airport."

"You mean they may try to squash us as we try to get away?" I asked. "And you're here to do what exactly?"

"Prevent that from happening, long enough to allow you to get in the Sandhog," Elias answered. "I'm here to buy you time."

"Cecil assured me you would be occupied elsewhere," Monty said, his voice hard. "This sounds like he put you on deterrence duty. I don't see how you intend to be out of harm's way while also buying us time."

Elias nodded.

"I intend to be," he said. "I will be occupied wherever there are creatures attempting to stop you. I fully expect that to be elsewhere from wherever you are."

"Cecil is just being careful," I said, before turning to Elias. "How populated is this part of the Black Forest?"

"How about you get the Sandhog out of sight and I'll brief you on your four mile hike to Shadowpeak?" he said. "I'll get the doors."

He moved over to open the doors with his hands.

"Really?" I asked, surprised. "Why not, you know?" I wiggled my fingers. "Open them that way?"

"Ambient magic this close to the Black Forest sets off some of the more sensitive residents of the Forest," Elias answered. "Better not use any abilities until absolutely needed."

"This is why you were masked," Monty said. "You were keeping a low profile."

"As low as possible," Elias said. "I don't know what is motivating you to go into this section of the Black Forest. I'm not questioning your motives. I know this is an old Montague property and you have your reasons for doing so, but I hope your mask is much better than mine."

Monty nodded.

"We should be able to enter Shadowpeak undetected," Monty said, looking around. "Are you here alone?"

"Yes," Elias said. "Mr. Fairchild felt having too many personnel on site would only attract undue attention. My team is stationed near where 500 South feeds into L86 East. About twenty minutes away."

"Twenty minutes away?" I asked. "That means you'd have to hold off whatever comes out of the Forest on your own, for twenty minutes—alone, before you had any backup."

"Hopefully, it won't take you that long to get in the Sandhog and beat a hasty retreat from here," he said. "If we're lucky, I won't need to hold off anything."

I gave him a look and a short laugh.

"This is us," I said. "With our luck, we'll have the *entire* Forest after us. There's no way you can stop that on your own."

"I don't intend to," he said. "My directives are clear. I'm to buy you enough time to get away, and then I'm right behind you. I'm going back on the same flight you are."

"Good," I said. "We don't leave people behind."

"Glad to hear it," he said, pulling out two packs from the garage. "These are yours. They should have everything you need for your hike. Food, water, supplies, and some extras in case your mask gets compromised."

He pulled out a small map and held it between us.

"We are here," he continued, pointing to a red dot on the map. "Shadowpeak is here." He pointed to a blue dot on the map. "As you can see, there is plenty of real estate between these two points."

"I'm not seeing any roads or trails," I said, peering closely at the map. ""Is that because—?"

"There aren't any," Elias finished. "Correct. It's why you can't take the Sandhog. You'd make it thirty feet before you'd have to stop. Also, the trees in this section of the Black Forest aren't stationary."

"What?" I asked, incredulous. "What do you mean they aren't stationary?"

"Exactly what it sounds like," Elias said. "They move. We tried taking in vehicles on our first sortie, within thirty minutes we lost the trail we had been following and found ourselves surrounded by trees."

"Surrounded by trees?"

"In fact, we had to abandon the vehicles," Elias said. "Another reason you can't take the Sandhog—you would lose it to the Forest like we did with our vehicles."

I glanced over to the edge of the tree line.

"This is really a haunted forest," I said. "Walking through it is fine?"

"See those concentric circles?" Elias pointed to the map. "They start at three miles out from Shadowpeak."

"Areas of influence," Monty said, examining the map. "Can I assume the creatures you encountered became worse as you approached Shadowpcak?"

"Outer circle, not too bad," Elias said. "By the middle circle, we started seeing ogres and something that resembled an ogre, only it was larger and mostly impervious to magic. We never made it to the inner circle."

"Did Cecil inform you of the four days?" Monty asked. "What are you tasked with doing in the event we don't return in the allotted time?"

"I get in the Sandhog and beat a hasty retreat to the junction of 500 South," Elias said. "There I rendezvous with the larger strike team. From there we initiate an exfil for the three of you."

"Let's make sure it doesn't come to that," Monty said, taking the map Elias gave him. "There's no need to put any more lives in harm's way."

"I agree," Elias said. "Mr. Fairchild believes like you do."

"Which is?"

"He leaves no one behind."

SIXTEEEN

After a brief conversation with Elias about the best way to enter the Black Forest, we headed in with our packs strapped to our backs.

"It seems we miscalculated the distance slightly," Monty said. "Probably due to the shifting nature of the Forest. How many miles is it?"

"Four miles to cover the entire distance," I said, remembering the map. "We encounter the first area of influence one mile in, right?"

"Yes," Monty said. "Think of Byron's defenses like concentric circles of deterrence. The outermost circle will warn us off, but not present much of a threat."

"So, we should be okay walking through that circle?"

Monty grew silent as he thought.

"No, I wouldn't underestimate the deviousness of Byron's mind," Monty said after a pause. "Even though it's the lowest threshold of danger, it still poses a considerable danger to us."

"You just said it shouldn't present much of a threat," I said. "Now you're saying it poses a considerable danger."

"The fact that it's the outermost circle means that the

danger is not immediate, not non-existent," he said. "There is danger in all of the circles. The closer we get to Shadowpeak, the more pressing, threatening, and immediate it becomes, but the overall danger has become present from the moment we stepped into this forest. We cannot be lax in our awareness."

"Understood, it's clear and present, just not instantaneous 'melt your face and disintegrate you' danger, right?" I asked. "I mean, it's the outermost circle. How bad can it be?"

Monty stopped walking and turned to look at me.

"The dangers that await us were created by an Archmage, who—according to every record I have read or been forced to memorize—was clearly certifiably insane," he said, as we moved forward. "If he wasn't of sound mind, then his defenses—"

"If you ask me, the words 'sound mind' and 'mage' should never be used in the same sentence," I said. "Present company semi-excluded."

"Thank you," he said with a slight nod. "I have to concur, I certainly have encountered plenty of examples of mages on the fringe of sanity."

"Some of them have gone beyond the fringe," I said. "Way beyond."

"The time and study required to become an accomplished mage is dangerous to a fragile mind," he said. "It breaks most."

"Are you saying Byron had a fragile mind?"

"No," he said. "To achieve the level of Archmage requires incredible mental fortitude. It was afterwards…after he attained the power that his mental acuity began to suffer. The records are vague on what caused Byron Montague's downfall."

"Was it the power?" I asked, concerned since we were

walking into Byron's creation which held immense power. "Did he fall to the temptation of absolute power?"

"I don't know if he was exposed to absolute power," Monty answered, his voice pensive. "As an Archmage, he must have commanded staggering power—I can't see him succumbing to the allure of more power."

"I can," I said, making sure to stay on the trail. "The powerful usually only want one thing."

"More power, true," Monty said. "But as an Archmage, he must have been aware of the danger of walking that path."

"My recent experience with beings of power is that they rarely think they will be tempted by more power—until they fall into the trap of wanting more power."

"Agreed," he said. "Let's make sure we don't commit the same error. We treat each circle—"

"As dangerous?"

"More than just dangerous. Assume *every* circle is the highest threat level," he said. "Keep your every sense on alert. Whenever you can, use your innersight within reason, and remain focused. Four miles may not seem like a great distance, but in this forest it may as well be forty miles through enemy territory. You heard Elias: two miles in, he had to pull his team out."

"Elias is an accomplished sorcerer, and yet he felt overwhelmed," I said "That can't be good."

"What does his action tell us?"

"That we should've taken the Shrike to Bermuda," I said. "Found a nice beach and a hammock. I'm partial to Horseshoe Bay, it has beautiful, pink sand and excellent food."

"Don't forget the hammock."

"Never," I said. "Pink sand, hot sun, calm water, a hammock, and I'm set."

"Somehow, I think they may frown upon a hellhound on their premises," he said. "You may want to reconsider

Bermuda, or *any* populated beach in existence, for the foreseeable future."

"I'd like to reconsider hiking through this scary forest to an even scarier castle or estate, whatever you call it," I said. "Not exactly a fan of the Montague Manor of Massive Monstrosity."

"It's estate, and reconsidering is impossible, as you know," he said. "But I think you may have hit upon the reason—fear."

"Are you saying Elias was scared?" I asked, glancing back to the hostel we had left behind. "He doesn't seem the type to faze easily—even in here."

"I doubt it was fear for his well-being," Monty said. "He had a team with him."

"Which is miles away right now."

"Yet, Elias chose to remain behind," Monty replied. "The fear that motivated him was fear for his team. Their survival, or lack thereof, is what drove him to pull out of the forest. It explains why he is still on site."

"Right, he removes them from the direct threat—"

"Yet opts to remain close by," he said. "Understanding the threat, the power within Shadowpeak presents, he gets his team to safety."

"Relative safety," I corrected. "They are still close to this place."

"Close but not in immediate danger," he answered. "He placed them where he felt they would be safer."

"He feared they would be killed," I said. "Sounds like a healthy fear to me. One I'm growing to appreciate with every passing second in this place—at night, mind you."

"Except *we* don't have the luxury of retreat," Monty said, moving forward. "We walk through the darkness to protect the light. It's what we do, what we have *always* done, and what we will always do. No sense in denying or refuting who we are."

"You know, I don't know if I will *ever* grow tired of these inspiring mage pep talks," I said, shaking my head. "I always feel so invigorated after your morale boosters."

"Mages do not do pep talks *or* morale boosters," he said. "You know this by now."

"True, mages do morale crushers," I said, peering into the night. "I know that much."

"Mages prefer to face things as realistically as possible," he said, keeping his voice low. "It serves no one to approach this task under the illusion that it will be easy or simple."

"Or survivable?"

"Survivable, yes," he said. "Easy or simple, no."

"Easy or simple?" I said. "Those thoughts never crossed my mind. In fact, I think I've eliminated those words from my vocabulary ever since I met you."

"You're welcome," he said, pausing and looking down. "We can follow this trail for some time before we enter the first area of influence."

"Will you know when we cross the outermost circle?"

"I will," he said. "So will you."

"Excuse me?"

"You can't hide in here, Simon," he said, extending an arm to the forest around us. "Your energy signature is quite prominent in this place. It's most likely an effect of Shadowpeak heightening your energy signature. You may not be a Montague mage, but your presence here is quite pronounced."

"Quite pronounced—that sounds hazardous to my health," I said. "Will you be able to mask us?"

"Yes," he said with a sharp nod. "We should be able to approach Shadowpeak itself without being detected."

"That doesn't exactly sound one hundred percent certain," I said. "Should be able?"

"I have full confidence in my masking abilities," he said, pulling on one of his overcoat's sleeves. "However, I always leave a percentage for unknown variables, say, two to five percent. Nothing is one hundred percent guaranteed. Especially not in here."

"So we're at ninety-five percent?"

"I think ninety-five percent is an excellent margin of error," he said. "Don't you agree?"

I gave him a look of disbelief.

"Is there any way we can increase it to one hundred percent?" I asked. "I'm asking for a friend."

"No," he said and paused, holding up an arm. "There are too many variables in play. Ninety-five is outstanding, considering what we're up against."

"While I agree, I also know that the way our luck goes, we are squarely in the five percent chance of chaos and disaster happening."

"Let's focus on the positive, shall we?" he said. "We haven't even reached the outer circle. No need to worry about the worst that could happen *before* anything has happened."

"You seriously didn't just say that," I said, looking around the dark forest. "Really?"

"I'm merely stating the obvious facts."

That was when the high-pitched screech cut through the night.

"What the hell was that, Monty?" I asked, lowering my voice. "Is it time to consider the worst thing that could happen now? I ask, because that sounded high on the list of worst things to run into while hiking through a haunted forest."

"That's...not good," he said.

"What is it?" I asked. "You recognize that screech?"

"Yes," he said, keeping his voice low. "No matter what you see, do not run or make any sound louder than your heartbeat or breathing."

"Louder than my heartbeat or breathing?"

He gestured quickly. Golden symbols floated over to land on Peaches and me. Within seconds, I felt the forest become muted around us.

He raised a finger to signal silence as he gazed into the forest ahead of us. After a few seconds, he began to slowly walk again. He released another set of golden symbols which floated over each of us before disappearing.

I felt my ears pop, as if I had entered a pressurized area and realized that it was now quieter than before, if that was even possible.

"That should allow us to speak without being heard."

"What did you do?" I asked. My voice sounded off as I spoke. "I sound strange."

"I altered the frequency of voices and our sensitivity to them," he said. "It's a short term effect, but should keep us hidden from any creatures that possess heightened senses of hearing."

"You muted us?"

"In a sense, yes," he said. "That doesn't mean we shouldn't exercise caution."

"We can talk, but keep it low?"

He nodded.

"Keep your weapons concealed," he said without turning, his voice barely above a whisper. "I created a wide mask around us, in an effort to diffuse our signatures. If that was what I think it is, I may have to rethink that strategy soon."

"You think?" I said, looking around again. "This is not a friendly Hansel and Gretel vibe I'm getting from this forest."

"The Brothers Grimm were hardly the creators of the friendly fairy tales most seem to believe," Monty said, almost whispering. "For example, the fairy tale of Hansel and Gretel deals with a cannibal witch, who imprisons children in an effort to fatten them up and eat them. Hardly heart-warming."

"You're seriously going there…now?" I asked. "While we're in *this* forest?"

"I'm merely sharing some pertinent information."

"Pertinent to who?"

"Whom."

I stared daggers at him.

"No need to go into the story of Hansel and Gretel—gore and death edition," I said, keeping my voice low. "I'm familiar with the general gist of the tale, thanks."

"By the end of the tale, Gretel kills the witch by pushing her into the oven meant for the children, roasting her to death," he continued, oblivious. "Eventually, they make their way back to their father, having escaped the evil witch and with her riches. Who knows how many countless children she devoured?"

"What you're saying is that the Brothers Grimm were twisted," I said. "How is that ever seen as a fairytale for children?"

"They have worse," he said, lowering his voice and coming to a sudden stop. "Stop moving."

I became absolutely still.

Peaches gave off a low rumble next to me as he dropped lower to the ground, freezing in place too. Monty looked down at him and shook his head. Off to our right, I could hear someone or something trying very hard to approach us silently.

Monty signaled for me to remain quiet as a large panther-like cat crossed several yards ahead of us. It was about twice the size of Peaches and barely made a sound as it sniffed the air around it.

It crossed directly in front of us and stopped for a moment, moving its head from side to side as if scanning the forest. Its entire body was coiled muscle, ready to pounce on whatever it considered prey. Its black coat gleamed in the dim light of the forest, but what threw me were its eyes.

The eyes gave off a milky white glow, which contrasted with the jet-black fur of the creature. A second later, it raised its head skyward and let out an ear-piercing screech that cut through the forest. Then it waited as it scanned the forest again.

My breath caught in my chest.

It sniffed the air for a few more seconds, before continuing to cross ahead of us. Monty had effectively masked our presence.

I exhaled when it stepped out of sight.

"Germany is not known for panthers," I said, barely above a whisper. "Since when does Germany have panthers with glowing eyes?"

"Ever since those creatures occupy the Black Forest around Shadowpeak," Monty said. "We're not even in the first circle of influence, why would it be patrolling out here?"

"Could it be because of Elias and his team?"

"Possibly," Monty answered. "If it's this far out, we must be wary."

"Wary?" I asked, incredulous. "How about petrified, does that work?"

"Not really," Monty answered as we started moving again. "You won't be at your best if you're paralyzed from fear."

"That was rhetorical," I snapped. "What exactly was that? It looked like an extra large panther with a side of mutated monster sprinkled in to make it interesting."

"That was a penumbral feline, more commonly known as

a darkcat," Monty said, his gaze fixed on where the large cat had disappeared. "Dealing with one is dangerous. Fortunately we didn't encounter a claw."

"A claw?" I asked. "We definitely didn't encounter a claw. I would know if I encountered a claw. I don't think we would be this calm if we had. What was with the eyes?"

"A group of darkcats is called a claw," he said. "That was the same screech you heard earlier. Darkcats are technically blind. They hunt by smell and echolocation. I managed to mask us enough to appear invisible to its heightened senses."

"Did Byron—?"

"Create it?" Monty finished, still looking off into the direction the darkcat had gone. "It was well within his capabilities to create or enhance such a creature. I don't know, but let's operate on the premise that he did and act accordingly."

"Is that supposed to make me feel better?"

"It's supposed to make you alert, more alert, if possible," he said. "Darkcats will be the least of our worries once we get closer to Shadowpeak. Let's move on."

He turned and started walking down the trail.

"How masked are we, exactly?" I asked. "How wide is this circle you cast?"

"As long as we maintain a relative silence, we should be able to progress to the outermost circle without encountering anymore of them—hopefully."

"Right, hopefully," I said, turning to look off in the direction the darkcat had come from. "Do you know offhand how many darkcats are in a claw?"

"Three to five," he said. "It's not well documented."

"Why not?"

"Because those who tried to study darkcats usually ended up as victims—dead victims," he said and glanced back at me. "Why do you ask?"

"I think we have company," I said.

"We have what?" he said, turning. "Company? What comp—bloody hell."

I glanced back at the three darkcats that were following us.

SEVENTEEN

"You think they see us?" I said, lowering my voice even more.

"No, I don't think they *see* us," he said. "Which explains why they haven't attacked or attempted to shred us to ribbons. Whatever you do, do not move."

"Oh, really?" I asked, stopping my hand from moving closer to Grim Whisper. "I was just about to attempt a hundred meter dash of death— of course I'm not moving; they look much faster than I am."

"They are and those claws are not decorative," he said, keeping his focus on the darkcats. "They will shred through skin and bone with ease."

"Maybe they can't see us clearly, you know being blind and everything?"

"If they can sense us, then they can 'see' us better at night, in this forest, than we can see with our eyes on a clear sunny day."

"Then why aren't they attacking?" I asked. "Not that I'm hoping they will, I'm just wondering."

"As am I," he said, crouching down. "Perhaps I was

mistaken? Is it possible they aren't sensing us, but some residual energy signature?"

Monty looked around the ground as the darkcats remained frozen in place. A few seconds later, the one in the middle let out an even higher and longer screech than the earlier darkcat we had crossed.

The other two darkcats looked up, sniffed the air and padded off silently into the forest, blending into the dark in seconds. "Can you explain what just happened?" I asked. "What were they doing?"

Monty pointed down at the ground.

I looked at where he pointed and saw a symbol that resembled a six-pointed star. In the center of the star, I saw a rune I couldn't decipher.

"It seems they were sensing this."

"Which is?" I asked. "Because from where I'm standing, that looks like a Star of David. Seeing as how we're standing in Germany in the middle of the Black Forest, I'm going to guess that I may be wrong."

"Yes and no," Monty said, touching the star which gave off a deep blue glow. "Let's move. I'll try to explain as we go."

He glanced at my side.

"You do realize you don't need a holster any longer?"

I glanced down at Grim Whisper. Wisps of black energy rose slowly from the barrel. I didn't know if I was ever going to get used to the new upgrade.

"I know, but I don't want to take a chance forming Grim Whisper and attracting even *more* attention," I said. "It's easier to just keep it in the holster. At least, for now."

"Understood," he said. "At some point you may want to store it internally."

"I will," I said. "Once it stops feeling off. I'm not used to this bond."

He nodded and picked up the pace.

We started moving faster, abandoning the trail to cross through the forest as fast as we could without making much noise. Peaches remained close to me as we moved, barely making a sound. If I didn't sense him through our bond, I would've lost him in the shadows.

As we moved, a cold chill raced across my body.

Monty stopped.

"We've crossed the first boundary," he said. "We're in the outermost circle of Shadowpeak. Let's take a moment to orient ourselves."

He took off his pack and placed it gently on the ground. He was still taking precautions not to make much noise even though we were masked.

"How did that symbol stop the darkcats?"

"It didn't, exactly," Monty explained. "The hexagram has a complicated history."

"I'm sure right now, right here, in this place, it has little to do with the Jewish faith," I said. "Am I right?"

"You are," he said. "The hexagram was only recently appropriated into the Jewish culture; its origins are much older than that. In fact, it can be found in the symbology of Hinduism, Buddhism, Jainism, Islam, early Christianity and more."

"All of those?"

"Yet it predates them all," Monty said. "You need to see past the modern symbology and look deeper. What appears to be a six pointed star is really two interlocking triangles, one pointing up and one pointing down."

He opened his pack and pulled out one of his mage bars, offering me one. I almost took one, when I remembered they tasted like pre-packaged dirt.

"Pass," I said and rummaged as quietly as possible through my own pack. I saw some sausages, pulled out one for my ever-starving hellhound, and took one for myself. "If I want to eat fresh soil, I can just take a handful of the dirt all around us."

"This," he held up the thin bar, "has everything the body needs."

"Only if that body has lost the use of its tastebuds, no, thanks," I said, feeding the larger sausage to my hellhound, careful to keep my fingers attached. "So what do the two triangles mean? I get that the symbol has been around forever, but what is the significance?"

"For mages and magic users it means balance and connectedness," Monty said. "As you know, everything is connected."

"So I keep hearing," I said. "These triangles mean everything is connected?"

"Indirectly," Monty explained. "*Sicut intra, ita extra sicut supra, ita infra.* That is the direct meaning and one of the first lessons a mage must internalize."

"And that means?"

"As within, so without; as above, so below," he said. "It is the guiding principle to all magic and casting, but goes much deeper than that."

"How old is this symbol, exactly?"

"That is unclear," he said, standing and placing the pack on his back again. "Some scholars have it dated to around 77,000 BC, but no one is certain."

"How did these triangles stop the darkcats from shredding us?"

"They're markers, of a sort."

"Markers of what?"

"Boundaries," he said. "I'm not entirely sure as to their purpose, but it seems like the darkcats are patrolling the outer edge of Shadowpeak, but are not allowed to engage in violence near that boundary. I doubt we will be as fortunate, now that we are well within the boundaries of Shadowpeak."

"But you're not certain?"

"I *am* certain any creature encountering us now, that can see through my mask, will attempt to shorten our lives," he said. "Of that, I have no doubt."

"Can't you just…I don't know create a mobile hexagram and trick the creatures into thinking they shouldn't attack?"

"It's not a creature repellant," Monty said. "Hexagrams can't be used lightly, especially not in this place. They are charged with immense power. Are you ready? We should really get moving. I'd like to reach Shadowpeak before sunrise."

"Sunrise?" I asked, surprised. "We have hours and it's only four miles."

"We don't and it's not," he said, pointing to his watch. "Check the time."

"No," I said in disbelief. "Are we in another temporal trap type of thing?"

"Time doesn't always operate linearly in the Black Forest, the same goes for distance," he said. "In fact, you could almost say that Shadowpeak influences time and relative distance in space throughout the Black Forest."

"This is just like the inside of the Shrike."

"On a much grander scale, done more subtly, and with considerably more power," he said as we started walking. "If we're not careful, we could wander the Black Forest for days or weeks, never getting closer to Shadowpeak."

"That sounds fun," I said, "in a hopelessly lost and trapped nightmare scenario kind of way. I'm guessing we wouldn't wander this place without being hunted?"

"Not even slightly," he answered. "We would be hunted, which makes wandering around hopelessly lost quite complicated—and deadly."

"About that," I said. "How are we not getting lost right now? How do you know we're headed in the right direction?"

"I'm a Montague."

"That's it? You're a Montague?" I asked. "What does that mean to us non-Montagues?"

"You remember how reluctant my uncle was about my coming here?" he said. "How he thought it was a bad idea?"

"He was clear about how much he disliked the idea, yes."

"Why do you think he finally gave in?" Monty asked. "He could have refused my offer. Could have used his position as my elder and shut the whole idea down. Why didn't he?"

"He's growing soft in his advanced age?"

"Uncle Dex is many things, soft is not one of them," Monty said. "It had to be a Montague because the physical location of Shadowpeak calls to those of the bloodline."

"The place *calls* to you?" I asked. "Are you saying only Montague mages can find Shadowpeak?"

"No," he clarified. "Powerful mages that are not from the bloodline can locate Shadowpeak, but it's easier for my family. We do not get lost in the Black Forest."

"Because Shadowpeak pulls you?"

He nodded.

"Yes, there is a definite pull from the presence of Shadowpeak."

"How strong is this call?"

"It's a fairly constant tug in a specific direction," he pointed ahead. "In that direction."

The question I needed to ask was on my lips, but I hesitated, fearing the answer.

I asked anyway.

"How strong is this pull and is it getting stronger?"

Fine, it was two questions, but they were important.

"Strong, but not overwhelming," he said. "And no, it's not getting stronger, nor is it overpowering my ability to think for myself."

"At least for now."

"I anticipated the pull will increase and I have taken measures to prevent any further influence," he said. "I do have mental shields in place. That pull is how we aren't getting lost in this Forest."

"It's probably why Elias had to retreat," I said. "He's not a Montague. Wait a minute."

"Dex mentioned that the rest of your family wasn't tripping over themselves to come to this place," I said. "Is that why? They wouldn't be able to resist the tug of Shadowpeak?"

"It's complicated," Monty said. "His exact words were: *It's not like Montagues are falling over themselves to go investigate Shadowpeak. Not everyone is keen on rushing to their deaths like you two.* The allure of Shadowpeak is the power it contains."

"It's really a death sentence?" I asked. "I mean you're already feeling the tug and we aren't even close. Will you be able to resist the call of the power?"

"I will and I have you and your hellhound in case I can't… Aspis," he said. "Besides, the alternative is roaming the Black Forest until we grow old, well until I grow old and you have to bury me in here somewhere."

"That's a depressing thought."

"Which will not happen," he said. "I just mentioned that it was the alternative to finding and entering Shadowpeak, or would you prefer to wander about lost, for days, weeks, or even years?"

"Wandering around lost and getting killed sounds much worse than trying to secure a haunted house," I said. "Even if the house is trying to kill you."

"We will do what we must," he said. "Right now, that means picking up the pace while remaining silent."

He gestured again and another layer of silence fell on us.

"Is this safe?" I asked as we picked up the pace. "I can't hear any of the ambient noise around us. We won't be able to tell if anything is sneaking up on us."

"The cast only mutes the sounds *we* create," he said. "You don't hear any ambient noise, because there isn't any to hear. Most of the creatures that inhabit the Black Forest operate by stealth out of self-preservation."

"There's always something bigger, stronger, and nastier in the Black Forest?"

"That would be fairly accurate," he said. "How about we don't run into any of those?"

"I'm on board with that plan," I said. "How far did Elias and his team get?"

"Two miles," Monty said. "About half-way in before they needed to extract from the Forest. Why?"

"Do your teleports work in here?" I asked, giving this idea some thought. "I know you said it was a bad idea, but is it only *your* teleports, or *all* forms of teleportation?"

"All teleports?" he said, glancing at me. "Have you suddenly acquired the ability to teleport?"

"No, not me, Peaches," I said, pointing at my hellhound. "Do you think he could blink us closer? Instead of one major teleport, he could do a series of smaller ones. Would that work?"

He paused and looked down at my hellhound.

"I'm not well versed in hellhound abilities, capabilities or limits, but it sounds like a solid theory," he said. "The only downside would be that we have no way of testing it. We either go all in or not at all."

"Why can't we test it?"

"The moment he does his first 'blink', which I assume entails carrying us with him, correct?"

"Yes, the whole point is to get us all closer to Shadowpeak before sunrise," I said. "If he goes alone, that would be bad, I think—mostly for us."

"Agreed," he said. "Well, once he attempts the first teleport, the outlay of power it would require to transport all three of us, even across a short distance, would alert most of the denizens of the Forest."

"Most of them?"

"As I said, I'm not entirely familiar with hellhound capabilities," he said. "Using my own ability as a baseline—if I attempted to teleport all of us, even a short distance, it would require a significant amount of power. It would be similar to lighting a beacon in the middle of this dark forest."

"Not good," I said. "We would attract all kinds of attention."

"No and yes," he said. "No, it would not be good; yes, we would attract all kinds of attention to our *current* location."

"That is exactly what I just said."

"Our current location," he repeated, ignoring my comment. "If it works, our current location would only be current for a few seconds, before we appear elsewhere."

I saw what he meant.

We could blink and even if we attracted the entire Forest, they would always be one blink behind us as we moved closer to Shadowpeak.

"But it hasn't been tested," I said. "This is beyond risky."

He nodded.

"True," he said. "It's a matter of which risk we want to undertake. Walking through the Black Forest using the best methods of stealth we can, without knowing if a creature that can see through my mask dwells in here, or—"

"Blink as fast as possible to Shadowpeak."

"Exactly," he said. "There are some things to consider. Is it possible, and if so, can he take all of us, and for how long?"

"Those are important considerations," I said, glancing at my hellhound. "Life and death even."

"There are more variables," he said, holding up a finger.

"Of course there are, why would I even think this would be easy or simple?"

"Can he do only one teleport?" he asked. "If it's only one, would that get us ambushed later rather than sooner?"

"I don't know, in fact I don't think he knows either."

"Or, if it's only one, can he take us all the way to Shadowpeak?"

"Too many variables," I said, shaking my head. "If Elias and his team made it two miles or roughly halfway, maybe we should attempt the same, and then try to blink the rest of the way?"

"It's a risk either way," he said. "I think we should try to get as far as we can while masked. Then once we cross into the innermost circle, we attempt your creature's method of teleport."

"What if it doesn't work?"

"We'll find that out soon enough," he said. "Along with the rest of the Forest who will arrive at our location to inform us of the folly of our ways as violently as possible."

"Very encouraging," I said, shaking my head. "You really should consider demotivational speaking. I'm positive you'd be great at it."

"I don't think I would find it very inspirational," he answered. "My heart wouldn't be in it."

"Oh, ha ha," I said. "Mage humor strikes again. I'm practically rolling on the ground with laughter from that answer."

"I thought that response was quite clever, if I do say so myself."

"Humble too," I said. "Will wonders never cease?"

"Of all the wonders that I have heard, it seems to me most strange that men should fear; seeing death, a necessary end, will come when it will come."

"Did you just Bard me?"

"I thought it apt, considering our present situation."

"Can we avoid the necessary end part for now?"

"It somewhat defeats the entire purpose of the...bloody hell."

"Defeats the entire purpose of the bloody hell?" I asked, confused. "That makes no sense."

He came to a sudden stop in front of me.

It was so sudden I nearly crashed into him.

"What the—?" I started and lost my words when I looked past Monty and gazed at what he was looking at. "What is that?"

Monty was looking up into the face of a monster.

EIGHTEEN

"It appears to be an ogre of spectacular dimensions," Monty said, taking a few steps back. "I don't think I've ever encountered an ogre this size."

"Or this ugly...wow."

The ogre turned to face me, narrowing its eyes as it glared in my direction. Monty was right, though. Outside of a troll-gre, I had never seen or faced an ogre this size.

"That...was quite rude, human," said the ogre as it kept staring at me. "My name is Obun the ogre."

"It speaks?" I said, shocked. "Since when do ogres speak? I mean besides, the usual: time to die or variations of the same message?"

"Since now, apparently," Monty said, without taking his eyes off the ogre. "You are capable of speech, how is this possible?"

"You smell," Obun said, looking at Monty. "A powerful smell."

"Now who's being rude?" I asked. "You just go around accusing people of smelling?"

"You smell of Montague," Obun said, ignoring me and

focusing on Monty. "A Montague...have you come here seeking death?"

"I smell of Montague?" Monty asked, his words pensive. "You know my family?"

"I do," Obun answered. "Many of your kin have died in this Forest. Many more have died inside Shadowpeak. Are you seeking death?"

"No," Monty said. "How do you know about Shadowpeak?"

"The First Montague formed me and shaped my tongue," Obun said. "Then he gave me words and power."

"Words and power?" Monty asked, entering professor mode, when I felt he should be entering unleashing armageddon mode. "He taught you to speak?"

"Yes," Obun said. "Then he gave me understanding and power."

"Monty, not really liking where this conversations is going," I said under my breath as I stood next to him. "Who is the First Montague?"

"I would assume it would be the first Montague it encountered, I would hazard Byron Montague," Monty answered under his breath, then raised his voice. "What was the name of the First Montague?"

"Byron Montague *is* his name," Obun said. "He formed me to protect the land around Shadowpeak. Why have you come?"

"*Is* not was," Monty said mostly to himself. "Why speak of him in the present tense."

"Does it really matter?" I asked. "If we keep this up, we are going to be past tense."

Monty raised a hand and remained focused on the enormous monster in front of us. He tapped his chin and took a step closer to the towering wall of muscle that looked anxious to get to the ripping and the shredding.

"You said he gave you power," Monty said, avoiding the ogre's question. "What power did he give you?"

"The power of Shadowpeak," Obun said, raising a hand and forming a flaming orb of bright orange in his open palm. "The power to protect and destroy. Why have you come to Shadowpeak, scion of Montague? Why are you here?"

"Monty, it just formed an orb," I said. "This ogre can...cast?"

Monty narrowed his eyes at the ogre, before glancing at the bright orb of imminent pain and destruction floating in its gigantic hand.

"This is not a typical ogre."

"What gave it away?" I said, taking a few steps back with Monty. "The orb it just formed, the fact that it can *smell* your Montagueness, or was it that we're here having a chat with tall, dark, and scary? Maybe you should offer it some tea and what do you call them—indigestives?"

Monty shot me a 'don't be completely foolish' look before returning his gaze to the ogre.

The ogre that was holding a flaming orange orb of energy.

"All of the above," he said. "I think the key is in the question."

"What question?" I asked, as Peaches rumbled next to me and I could, for the first time feel my hellhound gathering power. "I think it may be time to answer it with some darkflame rounds."

"No," Monty said, raising a hand to stop me. "Let me answer it first. If I answer incorrectly, we may need more than darkflame rounds."

"You only upgraded Grim Whisper to fire darkflame rounds," I said, staring at the oversized ogre. "I'm not carrying nuke rounds."

"You'd be surprised at the potency of darkflame rounds."

"Considering the size of this ogre, I hope you have something stronger than my darkflame rounds, if this takes a turn for the lethal."

"I think I know how to deal with this," he said, motioning for me to remain where I stood. "It's part of the lore of Shadowpeak. Byron created a fearsome sentry to control the entry to Shadowpeak. This must be it. If so, it's hundreds of years old, fascinating."

"You know, that's really amazing, this ogre being ancient and all," I said never taking my eyes off Obun. "You know what would be truly fascinating? Getting the ogre to leave us alone without ripping limbs from our bodies…that would completely captivate me."

"There is much to learn here," he said looking at Obun. "This is part of my family's legacy. If he wields the power of Shadowpeak, it means Byron bestowed this power upon it. That deserves further investigation."

"Of course it does," I said, shaking my head slightly. "I really hope you know what you're talking about."

He was still in semi-professor mode, wondering at the presence of Obun the ogre, designed to crush and maim, and given the power of words and casting to make its job easier. I was wondering when all hell would break loose, and we got to the part where we fought to stay alive.

"Why have you come here, Montague?" Obun the ogre asked again, its voice booming through the forest. "Have you come here seeking death?"

Monty took a few steps forward and faced Obun squarely. As a fighting stance, it was horrible; as a dying stance, it was perfect.

"I seek answers, for the deaths of the Guardian Monks placed to guard the property. I am here to secure the power dormant inside Shadowpeak," Monty said with conviction in his voice. At least he sounded like he knew what he was doing. I was just waiting for the giant fist to come swinging his way. "Weigh my words and see the truth."

"Monty, is that a good...?"

He raised his hand again and motioned me to silence. I kept my hand on Grim Whisper just in case things went sideways and Obun decided to smash and crush us to paste, right after it flamed us with that nasty orb of power.

Obun's eyes started glowing a deep green as he gazed at Monty. After a few seconds of the ogre X-ray, Obun nodded.

"Your words weigh true," Obun said. "Follow me."

I did a double take.

"Did it just say 'follow me'?" I asked. "Follow it where?"

"Closer to Shadowpeak, I assume," Monty said as we followed the enormous mobile mountain of muscle. "It's quite possible Byron created more than one sentry."

"More than one?" I asked, glancing up at Obun. "Why would he need more than one of these sentries? It's an ogre that can *cast*. One is more than enough."

"For centuries, mages and monsters have died in this Forest," Obun began, unprompted. "Both have sought the power within Shadowpeak. Only the blood of Montague is allowed inside."

Monty's expression darkened.

"We are all mages and monsters in our own way," Monty said his voice low. "It would seem there is no shortage of blood being spilled in the Black Forest."

"That sounds like I can't enter the special death club," I said. "I could always wait outside, it's probably safer outside."

"Rubbish," Monty said, waving my words away. "Obun, what of my companion? He is a brother to me, and I would have him enter Shadowpeak as well."

"He is not a Montague," Obun said, stopping to turn and face us. It gazed at me for a few seconds and then nodded. "You share a bond of brothers, yes. He may enter, but will be judged by his actions as a Montague. You will be mirrors to each other."

"What does that mean?" I asked as Obun turned around and kept walking. "Mirrors to each other."

"It doesn't seem open to conversation," Monty said. "I'm sure we can figure it out on our own. For now, we should keep pace."

After what felt like an hour, but was probably closer to thirty minutes, Obun stopped and turned again.

"The home of the monks lies to the East from Shadowpeak," it said, pointing off to the side. "To determine what ended their lives, you must venture into Shadowpeak."

"*Into* Shadowpeak, why?" Monty asked. "They lived outside of Shadowpeak."

"In the Black Forest, there is *nothing* outside of Shadowpeak," Obun answered. "If you wish to know what killed them, you must enter Shadowpeak."

"I have a question," I said, raising a hand. "Is that okay or do I need to have Montague blood to get information?"

"Ask, bond brother," Obun answered. "I will answer what I can."

That sounded vaguely specific.

"The thing that killed the monks, is it a being of magic, like you, or is it a human like us?" I asked. "Just so we know what we are up against."

"It is neither," Obun said and narrowed its eyes at me as they started glowing a soft green. "I *see* you. You are not entirely human, neither is the Montague Mage."

Neither? What was that about not being entirely human? I mean I understood the concept, but what exactly did it see, that made it answer that way?

"How much farther to Shadowpeak?" Monty asked since we were still standing in the middle of forest. "How much longer to the estate?"

Obun looked at Monty with some confusion in its eyes.

"You are *in* Shadowpeak," Obun answered, looking around. "All around you is Shadowpeak. You merely need to speak the words of command and it will appear to you—if you can."

"And if he can't?" I asked. "I mean what if he doesn't know these words of command?"

"Then he is not a Montague and he will die here," Obun said, gazing from Monty to me. "As will you and your hellhound, bond brother."

"Ah, got it, no pressure," I said, glancing at Monty. "I hope you know these words."

"I will return in the allotted time," Obun said.

"How long is that?" I asked. "Is there an actual time frame?"

"If the light of the sun rises upon you, or the encroaching darkness envelops you outside of Shadowpeak, you will never enter its walls...alive."

"That's some invitation."

"Thank you, Obun," Monty said as the ogre nodded in our direction. "Will we see you again?"

"Only if it is time for you to die," it said. "Think deeply on your words. You have only one opportunity to use the words of command."

"What happens if he gets it wrong?" I asked. "Does he get to revise his answer?"

"One opportunity, bond brother," Obun said. "An incorrect command activates the protective measures of Shadowpeak."

"Which I'm guessing are lethal?"

"You guess correctly."

Obun turned and walked into the Forest. For such a large creature, it was amazing how silently it moved. In seconds, it faded from sight into the shadows of the Black Forest.

"I'm not looking forward to seeing it again," I said.

"Considering it would mean our demise," Monty said as he took off his pack, "neither am I."

"I guess the most obvious question is: do you know these words of command?" I asked, taking off my pack as well. "Is this something they teach all the baby Mage Montagues as they grow up?"

"I have an idea what they may be," Monty said. "I also happen to have learned several words of command in my mage studies."

"That sounds like a bad thing—why does that sound like abad thing?"

"Potentially," Monty said. "I would have to eliminate the obvious ones, and filter all the words that have a direct link to my family *and* Shadowpeak."

"That doesn't sound so bad," I said. "How many potential words of command does that leave?"

"Not many," he said. "Only about one hundred words and phrases."

I stared at him for a few seconds.

"You only have one chance at this."

"I am aware," he said pulling on his sleeves. "There is no room for error."

"We're going to die, then, aren't we?"

"We have until dawn," Monty said. "I'm sure I'll figure it out before then."

"Don't forget the encroaching darkness," I said. "Do you know what it meant by that? It doesn't seem to make sense."

"I would imagine the darkness of the night, though it does sound somewhat vague," Monty said. "If the light of the sun rises upon us, or the encroaching darkness envelops us outside of Shadowpeak, we will never enter its walls alive. Does sound ominous. Unclear, yet ominous."

"Welcome to the Black Forest," I said. "Is it possible it meant a different kind of darkness?"

"What do you mean?" Monty asked, glancing at me. "What kind of darkness?"

"It said *encroaching* darkness, right?" I asked, looking into the Black Forest. "That means creeping or advancing darkness. How would we even see something like that? The pitch black night in the forest gets darker? Is that even possible?"

"Bloody hell," he muttered. "Encroaching darkness is not just darkness, it could also be referring to a Tenebrer—a bearer of darkness."

"This Tenebrer…is it currently a resident of the Black Forest?"

"Yes, I'm afraid so."

"How bad is it?"

"It was documented that during the Supernatural war, some of the Archmages unleashed an encroaching darkness," Monty said. "They were later classified as Tenebrer—creatures of darkness and were banned toward the end of the war as inhumane."

"Banned? Why?"

"It was a creature of darkness that was mostly impervious to magical weapons and attacks."

"A perfect weapon against mages, then."

"Indeed, its method of attack, aside from the physical destruction, was particularly devastating," he said as his expression darkened at the memory. "They would launch psychological attacks, driving mages to commit unspeakable acts of atrocity. Every victim ended up insane, their minds twisted and completely lost."

"Tenebrers drove mages crazy?"

He nodded.

"It was irreversible," he said. "Killing the mages was the only mercy that could be offered. They were too dangerous alive, turning into agents of death and destruction—if we didn't stop them."

"Holy hell," I said my voice low. "That sounds horrific."

"It was mostly hell, there was nothing holy about facing those monsters or what they did to their victims."

"You faced these Tenebrers?"

"More than once, barely escaping with my mind intact each time," Monty said. "Not a creature I want to face again—or ever."

"How do you stop them?"

"The simplest way is light," he said. "They abhor light, the brighter the better. I can't believe I didn't see that reference from Obun."

"Well, to be fair, you *were* having a productive discussion with an orb-casting ogre who could hold a deeper conversation besides 'I will rip your arms off and beat you to death with them,'" I said. "It was easy to get distracted, but if these Tenebrer hate light,"—I looked around the forest—"we are standing in the wrong neighborhood."

He nodded.

"Creatures of darkness in a place like the Black Forest would thrive," he said. "This is a perfect irony, when I think about it."

"Perfect irony?"

"It was rumored that the first Archmage to create a Tenebrer was—"

"Let me guess, Byron Montague?"

He nodded.

"It was never proven, of course, but there are strong indicators that the rumors are based in truth," he said. "Which is why it's not surprising to find them here in the Black Forest and near Shadowpeak."

"Fine, all we need to do is create large amounts of light—

say Luxor Lamp level," I said. "Can you do that with your finger wiggles?"

"First, no," he said, giving me a look that asked me if I had suffered a head injury recently. "Second, expending large amounts of energy right now would only attract the wrong attention. Even though Obun could see through my mask, it would be unwise and potentially lethal to dispel with it entirely."

"We need to stay under the radar?" I asked. "What about the Tenebrer? Would they see through your mask?"

"Yes," he said. "They are impervious to most magic, that includes offensive *and* defensive casts."

"Like a mask."

"Exactly like a mask," he said. "You and your creature can both produce light. I need to recall these words of command. Can you keep watch?"

"How much time do we have?"

"Not enough to engage in conversation—keep watch," he said. "I need to access these words of command, I will be right back."

"Be right back?" I asked, looking around the forest. "Where are you going?"

"Into my mind library," he said as he sat down on a patch of grass. "This will proceed faster if you could limit any interruptions."

"Will do," I said. "Try not to get lost in there."

He crossed his legs and closed his eyes. He slowed his breathing and seemed to enter a deep meditative state. A few seconds later, he was surrounded by a soft golden light as he started floating several inches above the ground.

I didn't know he could do that.

Peaches nudged my leg, nearly ripping my hip out of its socket as he let out a low rumble next to me. I looked down and let a smile cross my lips. I rubbed my hellhound's head and looked into the night.

<Hey, boy. We have to keep Monty safe.>

<He is safe. Is he tired? Does he need a nap? Why is he glowing?>

<No, he doesn't. He's looking for some information.>

<By taking a nap and glowing?>

<He's not napping, he's accessing his mind library. I think the glow is part of the process.>

<Where is his mind library?>

<In his mind, in a space in his head.>

<His head is not very big. How many books can he have in his head?>

<Not literal books, information. He is accessing information he has learned. He needs words of command to open the way to Shadowpeak.>

<I could speak. That can open many ways.>

<Usually by destroying everything in front of your bark. No, I think he needs actual words this time, not a sound that will obliterate everything—like your words.>

<My words are mighty like me.>

<I know. Right now our job is to keep him safe until he finds those words in his head.>

<There are many smells in this place. Some of them are bad.>

<I can imagine. Once Monty finds his words we can go into his family home and get out of this Forest. You let me know if any of those smells are getting closer.>

<Can I bite them?>

<No. This entire place is dangerous and I don't want you getting separated from me. I did want to ask you something, though.>

<You want to know how to become mighty? You must eat more meat, then you will get stronger. Once you are stronger, you must face dangerous monsters, like I do. Then you will become mighty—like me.>

<Thanks for the mighty tips, but that's not what I wanted to know. Do you know how far you can blink carrying another person?>

<I can walk in-between very far. With another it is harder, but I can go far. If you were mighty, I could explain it to you.>

<Meaning you can't explain it, because I don't understand hellhound speech?>

<Because you are not strong enough in our bond yet. Once you get stronger, you will understand me without words. This takes time, many years will pass before you get that strong.>

Wonderful, basically my hellhound was calling me dumb in the nicest way possible. It made sense though; when he hit XL, his speech level rose as much as his body expanded. Even in our battleform, his speech was becoming more and more elevated.

I figured it was only a matter of time before he didn't have to dumb down his speech so I could understand him easily.

<Are you calling me dumb?>

<No, you are very smart, just not very strong.>

<So, you're calling me weak.>

<Yes, as my bondmate, you are still weak. But I will help you become stronger—don't worry. One day you will be almost as mighty as I am.>

<Almost as mighty?>

<You are not a hellhound. You can be mighty, but never as mighty as me. I will still help you.>

Tact and nuance was lost on my hellhound.

It was a lost cause to try.

<Thanks, I appreciate it.>

<You are my bondmate. You do not need to thank me.>

<Still, I appreciate you making me almost as mighty as you.>

<The smells are getting closer.>

<Good ones or bad ones?>

Who was I kidding? We were in the middle of a haunted forest; there were no good smells in here. I let my hand rest on Grim Whisper as Peaches entered 'maim and shred' mode.

A low rumble escaped him.

<Bad ones.>

NINETEEN

<How many?>

<Too many to count.>

<Can you tell what kind of bad smell? Do they smell like darkness?>

<What does darkness smell like?>

He looked up at me and gave me a 'what kind of question is that?' kind of look. Which, coming from my hellhound, was a mix between confused and worried.

Not an easy look to pull off.

He was probably worried I was losing my mind, not a totally inaccurate assessment.

I guess I'd have to wait until I could qualify for my position of Zen Master which would let me ask questions like: *Do they smell like darkness?*

<How bad do they smell? Can you give me a range here?>

<Very bad. Biting bad.>

Okay, that was officially a threat.

I drew Grim Whisper.

<No blinking and no biting. If I tell you to use your fire bark or laser beams, you use only that, nothing else. Got it?>

<I understand.>

I heard the whispers first.

It was like hearing voices in the wind, except there was no wind. The forest had become still…too still.

At first it was just voices, loud enough to hear, but too low to make out distinct words. It was a jumble of words hovering at the edge of my understanding, like hearing a conversation from a distance.

"A Montaguuuue," one voice said. "He seeeeeks us."

It was bad enough I was standing in a haunted forest, now I had to deal with disembodied voices.

This was getting better by the minute.

I glanced at Monty, who still floated above the ground with his eyes closed. I didn't dare to interrupt him while he was browsing his mind library. I could only hope this mind library didn't come equipped with a cafe where he could sit and have a cuppa, while I faced whatever it was I was facing out here in the real world.

"He's not looking for any of you," I said into the night. "Why don't you go back to wherever it is you came from?"

Peaches let out a low growl next to me as I saw his eyes start glowing a deep red.

<Not yet, boy. Wait until they show themselves.>

"Where we came froooom?"

Laughter erupted all around me.

This wasn't the infectious kind of laughter where you couldn't help but join in out of reflex. No, this was the laughter that froze your blood and jumpstarted the fight or flight response, heavy on the flight.

"You are in our hoooome, human."

"Not human, otherrrr."

Great, now I had shadows calling me something other than human. Not that I had an issue with it, well, I *mostly* didn't have an issue with it. I enjoyed being human, but I was realizing it was becoming a liability given I moved in the world of creatures, monsters, and gods.

"That's right," I said, raising my voice slightly. "I'm an Other, which means I can kick your ass if I have to. So back off, no Montague snacks for you."

"He has powerrrr," another voice said. "Delicious powerrrr."

I was now on the menu, fantastic.

They all sounded alike, yet there were inflectional differences. One voice emphasized the ending consonants while the other opted for the middle vowels.

I don't know how my brain picked up on it, since it should have been thinking about exit strategies at this very moment, but there was no way I was leaving Monty alone to whatever had chosen to come pay us a visit.

"Power I will use to blast you to bits if you don't leave."

More laughter.

I slowed my breathing and began to focus.

I didn't know what I was facing.

The odds were great it was a Tenebrer or more than one. I had options, aside from my hellhound unleashing his baleful omega beams throughout the forest.

That would be a last resort.

The last thing I wanted to do was start a forest fire in a tree-dense area like the Black Forest. The destruction would be cataclysmic and I would have no way of putting out a fire on that scale, outside of a stormblood, which required the assistance of the glowing mage currently floating several inches off the ground in a deep meditative state.

I had never tried to contain my magic missile in orb form —actually I had, but I still recalled the Strix Experiment. Orbs and I were not friends, they had a tendency to want to fly away from my hands, not hover in my palms quietly.

I did have an idea to minimize any potential damage, but

that required whatever had decided to pay us a visit to show itself.

"Show yourself," I said into the forest. "You will not touch this Montague without facing me first."

A short burst of laughter followed by a low growl…that was *not* from my hellhound.

I know, I checked.

"You think you can face ussss?" the voice said. "Stupid childddd. We were old, when this forest was young. What do you think you can do against the power of darkness?"

I noticed the distinct change in speech, which concerned me. Not that I was an expert on monsters, or creatures of darkness, but when the voices that were previously softly murmuring and whispering, suddenly became clear and resonant, it meant trouble.

Trouble for me, that is.

"The power of darkness," I repeated, standing closer to Monty. "Is that what you are? Are you a Tenebrer?"

"A foolish name given to us by those who did not understand what they faced," it said. "We are darkness and shadows. We are the hidden desires of the heart, the thoughts and acts that lay buried and covered so deep that even you would deny their existence."

"I'm going to take that as a yes."

"We can show you," it said, its voice tantalizing. "We can show you what you *really* want. We offer you *true* freedom. You can do *whatever* you want, all you have to do is surrender."

"To you?" I asked. "You want me to surrender to you?"

"No," it said and I realized how dangerous this trap was. "Surrender to yourself. We can only give you what you possess. Surrender to us and we will show you what it is. Come closer."

I'd like to think I was the living example of virtue, but I

would be lying. For a few seconds, I was tempted and took a step toward the voice.

My world blossomed in pain, centered around my leg as I froze where I stood. I looked down to see my hellhound's jaws clamped around my thigh, preventing me from moving.

He gave me a quick shake for good measure and brought me back. I shook my head into clarity. The voice was some kind of cast. I should have expected something like that.

<*Do not listen to them. They lie.*>

I patted my hellhound on his oversized head and wondered why he didn't get affected.

<*Thank you, boy. You can declamp from my leg, I won't listen. I'm good.*>

He let go and I saw the figures hovering near the trees.

"Nice try," I said. "You almost got me. You used an auditory cast."

"Almost?" it said. "You are in the Black Forest. There is no escape for any of you."

It moved forward and I saw it appeared to be a large shadow in a vaguely human shape. There were no distinct features except for the glowing blue eyes.

"Give us the Montague and the hellhound," it said. "We promise to make your death swift. The destruction of your mind will be without pain."

"You know," I said, stepping even closer to Monty as I pulled my hellhound to me, "that sounds like a great deal, but I'm going to have to go with a hard no. You get no one."

"Stupid child, what could you possibly do against the darkness in this place?" it said as it started getting closer. "I am all around you."

"You are?" I said, noticing the change in pronoun. "*You* are all around me?"

"Yes, I am," it said. "And I will destroy you."

"Come try."

TWENTY

The darkness coalesced in front of me.

"A little closer," I murmured to myself. "Just a little closer."

The Tenebrer floated over as I took a few steps to the side. It changed trajectory and tracked me, exactly as I wanted. When it changed from 'we' to 'I', I figured it had condensed its consciousness into one form with a connection to the darkness around us.

This meant it could be trapped and extinguished.

I didn't think I could defeat it completely, but I could bruise it by giving it a bloody nose, figuratively, and send it packing or at least make it stay away until Monty came back.

It closed on my position as I shifted even more, away from Monty. When I felt I was far enough, I stopped moving and it raced at me.

It was nearly on me when I cast my dawnward around us. My violet dome of light exploded into being around us as the Tenebrer screamed with what I hoped was pain and rage.

<Now, boy! Hit it with your beams!>

Peaches unleashed his baleful glare into the center of the

Tenebrer, blasting a hole in its body. I focused energy into my body and whispered.

"*Ignis vitae*," I said the words as I shoved my hellhound out of the dawnward. "Move!"

He let himself be shoved out, as my magic missile exploded inside the dawnward. The explosion brightened the forest for a few yards in every direction.

The screams filled the forest all around us.

"The darkness fills the night, Other," it said as it retreated. "We are never far."

"I don't care if you're not far, just stay far away enough from us."

I heard fading laughter.

In that moment, I used my innersight to scan the forest and noticed that the shadows, the ones that were unnatural, were retreating away from us.

I had no doubts about what happened.

All I had done was buy us some time. My dawnward-missile attack was the equivalent of rapping it across the nose with a stick of light.

"I'm really glad that worked," I said to no one in particular. I noticed my hands were shaking slightly, before I formed fists to stop the shaking. "You'd think I'd be used to this sort of thing by now."

I looked around and noticed my hellhound next to me.

<Stay close to Monty, boy.>
<Where will you be? I go where you go.>
<I know. I'm going to be close, but if they attack me, I don't want to be close to Monty when they do. He can't protect himself right now. We only convinced them it was a bad idea to attack…for now. They may change their mind.>
<If they change their mind, I will speak with flames.>
<Not unless we have no choice. We're in a forest. If you flame the

trees, we are in serious danger. No flames unless you have to, understand?>

<I understand. Can I speak normally?>

I didn't think the word *normal* could ever be applied to a hellhound, but I wasn't going to dwell on it, not while I had hungry shadows in the forest.

<I don't see how sound will work against a shadow, but sure, we can try that if they get close again.>

<If we face them again, we will have to use our battleform.>

<That would make us super popular in this place. Not a good idea. We're supposed to be hiding or at least laying low.>

<We cannot lay low and protect the angry man. The shadows will return. I cannot bite shadows, but I can destroy them.>

<Again, that would attract more attention than we want.>

<What do you think you did?>

<Excuse me? I did?>

He sniffed the air.

<You exploded light in the dark forest. That will attract more bad smells.>

Well, damn.

He had a point.

<Fine, if we get more guests, we go into our battleform to deal with the threat. How long can you hold it?>

<I need meat.>

<I know. One sec.>

I rummaged through my pack and found more sausage which I gave him. He inhaled the meat in record time, as I shook my head in surprise.

<Is that enough?>

<No, but it will work...for now.>

<Is it ever enough?>

<I am a growing hellhound. There is never enough meat for a growing hellhound that is mighty. To be mighty means I must eat plenty of meat. Meat is life.>

<I don't know why I even ask.>

<Because you are not mighty. When you become mighty, you will not have to ask.>

Another growl, this one louder, filled the forest.

"You have got to be kidding me," I said, glancing at Monty. "What is it now?"

I looked off into the distance and saw a pair of bright yellow eyes looking back. Not exactly surprising considering where I was, except that these eyes were a good eight feet off the ground and headed my way.

It was hard to tell what it was, until I used my innersight.

Then it was hard not to run away in the opposite direction. We were being approached by what appeared to be a large black wolf. Part of my brain saw it as a wolf. The other part, the part that had processed ogres and talking shadows, knew this was no ordinary wolf.

In fact, this wolf had left ordinary so far behind it was firmly standing in the mind-melting area of my brain as I tried to make sense of what I was seeing. I took a few steps back as Peaches stepped in front of me, letting out a low growl in response.

The immense wolf stopped and sat on its haunches, staring at Peaches and then, slowly turned its piercing gaze to look at me.

Peaches slowly increased in size until he matched the size of the wolf in front of us. I had never seen him alter his size this way. It was usually done in a battleform, or when he went Peaches XL.

Both modes were fast, not gradual transformations like what I was seeing right now.

The wolf growled again and then let out a short bark, which Peaches echoed, adding a low growl of his own.

"You would sacrifice your life for this human?" the wolf said, its voice low and dangerous as Peaches growled again.

The fact that it spoke took me completely off-guard. "Bondmate?"

The wolf looked at me for a few seconds.

"You are bonded to this hellhound?" the wolf continued, focused on me. "Stand before me, human."

I realized it meant that it wanted me to step closer, something I definitely did not want to do.

<*You must get closer, bondmate.*>

<*Not the best idea. Do you see how large this wolf is?*>

<*Yes, my eyes are working.*>

<*And you want me to get closer?*>

<*If you do not get closer, he will get angry. If he gets angry, he will attack. He is as strong as my sire. It will be bad to fight him. I will not win and you will get hurt. I do not want you to get hurt. Step closer.*>

<*Strong as your dad? I think I'll step a little closer, then.*>

Against every instinct in my body, I took a few steps closer to the monster wolf that stood still, looking down at me approach. I took special note of the fangs I could see, and the long claws that dug slightly into the earth.

Even if I could run, how far could I get? It looked like this wolf could catch me in a bound and tear me to shreds without much effort.

The wolf continued to look at me as I approached.

Its yellow eyes gave off a soft glow as it stared. I could feel the incredible energy signature around the wolf and realized that it drew energy from the Black Forest itself.

The energy signature was vaguely familiar; it felt like standing too close to an angry Kali—raw, primal, and overwhelming.

"Why are you here, hellhound-bound?" the wolf asked me. "This land is dangerous for you and your hellhound. You must leave."

"You can speak," I said, still surprised. "I didn't expect—"

"Do you always state the obvious?" it said. "Of course I can use the primitive method of communication you call speech. It would be too much to expect that you communicate in my tongue."

"I meant no disrespect," I said, figuring it would be a bad idea to anger the very large, intelligent wolf. Time to break out the tact and diplomacy. "I can't leave."

"You can't or won't?"

I pointed to Monty.

"Can't," I said. "Not until he finishes."

The large black wolf narrowed its eyes at Monty.

"A Montague?" it said with some surprise in its voice. "You are staying by his side voluntarily?"

"Yes," I said. "What do you mean, 'voluntarily'? How else would I be staying by his side?"

"Do you not understand the words I am using?" it asked. "Are you here of your free will? Or does the Montague coerce you to remain by his side with magic?"

"He is my friend—and brother," I said. "Why would he coerce me?"

"It has happened in the past with other Montagues after the power of Shadowpeak," it said and gazed at me hard. After a few seconds, it shook its head and rumbled. "You speak truth. You share a bond of brothers."

"That's what I said," I answered. "What would you have done if he was coercing me?"

"I would have ended your life where you stood—a small mercy—followed by ending the life of the Montague," it said. "As I have done in the past. Not all Montagues were honorable, and power...power twists the minds of men—especially when those men are mages."

A thought crossed my mind.

"Did Byron Montague make you too?" I asked, wondering

if this was another situation like Obun. "Did he give you the power of speech?"

A low growl escaped the wolf and I realized I may have made a fatal mistake in my tact and diplomacy strategy.

"Byron Montague?" it asked. "*Make* me?"

It growled again and Peaches returned a growl.

"I meant no insult," I said, raising my hands in surrender, "it's just that we ran into an ogre that could speak and cast—"

"Obun," the wolf said with contempt. "*He* is a creation of Byron Montague. I wandered these woods before Byron Montague was a pup. I was here when the foundations of Shadowpeak were formed and I roamed the night when Byron Montague, First of the Mages of the Order, imbued Shadowpeak with his power. No Montague *made* me. I was, before any Montague entered this land. Now, hellhound-bound, tell me why you are in *my* forest."

"This is *your* forest?"

"My name is Udolf. Do you understand the significance of this name?" it asked. "Do you comprehend the power you face?"

These comments were unlike the many times I faced megalomaniac mages trying to convince me of their innate greatness. No, these words were being said the way a master informs the beginner of how outclassed they are.

It was merely stating facts.

I was standing in front of incredible power I couldn't grasp.

If I gave it the wrong answer, there was a good chance it would shred me on principle alone. I opted for advanced tact and hoped it didn't get me killed.

"No, sorry, I don't," I said, making sure I kept some distance from the enormous wolf. "Does it mean fearsome wolf?"

"I will excuse your lack of knowledge, because of the limitations of your kind," it said. "It means *wolf ruler*. Where *exactly* do you think I rule?"

It lowered its head a bit and narrowed its gaze as it asked this question.

I looked around cautiously.

"The Black Forest seems to be the most logical answer."

"Correct. You are not as simple-minded as you appear," Udolf said, raising its head. "Now to my question. Why are you in *my* domain?"

I looked over to where Monty hovered.

"We need to enter Shadowpeak," I said. "Monty needs to get inside and secure the power that lies inside the estate."

"Monty?" Udolf asked. "Who is Monty?"

"Tristan," I said, pointing at Monty, before turning back to the intimidating, oversized wolf. "Tristan Montague. I call him Monty."

"And he allows this?" Udolf asked. "Is he not a mage?"

"Yes, he is a mage," I said. "One of the best I know."

The wolf took one step forward, causing mini-tremors in the forest all around me as it focused its piercing gaze on me.

"Does he not understand that names have *power*, that names *are* power?" Udolf asked. "Why does he allow this twisting of his name? Is his mind addled?"

"We are bonded as brothers," Monty said from behind me, nearly giving me a heart attack as he stepped close. "He means no insult to me, my family, or my status as a Montague mage."

"I see," Udolf answered. "For what purpose have you entered my domain, Mage Montague?"

"To ensure that it remains your domain," Monty said from behind me. "Well met, your Majesty."

Monty gave the wolf a short bow.

"A Montague with manners who remembers the old ways,"

Udolf said, returning Monty's short bow with a nod. "Explain your words, are you implying my domain is in danger?"

"There is no external threat that could challenge your sovereignty," Monty said. "This threat comes from within."

"From within?" Udolf said, narrowing its eyes at Monty. "From where, exactly?"

"From the only place that could present a threat to your power and domain," Monty said. "The threat comes from within Shadowpeak."

TWENTY-ONE

"Shadowpeak," Udolf said the name with thinly veiled anger. "You give me veiled truths and twisted words. Speak true, Montague, or look clearly around you, for this will be the last scene your eyes see."

Monty stepped forward and stared hard at the large wolf. Either he had found some new power in his mind library, or he had lost what little mind he had left and had come back choosing violence and death—ours.

"The threat to your domain comes from *within* Shadowpeak," Monty repeated. "The failsafes have fallen and killed the Guardian Monks which kept it in check."

"Failsafes and guardians placed by Montagues," Udolf answered, the menace in its voice growing. "Are you here to claim the power? The power your ancestor unleashed in my land?"

"No," Monty said. "I lay no claim to this power."

"You refuse your birthright?"

"It is true, this power was placed by Byron Montague," Monty said. "And it is also true I have a claim to it."

"Yet you refuse?" Udolf said. "A mage refusing power?"

"This power is not mine, though I have a claim to it," Monty said. "Every Montague that has tried to appropriate this power has failed. I will not be the next in a long line of deluded mages, even if it was my bloodline which poisoned this land—your land, your Majesty."

Udolf remained silent for a few seconds then growled.

"Your words weigh true, scion of Montague," it said. "What is your purpose here, then? Why have you come to my domain?"

"I must secure the power in Shadowpeak before it causes irreparable harm, or another tries to claim it for themselves," Monty said. "I must discover what killed the Guardian Monks."

"Do you have the words of command?" Udolf asked. "Shadowpeak will not appear to you without the words of command. Being a Montague is not enough. You must have the words and command the power that lies dormant within."

"I have the words."

"You do?" I asked, surprised. "Really?"

Monty nodded.

"I have a very good guess," he said under his breath. "If I'm wrong, we won't be here to discuss my error."

"You have only one opportunity, Montague," Udolf said, taking another step forward, placing Monty firmly in chomping range. "If you utter the wrong words of command, they will be the last words to escape your lips. Your life will end here."

"No pressure," I muttered. "What happened to giving you three chances?"

"Three chances?" Udolf echoed and growled as it shook its head. "A Montague needs only one opportunity to prove they are a Montague."

"How do you expect him to know these words of

command?" I asked. "He's not from here and he's never met Byron Montague."

"Irrelevant," Udolf said. "Montague blood runs in his veins. If he fails the command, his blood will flow into the forest floor."

"Simon, there is no negotiating here," Monty said. "I have one opportunity. I'm fairly certain I have the words I need."

"Fairly certain?" I asked, giving Monty a 'you can't be serious look'. "I'm fairly certain if you get this wrong, we get to die a few seconds later."

"Yes," Udolf answered. "Though your demise will be interesting to witness, Deathless one. How many deaths will it take before your goddess appears, I wonder?"

"You know?"

Udolf cocked its head to one side and looked at me.

"Did you think you could hide your signature from *my* eyes?" Udolf asked. "I am older than the oldest trees around you, older than the land that sustains this forest, human. You may have power, but it will not save you, if the mage fails to command Shadowpeak's presence."

I glanced at Monty.

"I really hope you found those words in your library," I said. "That sounds like a good inscription for a tombstone: he had power but it didn't save him."

"If I get this wrong, there will be no tombstones," Monty said, lifting up my spirits in a way only a mage could. "He would end us instantly. Only the memory of us would remain."

"I'm feeling so much better about this now, thanks."

"You're welcome," he said, pulling on his sleeves, then focusing on Udolf. "I am ready."

"Very well, Montague," Udolf said. "I will guide you to Shadowpeak's location. Speak the words and summon the estate…or perish."

Udolf turned and started walking into the forest with us in tow. Peaches returned to normal size as we followed the huge wolf.

"I'm getting serious 'do this or die' vibes from everything in this forest," I said, keeping my voice low. "First Obun, now Udolf. What is with these warnings?"

"It's the old ways," Monty said. "This place is designed to dissuade outsiders, even those from my family. Being a Montague wasn't enough to get into Shadowpeak, as I'm sure you've noticed."

"I've noticed," I said, keeping my eyes on Udolf ahead of us. "I'm noticing you also need a healthy amount of psychosis to even attempt this. No wonder Dex was against you coming here."

Monty shook his head slightly.

"Not psychosis, exactly," Monty said. "Confidence and resolve. Your will must be unshakeable. You must believe in your capacity and ability as a mage. Without all of that, well, it never ended well for those who only came here seeking power."

After some time—it made no sense trying to gauge exactly how much time had passed in this place—I only knew we had been walking longer than ten minutes and shorter than two hours, give or take.

Udolf came to a stop in front of a large clearing and growled again, motioning forward with its snout, pointing to the open space ahead.

"This is where the words of command are spoken," Udolf said, sitting on its haunches, motioning to a spot on the ground. I noticed that the spot it indicated was a large hexagonal-shaped slab of black stone. "Stand there, Montague."

I looked at the hexagonal slab and saw the white runes all along the edge. The stone was polished to a mirror finish and seemed to disappear into the night with only the glowing runes marking the boundary of where the stone ended and the forest floor began.

"Can you read those runes?" I asked as Monty looked down at the stone. "What does it say?"

"Do you really want to know?"

"Depends," I said, glancing at the stone. "How bad is it?"

"Very," Monty said, still glancing at the runes on the stone. "The usual warnings about failure meaning death, annihilation, and complete destruction."

"That's all?" I asked. "That's the fine print on everything we do, isn't it?"

"More or less," Monty said. "I won't bore you with details, except to say that these conditions apply to us, and your hellhound, according to our bond."

"No exemptions?"

"None."

"Is it too late to renegotiate this whole thing?"

"It was too late the moment we stepped into the Black Forest," he said. "Do you really want to?"

"What and miss the tour into the extremely-out-to-kill-you haunted mansion?" I asked, giving him a look. "Who would want to pass up that opportunity of a lifetime?"

"Most, if not all, of my family," he said, his voice dark. "They will not come to our aid. In fact, no one will come to our aid should something go wrong."

"Cecil has an exfil plan in place, doesn't he?" I asked. "Four days and he arrives to get us out?"

He sighed and glanced into the forest.

"I care deeply for Cecil, he's family to me," Monty said, "but on occasion, his assessment of the danger of a situation is somewhat misguided. If we aren't out of Shadowpeak in four days, it would be better to unleash my uncle on the place, not wait for Cecil and his rescue."

"That's sounds like you're saying no exfil."

"That is exactly what I'm saying," he said. "Cecil is powerful in his own right, just not when it comes to storming a castle—especially not Shadowpeak. It's too strong for him."

I looked down at my hellhound and rubbed his oversized head, then glanced up at Monty, before looking over to the wolf of imminent destruction sitting close by.

"We're much stronger these days," I said. "Who would we count on to come save us anyway? We're in the middle of the Black Forest, being guarded by Udolf the Uberwolf, no one could aid us, I think, even if they wanted to. This isn't something new, we call this Tuesday."

He nodded.

"True," he said. "I just want you to know—"

"Nope," I said, cutting him off. "Get the words right and get us into Shadowpeak. No heartfelt expression of gratitude until we're sitting in that hammock on that pink beach, someplace warm without supernatural creatures."

"Your hellhound is a supernatural creature, by the way," Monty pointed out. "You plan on leaving him behind?"

"Never," I said, scratching behind Peaches' ears. "Wherever I go, he goes. He gets an exemption. Now stop stalling and let's do this. Rip off the bandaid and get to the commanding."

With a nod, he stepped onto the hexagon of black stone.

TWENTY-TWO

The runes erupted with white light.

It was so bright that for a few seconds I worried it would signal to all of the creatures in the forest that this was where the buffet was taking place, by sending a rune-signal into the sky.

Then I remembered Udolf.

It didn't matter which creature in this forest could see the light from the runes—Udolf's energy signature increased as the light intensified.

If I was a resident of this forest and sensed that energy signature, I would be looking for the farthest edge opposite of that power to inhabit.

There was no way I would be getting closer to come investigate what this light or energy signature was. I would stay far, far away.

Which is where I wanted to be right now.

I looked at Monty who was bathed in the white light from the edge of the speaking stone. I saw the runes start to shift and move around the six edges of the stone.

He closed his eyes as the energy around him increased.

It was slow at first, but started to pick up speed with each passing second. The runes started moving faster and faster until they were a blur of white light around the edge of the stone.

The light flowed upward and then crashed into Monty, impaling him from six directions at once, slowly lifting him off the stone.

His eyes were still closed, but I could see the power coursing through his body. The sheer pressure of the power made me take a few steps back.

Even Peaches, who was usually unmoved by the displays of power, moved back to stand next to me. Only Udolf remained where it sat, undisturbed by the explosion of raw power all around us.

Monty's eyes shot open and beams of white light shot upward as he screamed. I didn't dare take a step forward because in that moment I knew a few things: There was nothing I could do to stop this process—it had to play itself out to the end. Also, if I tried to stop this process, there was a good chance something painful and final would happen to me, making sure I couldn't stop or interrupt the process.

All I could do was watch.

Watch and hope.

Hope that Monty would survive this and hope that he knew the right command words. Actually, it was more a hope that he knew the right command words, or survival was off the table.

A few moments later, Monty stopped screaming and the beams from his eyes had become a bright glow. He looked down, since he was still floating about four feet from the stone, and Udolf let out an ear-splitting roar.

Not a bark, not a growl, an actual roar.

"Speak, Montague!"

"*Sicut supra, ita infra,*" he said in an otherworldly voice that reverberated all around the forest. "*Lux et tenebrae sunt una.*"

I held my breath.

As above, so below. Light and darkness are one.

It sounded good in my head, but I didn't know if these were the words of command we needed. For all I knew, these would be the last words I heard before Udolf erased us from existence.

Udolf took a step towards Monty and I reflexively let my hand drift to Grim Whisper. I didn't know what I was going to do exactly. Even with darkflame rounds, I doubted I would do more than annoy the enormous wolf, but if these were the wrong words, we weren't going down without a fight.

"Stay your hand, hellhound-bound, the mage has spoken true," Udolf said. "He *is* a Montague."

"It took all *that* to prove he was a Montague?" I asked, still keeping my hand close to my weapon. "You could've just asked me."

Udolf stared at me for a few seconds, before returning its gaze to Monty, who was still trapped in a column of light.

"Why is he still in there?" I asked. "You said those were the right words."

"Shadowpeak must appear before he can be free," Udolf said. "It must phase into this plane, then the command stone will release him."

"What would've happened if he got it wrong?"

"The mage would have perished shortly after giving the wrong command," it said, giving me a glance. "You would have died shortly thereafter. Your hellhound…he would have been banished from this land."

"Banished?" I asked, somewhat surprised. "I thought he would have been eliminated?"

"He is a hellhound," Udolf said. "If I could send him back, I would."

"That wouldn't end well either," I said, glancing down at my hellhound and rubbing his head. "He doesn't exactly get along with his sire."

"Nevertheless," it said. "I would prefer to remove him from this land rather than end his life. As a hellhound, he is a distant relation to my kind. I would not take his life."

It was good to know Udolf wouldn't kill Peaches, at least not directly. Sending him back to the Gates of Hades would probably be a death sentence, but at least he had a chance at survival if Hades managed to get involved.

The fact that there was no such consideration for Monty or me did bother me a bit, but something told me that filing a formal complaint with the large, menacing, and powerful wolf would be a mistake.

I opted to keep that thought to myself.

I was about to mention how quiet the forest was, when I felt the first tremor. The ground began to shake and I noticed cracks in the ground began to form.

"Shadowpeak?" I asked as I hung onto a nearby tree to keep from being thrown. "Is it going to destroy the forest?"

"It is phasing into this plane," Udolf said, walking across the shaking ground unbothered. "Brace yourself."

Udolf walked a few feet away from Monty and stood looking out over the clearing. There was nothing there except plenty of open space.

In an instant, the column of light exploded, sending beams of light in six directions, as Monty descended slowly to the ground. I ran over to him and he staggered forward a step.

He leaned on me as he regained his balance as the tremors calmed down. An undercurrent of power filled the area with a low-level thrumming.

"Looks like those were the right words," I said. "How did you know?"

"I didn't," he said, keeping his voice low. "Those were the words that made the most sense, considering our situation."

"You guessed?"

"It was an *educated* guess," he said with a slight nod, "but yes, still a guess."

"You would've died, we would've died, if you had gotten it wrong."

"I know, but it was a risk I had to take," he said and placed a hand on my shoulder. "Thank you for standing with me."

"No worries," I said, glancing at the wolf. "He was kind enough to inform me that if you had messed up and used the wrong words, he would've dusted us, but, my hellhound, he would be banished, not disintegrated. Isn't that nice?"

"I don't know if *nice* is the word I would use," Monty said, glancing at Udolf. "I suppose he is taking into consideration your creature's lineage and the fact that he is a hellhound."

"That's what he said," I answered. "We had a nice chat while we waited for you to finish your light show."

"A nice chat?" he said, still staring from me to Udolf. "Somehow, I find that unlikely."

"Fine, it wasn't much of a chat," I said. "I don't speak the superwolf language and I think he holds having to speak English against me."

"That seems more likely."

I looked past Udolf into the clearing.

It was still dark, which made it hard to see much of anything.

"You sure you used the right words?" I continued, peering into the darkness. "I'm not seeing anything."

"We wouldn't be here to have this discussion if I had used the wrong words," Monty said, pointing ahead into the clearing. "Use your innersight—gradually—or your brain may recoil at the image and send you into shock."

"Send me into shock?" I said as I used my innersight in stages. First, I kept my vision low to the ground. As I let more of it take over, I began to see the estate. "What the actual—?"

The large estate began to materialize before my eyes.

At first I didn't understand what I was looking at, but slowly the image came into focus. Shadowpeak was a wide, squat building about three stories tall, shaped as a hexagon. On each point of the hexagon, stood a tower.

The entire estate was made of a dark stone which glimmered in the night with violet accents. The speaking stone rested on an elevated section of land, and we were looking down at Shadowpeak from where we stood.

I know Monty had called it an estate, but I was looking at a cross between a stronghold and a castle. Shadowpeak looked like it should be defending something.

Except we were standing in the middle of the Black Forest.

Once it came fully into view, I felt the power wash over me in waves. It wasn't oppressive, but there was no ignoring the presence of deep ancient power coming from the castle.

"That's—?" I started, pointing at the castle

"Shadowpeak," Udolf finished. "Gaze upon your home, Montague."

Monty walked up to where Udolf was sitting. I followed reluctantly with my hellhound by my side.

"That is my family's estate, but it is not *my* home," Monty said, turning his head to the side. "Where did the monks live in relation to Shadowpeak?"

Udolf turned its head and pointed with its snout.

"They were housed in the first tower on the right," Udolf said, completely throwing me off. "From there, they kept guard on the runic receptacle in rotations."

"Wait a minute," I said. "I thought the Guardian Monks

lived outside of Shadowpeak? In some other building? Not in one of the towers."

"Some did, yes," Udolf said. "At every determined interval of nine days, the three monks who were inside Shadowpeak, would exit and be replaced by three others. Always three to maintain the balance—which has been lost since their deaths."

"How long has the receptacle remained unguarded?" Monty asked. "How long do we have until the imbalance destroys Shadowpeak and the power is released?"

"Six days it has been left unguarded," Udolf said. "That leaves—"

"Three days," I said. "What happens in three days?

"The rite of sealing must be performed," Udolf said, looking at Monty. "Montague, you have three days before this place must be sealed away from this plane."

"When you say sealed away—?" I started.

"The power within Shadowpeak must be contained off this plane," Udolf answered, turning to me. "The monks were not mages, but they *were* attuned to this land and this place. They kept the power in check. With their absence, the power, unchecked, will destroy Shadowpeak, then the Black Forest, then—"

"It doesn't stop, does it?" I asked, understanding what it was trying to say. "If the power isn't checked, it just keeps going and destroying everything in its path."

"Worse, Deathless," Udolf said, turning to face Shadowpeak. "It is out of balance and will corrupt everything it touches, first, then...it will obliterate this plane."

"The entire plane?"

Udolf looked away from Shadowpeak to stare at me again.

"If the power escapes the runic receptacle, even I will not be able to contain it," Udolf said, its voice low and ominous.

"It will devastate this plane, eventually corrupting and destroying it…all of it."

"Damn," I said, looking at Monty. "Isn't this one a little above our paygrades? I mean shouldn't we get the divine division in on this whole 'plane destroying prevention plan'? I mean it's just us. Are we enough?"

"We will have to be," Monty said. "The condition hasn't changed. It still needs to be a Montague."

"I know one Montague that is much stronger than the both of us put together," I said. "I vote for calling Dex."

"We can't."

"Can't or won't?"

"He cannot," Udolf said. "Dexter Montague did not speak the words of command. He cannot help in this matter, despite being a Montague. Shadowpeak would not respond to his presence."

"It was the same mistake many mages made trying to get access to the power of Shadowpeak," Monty answered. "That error cost them their lives."

"Is that why it killed the mages who tried to take it?" I asked. "It was corrupted power?"

"No," Udolf said. "It killed the mages because *they* were out of balance with the power they tried to usurp. Even those of the bloodline had little understanding of what they were trying to do. They only sought to take, forgetting that as it is above, so must it be below, as it is within, so must it be without. Everything has a cost that must be paid."

I looked at Monty, hoping to express that I understood nothing of what Udolf had just shared, except the last part. I understood that part, about how everything had a cost.

"Is that another type of command to access the power inside Shadowpeak?" I asked. "What does that mean?"

"The mage can explain it to you," Udolf said. "I urge

haste. Time flows in its own way inside the Black Forest. It would be best not to waste any of it."

Monty nodded.

"Thank you, your majesty," Monty said with another short bow. "I will strive to fulfill my duty as a Montague and secure the runic receptacle to prevent any harm coming to this land."

"You have three days, scion of the Montagues," Udolf said. "If you have not succeeded by then, Shadowpeak will be sealed away in outer darkness. Whether you are sealed away with it, depends on your will and the choice you must make. Choose wisely."

Udolf turned and began walking away, disappearing into the night a few moments later.

"Choose wisely?" I asked, turning to Monty. "What did it mean by that?"

"I thought that was fairly self-explanatory," Monty said as he started heading toward Shadowpeak. I remained where I stood. Monty glanced back at me. "Do you plan on staying there?"

"What did he mean about choose wisely?"

"In order to secure the runic receptacle, there is a chance, a slight one, that I may have to...run the gauntlet," he said, pulling on a sleeve. "That in itself is not inherently dangerous. It's what can occur during the gauntlet that poses the major threat."

"Run the gauntlet?" I said in disbelief. "You said we were *not* going to run the gauntlet. Dex warned us against running the gauntlet. Why are we running the gauntlet?"

"He warned us, and yet, he gave me this," Monty said, showing me the Radiant Star around his wrist. "The only reason for giving me this was to survive the gauntlet."

"How did I know we were going to run this gauntlet

thing?" I said, giving him a hard stare. "Why do you have to run the gauntlet? Just seal this receptacle remotely."

"First, there is no such thing as remotely sealing the runic receptacle," Monty said. "If such a thing existed, we wouldn't need three monks on site constantly. There is a chance you may not have to run it with me."

"You must have lost your mind," I said, staring at him." That light show"—I pointed to the command stone—"did it microwave your brain? I'm not leaving you to run the gauntlet alone. We all run it or it doesn't get run. Just tell me *why* we have to run it."

"In order to uncover what happened to said monks, I need to run the gauntlet," Monty said. "I have a suspicion that whatever killed the monks originated with the gauntlet."

"In the gauntlet?"

"Inside Shadowpeak—the runic receptacle to be precise," he said "It's quite possible one of the monks managed to tap into the power of Shadowpeak and became corrupted, which resulted in the deaths of all the monks."

"They weren't mages," I said. "How would they tap into the power?"

"They were still at risk," he said. "It was why they were rotated out every nine days, to avoid any contamination. Something must have happened, something that shouldn't have happened."

I looked over to Shadowpeak, where it sat giving off death vibes.

"What exactly is in this place?"

"There's only one way to discover that," Monty said, glancing over at Shadowpeak. "We need to go inside. Are you coming?"

"Like I have a choice."

"There is always a choice," he said. "Even when it feels like there isn't one."

He turned and we started to walk toward the main entrance.

TWENTY-THREE

We stopped in front of the enormous main entrance.

The door gave off definite 'storm the castle' vibes. It looked ancient and weathered, but was also polished and impressive in its age. I could tell it was old, but there were no marks or damage on the door itself.

It appeared to be entirely wood, which surprised me. Usually these ancient doors had some metal keeping them together. That was the other odd thing—this door wasn't made of pieces of wood joined together.

As far as I could tell, it was one large slab of material.

That seemed impossible, considering the age of Shadowpeak.

"What is this door made of?" I asked. "Is this Australian Buloke?"

The door looked like wood, but I could feel something different about the 'wood'. It gave off a powerful energy signature of 'try to get by me, and see how short your life will be' kind of energy signature.

"Not normal Buloke, if there is such a thing," he said.

"This door is made from the trees of this very forest. It is much stronger than Australian Buloke, holds more runic properties, and I think, is the only door in existence made from Black Forest wood."

I glanced at the door again.

The feeling was bizarre.

It felt like it was daring me to try and breach it.

I shook my head to clear my thoughts.

"What is it?" Monty asked. "You sensed something?"

"You won't believe me if I told you."

"Try me."

"It feels like this door is daring me to try and break it down," I said. "I know that sounds crazy, but for a moment, I had this brief feeling of blasting it with a magic missile."

"No," he said, glancing at me. "That's not crazy. Has the feeling passed?"

"Yes," I said, glaring at the door suspiciously. "What was that?"

"What you felt were the runes—the antagonistic runes—inscribed into the door," he said. "They're designed to prompt an attack on the door. A short-lived and fatal attack."

He pointed to several sets of runes spaced out around the surface of the door.

"Antagonistic runes?" I said. "It wanted me to attack?"

"And die in the process," he said. "It's a failsafe to weed out the more impetuous of the visitors."

"What would've happened if I had attacked?"

He pointed to a set of runes, one on each corner of the door.

"You see these sets of runes?"

"I see them but can't make out what they mean."

"I'd be surprised if you could, these are protorunes dating back to the formation of Shadowpeak," he said. "These four runes are called reverberating runes. They would take your attack, amplify it, and then reflect your now considerably stronger attack back at you."

"How much stronger would the attack be?"

"I've never had the opportunity to study the amplification process, but my uncle mentioned it once that the increase is exponential, something to the power of ten."

"Not ten times more powerful?" I asked, surprised. "You mean it's multiplied by itself ten times?"

"That would be what exponentially to the power of ten means, yes," he answered. "It would be fatal, if you used a magic missile."

"Why did I feel that urge?" I asked. "Not being a mage and all."

"You do wield power," he said, glancing at the door. "I don't think Shadowpeak makes a distinction."

The entrance was large enough to allow the massive Udolf to walk into Shadowpeak with room to spare. The door was covered in runes that gave off a soft violet glow in the night. These runes were beyond me, which I figured was due to their age.

"Are most of these protorunes?" I asked, pointing at the door. "Can you read these?"

"Yes and no, I can't read most of them," Monty said, shaking his head. "Apparently these runes were inscribed by Byron Montague himself. I can only read the inscription above the door. I'm sure you can, too."

"I doubt—"

"Try it," Monty said, pointing to the runes above the door. "Those are not ancient."

I looked up at the runes above the door.

For a few seconds, it was indecipherable. Then, slowly the words shifted and began to make sense.

"As above, so below?" I said as I read the runes out loud. "As within, so without. I think that's what those runes say."

"Precisely," Monty said, looking at the runes. "However, the words of command alluded to light and darkness being one."

He tapped his chin.

"That part isn't here somewhere?" I said. "Maybe on another part of the door?"

He looked around the entrance, carefully examining the runes.

"I'm not seeing it elsewhere, perhaps it's inside?"

"I understand the concept," I said, looking at the runes above the door. "I mean loosely. I don't get how it applies to being a mage, since you know—that's not what I do, or am."

"Understood," he said. "I'll try and explain."

"That would be helpful," I said. "In English and not magespeak."

"I am currently speaking English."

"Sometimes, you use words that are in English, but mean something completely different than what I expect."

"I'll use small words and simple concepts."

"Both would be appreciated."

He pointed to the runes above the door.

The only runes I could read.

"At its core, this statement is an expression of connectedness and balance," he said, joining his hands together and stepping into full-blown professor mode. "Every mage understands this principle inherently. It is what allows us to tap into power, to cast, and to manipulate energy."

"What about that part Udolf mentioned about being out of balance with the power?" I asked. "The part that killed the mages coming here?"

"That," Monty said as his expression darkened slightly, "is more complicated. In order to tap into the power of Shadowpeak, a mage must be aligned to the power in the runic receptacle."

"The power which is neither good nor evil," I said. "*That* power?"

"Normally, I would agree with you," he said, glancing at the door again. "But when it comes to Shadowpeak, I think the mage in question needs to have faced whatever darkness may lie within, and be reconciled with it."

"Are you saying this place is evil?" I asked, concerned. "That it requires darkness to access the power?"

"No," he said, shaking his head. "I'm saying that this place —Shadowpeak—will see through any deception, especially self-deception."

"You can't pretend to want the power for good, when you really want it for yourself," I said, following Monty's gaze with my own and looking at the door. "If you try and grab the power while lying to yourself, it blasts you to nothingness?"

"I don't know if it's *that* extreme."

"What if I'm evil, and I'm okay with being evil, meaning I've made peace with my evilness," I said. "Then I come here and I have no illusions about why I'm here. I want the power to further my evil plans in the world. Would it let me tap into the power?"

"I...I don't know," he said, his voice pensive. "Presented that way, I would think you would be able to access the power. Leaving Shadowpeak with the power would be another matter entirely."

"How many evil Montagues are there in the world?"

"In the world?" he asked. "Why do you ask?"

"You mean aside from the scenario I just presented with an evil Montague mage coming here, tapping into Shadowpeak and growing powerful enough to take over the plane?"

"Yes, besides that scenario," he said, looking at the edge of the door. "Why are you asking about evil Montagues?"

"Something Udolf said," I answered. "It asked me if I was by your side of my own free will."

"Why did it ask you that?" he asked. "Did you appear to be under duress?"

"Not to my knowledge, but it made reference to other Montague mages in the past. Its exact words were: Does the Montague coerce you to remain by his side with magic?"

"And you said?"

"No, why would you coerce me?"

"I wouldn't."

"Udolf said it had happened in the past with other Montagues after the power of Shadowpeak."

"I have no reason to believe Udolf is lying," Monty said. "I'm certain there were some unscrupulous mages in my family that attempted to attain the power within these walls, using duplicitous tactics."

"Udolf ended them," I said. "It said their minds were twisted by the pull of the power and they were retired permanently."

"Power has a way of doing that," Monty said, standing in front of a section of the door. "Not all Montagues were honorable."

"That's what Udolf said."

"It was right," Monty said, placing a hand on the side of the door. "It wasn't the only one that had to cut the lives of some mages short due to what happened at Shadowpeak."

"You...?"

"No," he said, touching several runes in sequence. "My Uncle, or rather, the Harbinger."

"Well, shit."

"Indeed," he said as the door slowly swung inward. "I told you, attaining the power was only half of the goal. The mage in question also had to leave Shadowpeak with the power...alive."

"You opened it?"

"I'm a mage with power," he said. "Shadowpeak will allow us entry."

"It's the exit I'm concerned about."

"As am I," he said. "Let's go."

We stepped into Shadowpeak.

TWENTY-FOUR

The reception area of Shadowpeak was as grand as I expected.

Outside, the dark stone gleamed with an inner light, blending the violet and black. Inside, it was an entirely different feel.

Warm lighting filled the reception area, which was mostly empty except for some low lounges along the walls. Most of the space was dominated by a large rug and portraits on the walls.

"This is the minor reception room," Monty explained. "The Grand Reception room is upstairs."

"This is minor?"

"Minor as in smaller," Monty clarified. "Not minor in the sense of importance. In fact according to my studies, this room was used more than the Grand Reception room."

"These paintings," I said, pointing to some of the large frames hanging on the walls, "are any of these of Byron?"

Monty looked down the room to an oversized painting of a fierce-looking man that stood glaring at the painter. His body was bladed to one side and he wore a violet cloak over a dark ensemble of what looked like riding clothes.

The family resemblance was incredible.

I glanced at Monty for a moment, before looking back at the portrait. Byron looked like a Monty that had focused all his spare time in the gym. He was tall, broad-shouldered and imposing. The most telling Montague feature was the hair.

He wore his hair exactly like Monty, going for the long, disheveled, 'never touched by a brush or comb' look. Monty made it look stylish, Byron made it look dangerous.

This was not an Archmage I would ever want to face.

"Byron Montague," Monty said, motioning with a hand. "I can only imagine the level of composure needed by the artist to paint that portrait."

"If I was that artist, I would've retired after that painting," I said, gazing at the large painting of Byron Montague. "He looks upset. Has anyone ever told you that you look like… what exactly is he to you? Your great great great great—?"

"Ancestor, and yes, it has been mentioned that I bear a striking resemblance to Byron," he said, gazing at the portrait. "Especially the hair."

"I wasn't going to say anything, but the hair and scowl are very Montague," I said. "Smiling every so often isn't going to hurt, you know. Your face can handle it."

He scowled at me in response.

"It's my understanding Byron Montague had a spectacular resting murder face," Monty said, walking down the room to stand in front of the painting which towered over the floor. "He was not a pleasant man."

"I kind of get that impression from the scowl of irritation," I said, as Peaches nudged my leg next to me. "He seems like he's barely holding it together, the rage is strong."

I noticed that many of the features of Shadowpeak had

been modernized. The light fixtures for example were using bulbs, not candles.

"I didn't notice these lights from outside," I said. "How are they on?"

"They were activated when we entered Shadowpeak," Monty said. "The modernization was done several years ago, by my uncle, against the wishes of the family."

"They didn't want this place modernized, why not?"

"They felt it would fundamentally change Shadowpeak," Monty said. "My uncle felt that we should, as a family, spend more time in our ancestral home."

"Let me guess, the Montagues aren't big on family get-togethers?"

"Not in the slightest," Monty said. "My family, aside from being intensely private, actively dislikes my uncle, disowned my father, and abhorred my mother. They refused to acknowledge my mother when my father chose her as his wife. It caused a major rift in the family, even to this day."

"Does that mean they don't like you?"

"As the product of that union, I have been the target of considerable vitriol from my family," Monty said, his words clipped. "No...they don't like me."

"Why?" I asked, looking around at some of the other portraits around the room. "Why didn't they like your mother?"

"My mother didn't fit in with the Montagues," Monty said. "She loved my father fiercely and he loved her just as intensely, but she could never be a Montague, she was brilliant, never afraid to show her emotions or express her thoughts, and what really turned them against her, she was staggeringly powerful."

"How powerful exactly?"

"Only my father and my uncle Dexter could rival her in

magical power," Monty said. "Needless to say, their insecurities caused petty rivalries and family drama to form."

"They felt threatened by her."

"Yes, my family feared her, all except my uncle, who formed a close friendship with her. That probably didn't help her case, either, since my family never liked my uncle."

"I'm sorry your family never accepted her," I said. "That must have made life hard."

"We only came here twice when I was a child," he said, his voice low. "On the English side. After that, my father felt the strife was not worth the trip."

"Family can make life difficult," I said with a sigh. "They know which buttons to push, because they're the ones who installed them to begin with."

He nodded.

"It's not the family you're born into that matters most, but the one you create," he said, glancing at me and Peaches. "I have my found family and I am content. Besides, my uncle is still very much a part of my family and that's all the Montague family I need in my life."

"Are you going to get any blowback by doing this?" I asked. "Securing Shadowpeak?"

"From whom? My family?"

"Yes," I said. "They're not going to come out of the woodwork to attack you because you did this?"

"Unlikely," he said, pulling on a sleeve. "They dislike me, but they fear me. More than that, they fear my uncle more than they are willing to take me to task over my actions here. They will voice their objections in the whispers, or if I ever attend the annual Montague Family gathering."

"Your family gathers every year?"

"Yes, and each year, I am invited," he said. "I don't know what possesses them to send me an invitation. I have never accepted."

"Maybe they want to mend fences?"

"Ten minutes," he said. "That's how long uncle Dexter lasted at the last family gathering before he nearly teleported some family members to Antarctica, after they brought up my father and his poor choice of picking my mother as his wife. Had I been there, it would have gone…poorly."

"It sucks when your family acts like that," I said, looking around the room. "I think its better you stay away from them."

"As do I," he said, still gazing at Byron's portrait. "It's safer that way—for them."

"Where exactly are we going in here?" I asked. "I know this place is amazing, but we aren't sight-seeing. We're on the clock."

"Agreed," Monty said, shaking his head and turning from Byron Montague's painting. "We must head to the lowest level. The design of Shadowpeak embraces the saying on its doorway. It has three levels above ground, which means—"

"It has three levels below ground?"

"Exactly," he said. "Each of those sub-levels is guarded, with the runic receptacle on the lowest level."

That was when I heard the whispers.

Montague…a Montague has entered Shadowpeak.

"Tell me you heard that," I said, staring at him. "You heard that, right?"

"Heard what?" Monty deadpanned. "Are you hearing things now? What exactly did you hear?"

"That is not funny," I said, raising my voice. "You heard that, right?"

"Yes, calm down," he said, raising a hand and looking around. "Those are just echoes attuned to my particular signature, or rather the signature of any Montague that enters Shadowpeak. They're harmless."

"Harmless echoes," I said still looking around. "Are they planning on staying harmless?"

"I see no reason why they would present a danger to us."

"The sooner we do what we came here to do, the sooner we can get out of your haunted castle," I said. "No need to spend any extra time in here."

"It's not *my* haunted anything," Monty said. "This place is not inhabited by ghosts, it's just very old."

"I don't mind old things," I said glancing around. "I do mind dead things that don't stay dead."

"You wield a necrotic blade," Monty felt the need to point out. "You *literally* communicated with the dead at Iron Fan Mountain when you confronted the Emissary...did you forget?"

"No, I did not *forget*," I said. "Just because I communicated with the dead on the mountain, doesn't mean I want to communicate with them *all* the time. I especially don't want to communicate with the dead ghost of an angry Archmage."

"I find that unlikely," Monty said, glancing at the portrait of Byron again. "I highly doubt Byron's ghost is lingering about Shadowpeak waiting to have a word with you, or me, for that matter. Despite what my uncle says, Byron Montague is long dead and gone."

I glanced around nervously.

"Not that I don't believe you, but how do we get downstairs to this runic receptacle thing?" I asked. "The fastest way possible would be good."

"You didn't want the grand tour of Shadowpeak?" Monty asked. "The history contained in these walls is quite amazing."

I gave him a hard stare.

"No, thank you," I said. "You can save the tour for another day or century. We have three days before Udolf comes back to evict this place from the plane permanently. I don't want to be inside when it does that, do you?"

"No," he said pulling on a sleeve. "You're absolutely right, we have no time to waste. I do have to warn you, though. "You may hear more than those echoes, more…personal things."

"Personal things?" I asked wary. "Personal things like?"

"We have to run the gauntlet," he said. "It's not just a physical event. It's mental—a psychological test of your will and determination in addition to a physical testing that will push us to our limits. Are you certain you want to go through with this?"

"Are *you* doing it?"

"Yes, I think I must."

"Then I'm doing it," I said. "Last thing we need is for you to be in the middle of this gauntlet and then you lose it. That would be bad for everyone."

"Lose it?" he asked. "I have no intention of *losing* it."

"No one ever has an intention of *losing* it, Mage Montague," I said, emphasizing his title. "But if I have ever seen a more perfect setup for losing your mind—it's this place. You will *not* be doing this gauntlet alone."

"Thank you," he said after a short pause. "I apologize beforehand for any discomfort you will experience as you undertake this ordeal with me."

"Way to sell the gauntlet, thanks."

"Realist, remember?"

"What about Peaches?" I said, glancing down at my hellhound. "Will he undergo *discomfort* too?"

"I'm not sure," Monty said, looking at my hellhound. "It's never been documented for a familiar or a creature of his type to undergo the gauntlet. He has a unique physiology that would require extensive study to understand the stresses a gauntlet would subject him to. That…would take time."

"Time we don't have," I said, rubbing my hellhound's oversized head. "I'll have to keep an eye on him."

"Do not hesitate to inform me the moment you sense anything amiss through your bond," Monty said. "You may even notice it before he does, so remain vigilant."

"I will," I said, noticing a staircase going down at the end of the next room. "Are we headed to those stairs?"

"Yes," Monty said, turning in a slow circle. "If memory serves, that would take us to the first sub-level."

"You're not sure?"

"I didn't exactly spend summers here as a child," Monty snapped. "This place...certain aspects feel familiar, while others feel alien. It will take a while to find my footing."

"Are you sure you're okay?" I asked wary. "I mean, are you hearing any more voices, is anyone telling you to blast this place apart in a ploy to get you to destroy yourself?"

"The antagonistic runes are only on the door, as far as I know," Monty said. "To answer your question, no, I'm not hearing any voices, besides yours, that is."

"Well, that's good. Lead the way."

TWENTY-FIVE

We entered the next area, which was joined to the minor reception room by a small hallway and a large entrance. I had been in castles before, they all had the feeling of being inside a museum.

Shadowpeak felt different.

"This place feels lived in," I said as we walked. "It's not stuffy or cold. It feels like there could be people—your family, in the next room having a discussion. Why is that?"

"Shadowpeak is not just the estate, the building," Monty explained. "It's also the aggregate of the people who did live here long ago. Every Montague from Byron on, who lived in this space, left something of themselves inside the walls of Shadowpeak."

"But this place isn't alive, right?" I asked. "Shadowpeak isn't sentient, right?"

"No," Monty said. "It is not sentient, it's a castle. What it is, is imbued with power from centuries of mages incrementally, over time, depositing power into the runic receptacle."

"How many mages are we talking about?" I asked. "Over how long a time period?"

"All I have is a rough estimate," Monty said. "According to the notes, Byron founded Shadowpeak around two millennia ago. The world was a much different place back then."

"Two thousand years ago?"

"Yes, since that time, some branches of the Montague families have stayed here, but never for long," Monty added. "Prolonged exposure to this place seems to make mages uncomfortable."

"Could it be all the homicide in the air," I said. "Centuries of mages dying here makes an impact to the energy of a place."

He gave me a look.

"You almost sound like a mage," he said. "You're not wrong."

"Killing fields are never pleasant," I said. "This may be your ancestral home, but living here would expose anyone to years of death. It would take a toll."

"There is that," he said. "Over time, less and less of my family would occupy this place until one day, no one from my family did, and it was closed. That was when the words of command, the Guardian Monks, and the initial sealing were instituted."

"Now no one stays here…ever?"

"No," Monty said. "The cost is prohibitive."

"Your family is wealthy, isn't it?"

"Part of that wealth was accrued when they stopped living here," he said. "My personal wealth was created through intelligent investing, owning properties and being part of a select group of entities throughout the world."

"Like SuNaTran?"

He nodded.

"Like SuNaTran."

"I could see how this would be an expense," I said. "I would never have or live in such a large place."

"Nor would I, this place would be enormous for ten families, much less for one branch of mine. Not to mention the upkeep would be considerable, you would need a steward to oversee the property, groundskeepers to maintain the grounds, kitchen staff with a dedicated chef, butlers and maids, a significant amount of carpenters and masons to maintain the actual structure, and if they brought horses, you need a dedicated group of stablehands. That would just be the immediate staff—a small army of people."

"And they would have to relocate to live in the Black Forest."

"There is that, too," Monty said with a nod. "All of these people would have to be comfortable with the energy of Shadowpeak, which, as you may have noticed, is not exactly what I would call normal or welcoming."

"That sounds impossible," I said. "Is that how it was in Byron's day?"

"I'm sure there weren't that many people in his time, but not everyone who lived here was a Montague," he said as we slowed to admire the next room. "Even so, it must have been quite the undertaking—even for an Archmage."

"Why hasn't this place fallen apart?" I asked as I looked around this new room. "I mean no one is maintaining Shadowpeak right now. Why does it look so...I don't know—intact?"

"Part of that was the monks who maintained the estate and the other part is the stasis cast that rests on all of Shadowpeak," he said. "It's one of the reasons the flow of time has been affected here."

"Stasis cast?" I asked. "You mean most of Shadowpeak is frozen in time?"

"No, not really," he answered as we crossed the room. "For example, take this room."

"What is this place?" I asked, looking at the set up. "This seems like a cozy room."

This room we walked through was furnished with plenty of comfortable chairs and small tables, each set creating a small environment for more intimate conversation. In the middle, were several long sofas placed back to back. In front of each of the sofas were low tables where I guessed you could place whatever you were drinking at the moment.

In one corner, I noticed the grand piano. What impressed me was that the piano was polished and looked ready to be played.

"This is one of the main drawing rooms," Monty said. "Guests would withdraw here after dinner for conversation or entertainment."

"Entertainment being the piano I assume?"

"Not always," Monty answered. "There were poetry readings and other forms of entertainment. Although many of the guests weren't Montagues, there were still some mages who visited the family here."

"What exactly does a mage consider entertainment?" I asked taking in the room. "Who could explode an orb better?"

"There was no orb exploding conducted inside Shadowpeak," Monty said. "Entertainment for a mage with regards to magic would be somewhat more esoteric in nature. If all of the guests were from the magical community, they would most likely discuss the nature of casts, their origin and their potency."

"And if they weren't all magical?"

"Then the piano, some singing, and poetry would serve as entertainment for the evening," Monty said. "I don't think the Montagues entertained all that often, as I said, my family valued their privacy, even back then, and the location of the Black Forest, made it inconvenient to visit Shadowpeak."

"Was that intentional?"

"Of course," Monty said. "Left to his devices, Byron wouldn't have visitors. In case you haven't noticed, most Archmages are not social butterflies."

"True, the few I've met seem pretty antisocial."

Monty paused in his steps and looked around the room.

"It's a shame we don't have time to explore more of the property," he said. "I would've liked to examine the entirety of Shadowpeak. This is a singular opportunity."

We arrived at the stairs and I noticed that the part of the staircase that was on this floor was ornate wrought iron, but as it descended it became plainer and less decorative.

"What happened?" I asked, looking down the stairs. "The designer got tired halfway through creating these stairs?"

"It's all about appearance in Shadowpeak," Monty said. "If the stairs were going to be visible on this floor, they had to fit with the decor. Once they were out of sight, the decor was no longer needed."

We took the stairs down.

I expected to hear our footstep on the iron stairs, but any sound we created was muffled as we descended. I stomped on the bottom stair, but the sound barely registered.

That's when I noticed the runes along the edge of the stairs.

"They're runed silent?"

"Yes," Monty said with a nod. "Again, it's about the appearance, it would be unseemly to have footsteps echoing through the drawing room while guests were having their conversations."

"It also allowed for stealth approaches," I said. "You could go up or down and no one would hear you. Pretty effective for staying undetected."

"Not in Shadowpeak," Monty said as we continued down

a plain corridor made up of gray stone. "It would be difficult for anyone to hide from Byron in this house."

"Why?" I asked, curious. "Cameras didn't exist in Byron's time."

"He didn't need cameras, he was attuned to Shadowpeak," Monty said as we approached a large door. "In a way, he was part of Shadowpeak. He was aware of what happened in every inch of this place."

"That's what Udolf said about the Guardian Monks, they were attuned to Shadowpeak," I said. "Were they all attuned to the entire place?"

"No," Monty said. "Only Byron could manage that amount of information at once, he was an Archmage, after all. Two monks were attuned to a particular area, dividing Shadowpeak into six sections. It made it easier to maintain the property and didn't overwhelm the monks."

"Makes sense," I said, looking at the door. "First sub-level?"

"First sub-level," Monty said. "The actual gauntlet is on the lowest level, but all of the sub-levels are a gauntlet of sorts. Be on your guard."

"I've been on my guard since we stepped into the Black Forest," I said. "How dangerous are the sub-levels?"

"That depends on your definition of danger," Monty said, placing his hand on sections of the door. "This was the home of an Archmage, what he considered the norm could be deadly for us."

"Right, so sub-levels are probably lethal?"

"I think it would be wise if we operated under that premise," Monty said, taking a step back as several runes formed on the door, glowing in a subtle golden light. "That should be it."

The door swung in silently and opened into another long dark hallway. I could see about five feet down the hallway before it became pitch black. I was about to walk in, when Monty held me back, shaking his head.

"Wait," he continued. "You don't want to go in there while its dark."

"Can't you form one of your lightbulb orbs?"

"I could," he said, still staring into the hallway. "It would be better if I showed you."

He formed a bright white orb and let it go into the corridor. It illuminated the hallway for about three seconds before it was enveloped by darkness and swallowed.

"What the—?"

"It's a shadow passage," Monty said. "Dangerous while dark. They take a few seconds to illuminate. Watch."

"Where did that orb go?"

"I don't know for sure," Monty said, peering into the darkness. "Probably the same place Shadowpeak goes when its not entirely on this plane."

"What happens if we step into this shadow passage?"

"From my studies, it seems shadow passages are not particularly kind to organic material," he said. "The outcomes are grisly and fatal. A few mages discovered that the hard way."

"I'd like to keep my organic material intact, thank you."

"As would I," he said, pointing to the hallway. "Avoid any passage that looks like this one."

"Byron created this?"

"Yes," Monty said as small orbs of light began to glow inside the passage. "It is a passive and effective failsafe regulating traffic throughout Shadowpeak. He also had the ability to remove the lighting from any of the shadow passages whenever the mood struck him."

"These passages are all over the house?"

"No," Monty said, taking a step forward into the now brightly lit hallway. "Only on the sub-levels. It was a way for him to create privacy. No one could follow him into the sub-levels if he didn't want them to."

"He really took his privacy seriously," I said, looking around the hallway as we walked down its length. "Let's not take the scenic route okay?"

"There is no—oh, you want us to hurry."

TWENTY-SIX

We arrived at the first sub-level and another door.

"There's no going back now," Monty said as he touched sections of the door. "Brace yourself. The failsafes of the house will be active from this point on."

The door swung inward, opening into a large space.

The contrast was immediate.

Where the upstairs was furnished and inviting, this space was an empty floor. As the lights increased in intensity, I noticed the circles on the floor.

This floor wasn't empty.

It was a training floor.

"This is a training floor?"

"Not a normal one," Monty said warily as he looked around. "These circles, do you recall the obliteration circles we've encountered?"

"Yes," I said, worried about the tone in his voice. "Are you saying these are—?"

"Some of them, yes," Monty said, pointing. "There's a pattern. Avoid the ones with the blue glowing runic script."

"What about those with the green glowing script?" I

asked, pointing to the other circles that were spread out all over the floor. "Are those safe?"

"No," Monty said. "Avoid those too."

"You realize that leaves us with nowhere to walk," I said, scanning the floor. "The entire floor is covered in circles."

"Correct," a voice said from the corner of the room. "You must disable the circles in the proper sequence if you intend to cross the level."

A figure stepped into the center of the room.

Byron Montague.

"That can't really be—?"

"It's not," Monty said. "This must be some kind of avatar for Shadowpeak. A construct. The essence of the power of Shadowpeak given form."

"And you…are a *Montague*," Byron said, looking at Monty. "After all these years, it is refreshing to have a Montague within my walls again."

"That's not Byron?"

"No, it's not."

"Then, what is it?"

"I am, for lack of a better term, the essence of Shadowpeak," Byron said. "I am here to ensure that the gauntlet is performed according to the precepts instituted by the original Byron Montague."

"The original?" I asked. "This is a copy of Byron?"

"A poor one at that."

"Ah, a feisty Montague," Byron said, with a smile. "I will enjoy watching you fail…and die."

"A morbid one too," I said. "That's not even remotely funny."

"What are the precepts?" Monty said, looking at the circles that filled the floor in front of us. "How many are there?"

"There are three precepts that must be followed," Byron

said. "The mage attempting the gauntlet must be of the bloodline. He is not of the bloodline, in fact,"—Byron pointed at me—"I'm not quite sure what he is."

"I'm complicated," I said. "That's what I am."

"Be that as it may, you are *not* a Montague," Byron said, then looked at Monty. "Do you place him under your aegis as a Montague of the bloodline?"

"I do," Monty said. "What are the other precepts?"

"You must abide by the outcome of the gauntlet…if you survive," Byron said. "Do you abide by the outcome?"

"You want me to abide by an outcome without knowing the outcome?" Monty asked. "Isn't that somewhat premature? Who determines this outcome?"

"You do…of course."

"That doesn't make sense," I said. "How do you determine the outcome when you haven't even run the gauntlet yet?"

"I see," Monty said. "Very well, I accept the second precept. What is the final precept?"

The avatar of Byron smiled at Monty.

It wasn't a pleasant or welcoming smile.

"Only wits, will, and abilities may be used to overcome the gauntlet," Byron said. "This is a rite of passage for mages seeking to increase their power. Anything artificial to your being will be nullified. Do you accept?"

"Wits, will, and abilities," Monty echoed. "You're stipulating we cannot introduce anything foreign to our beings, correct?"

"Correct, do you agree?"

"One moment," Monty said and turned to me. "Are you carrying any device that's foreign to your body?"

"Like my phone?"

"No," he said. "Your phone won't work in here, regardless. I mean weaponry. Do you have any weapons on you that are not a part of you?"

"No," I said. "Everything I'm carrying is part of me...now."

I was thinking about the recent addition of Grim Whisper and was thankful Monty had upgraded my gun on the Shrike.

"Good," Monty said then turned to Avatar Byron. "We only carry that which is part of our being. We accept the third and final precept."

"Very well," Byron said with a short nod. "If you survive the gauntlet, you will face the Well of Pain and make your final choice. Choose wisely."

"Well of Pain?" I asked, concerned. "What choice?"

Byron Montague vanished from sight, leaving me with my questions. I turned to Monty who was examining the circles.

"You never mentioned a Well of Pain—care to elaborate?"

"I can only assume he was referring to the runic receptacle," Monty said, still looking at the circles. "It's just a name, don't read too much into it."

"Just a name? Then why didn't they name it the Well of Joy?" I asked. "The Well of Pain doesn't sound like a well I want to visit."

"Right now, we have to get past these circles," Monty said. "I would hazard a guess and say this is the physical aspect of the gauntlet."

"I thought the gauntlet was only on the lowest sub-level," I said, looking at the circles. "Now it sounds like all three sub-levels are part of the gauntlet. Which one is it?"

"Both," Monty said, gesturing. "The material on Shadowpeak was sparse on details about the gauntlet, as you can imagine."

"Sure, because who would document in detail that they set up their own psychotic home dungeon, not on one level, but three."

"It was sparse to avoid other mages from trying to access

the power of the runic receptacle," Monty said. "And no, before you ask, I am not going to call it the Well of Pain."

I was getting predictable.

He must have read my expression as he said runic receptacle.

"You said Shadowpeak wasn't sentient," I said, changing subjects. "That Byron seemed plenty aware."

"It wasn't," Monty said. "Think of it as a kind of computer program. One designed to protect the house and enforce the rules of the gauntlet."

"How strong do you think this 'program' is?" I asked. "Do you think it will attack us?"

"I didn't pick up an energy signature, but that could have been due to the dampening effects of Shadowpeak itself," Monty said. "It reacted predictably to my presence, but had some trouble ascertaining your level of ability."

"It couldn't read me clearly."

"That could work to our advantage," he said. "I noticed it made no mention of your creature, which was curious."

"Maybe it thinks Peaches is just an oversized canine?" I said, glancing at my hellhound. "Maybe he doesn't present much of a threat?"

"I highly doubt that," Monty said. "Remember this was a failsafe created by an Archmage. Even two thousand years ago, there was such a thing as having contingency plans for unexpected events. Keep your eyes open, all of them."

"I will," I said. "Do you have a plan to get past these circles?"

"I do," he said. "The green circles are tied to the blue circles through lines of energy."

"Like ley lines?"

"Precisely," he said. "Upon closer inspection, we can step on the green circles—"

"You said they were dangerous too."

"They are, if you remain on them for longer than five seconds," Monty said. "The blue ones will give us three seconds and they will rotate colors. The only danger will be if we encounter red circles."

"How bad are the red circles?"

"Red circles will produce an instantaneous reaction, no delay."

I looked out over the floor again and only saw blue and green circles, but I knew it wouldn't remain that way for long.

"Okay we avoid the red circles," I said. "I'm only seeing blue and green, so it shouldn't be too bad."

"We both know it won't remain this way," Monty said, scanning the floor. "The logical pattern is we step on a green, wait two seconds, then move quickly to a blue without pause, using it as a bridge to the next green."

"That sounds like it can work. Where's the twist?" I asked. "This is a test for mages. No way is it going to stay *that* simple."

"This is very similar to a mage test I took early on as an apprentice mage," he said. "In fact, it's quite possible that test was based on this exact test here."

"Focus, Monty," I said. "The twist?"

"Right," he said. "Since the circles are connected by ley lines, it's quite possible there is an element of randomness, causing some red circles to appear."

"Why can't we just teleport to the other side of the floor?" I asked. "That seems like the easiest way across."

"I'll show you why not."

He formed a green circle of teleportation and sent it in the air across the floor. Black beams of energy intercepted and disintegrated the circle before it got halfway across.

"It can read energy trying to bypass the circles," Monty said. "If it can reduce an energy circle to nothing in seconds, what do you think it will do to us?"

"Right, we use the circles then," I said, still looking at the point where the green circle was blasted. "We'll have to test your color changing theory."

"As well as if we can reverse course to go forward," Monty added. "We won't have much room for error."

"We can try on the second circle and see what happens," I said. "I also think to keep our footprint small, we all go for the same circle. That way we don't flip too many circles."

"Good point," he said. "We'll start with this one here in front of us, ready?"

"As I'll ever be."

TWENTY-SEVEN

There were three green circles in front of us with blue circles connected to each of them, and green ones connected to them. The pattern expanded and spread out all over the floor, until it reached the other side of the level and a door on the far end of the floor, which I guessed led to the second sub-level.

We stepped on the middle green circle.

We waited a few seconds, moving to the blue circle on our right, before jumping back to the green circle we started on and then off the floor.

The green circle turned blue by the time we left it, and the blue one had turned red. It was good we had left the circle by the time it changed colors.

As we jumped back to the original circle, now blue, we had to get off right away as it began to turn red.

"Whoa," I said as we stepped off the floor. "That was close. We only have two green circles to use now."

"One really," Monty said, pointing. "If we take the left green circle, it will lead us to a dead end. The pattern will force us to a red circle."

"A literal dead end," I said, looking at the pattern of circles. "At least now we know the pattern, right? Green to blue to red. As long as we avoid the red circles, we should be good."

"That is the key to this entire test," Monty said. "But it's never that easy. There is always an unexpected element introduced into this test."

"The randomness aspect?"

He nodded.

"It forces the mage to adapt to unforeseen circumstances," Monty said. "It's an attempt to mimic actual battle or a real life confrontation, not a test."

"I'm not seeing the red circles turn back to another color," I said. "Once they turn red, they seem to stay red."

"Which means they're out of play."

"Are they?" I said. "We should test the theory before accepting that red means dead."

"Fair enough," he said, producing a quarter and materializing a shield in front of the closest red circle. "Ready to see how volatile these red circles are?"

I nodded and moved back a bit more.

He tossed the quarter into the red circle, which exploded the moment the coin touched the floor. A beam of red energy the circumference of the circle shot up into the ceiling. The beam lasted five seconds, yes, I counted, before disappearing.

The circle was gone, the quarter was gone too.

"Five seconds," I said. "That's how long the beam lasted. Were you able to gauge how strong that beam was?"

"Strong enough to render us into memories."

"Okay, so the red circles are real threats and stepping on one—"

"Red means dead," Monty said. "It didn't destroy my shield however, so the blast is directed straight upward. As long as we're out of the circle—"

"We're safe from the blast."

"Yes," he said. "Ready?"

"Absolutely not, but we don't have much of a choice in this one," I said. "It's not like we can stay here and just look across this floor, we need to cross it."

"We do *need* to cross it," he said. "There's a pattern, but we don't necessarily have to follow the established pattern. The floor is inert after that blast. The circle is gone."

"What are you saying?" I asked, glancing at him. "That we should detonate the pattern in order to cross the floor? Because that sounds suicidal."

"Wits, will, and abilities," he said. "There is a pattern, but we can make our own pattern. We also have a safe area to stand now."

He pointed to the burnt-out section of the floor.

"How exactly is that spot safe?" I asked. "It's surrounded by circles. Are you seeing the other circles around it?"

"I am, but I have an idea."

"Oh, hell, every time you say 'I have an idea', it sounds like pain."

"This should work with no to minimal, pain," he said. "We stand on the disabled circle, you cast your dawnward, I will reinforce it with a shield of my own."

"Will that be enough?"

"I believe so, yes," he said, giving me no confidence whatsoever. "Remember the blast goes upward not outward. Our shields should protect us."

"Then what?" I asked, unsure of where he was going with this idea, but not exactly a fan. "We are standing in the middle of deadly circles."

"Once our shields are in place, I will unleash two barrages of orbs across the floor to impact all of the circles at once. One barrage to prime them to red, and the other to detonate them all."

"All the circles at once?" I said. "That would cause one enormous explosion of beams."

"As long as we remain in our circle for five seconds, we will be safe," he said. "It can work."

"It sounds like it could work," I said. "But if that's a solution, don't you think another mage would've figured that out? There has to be a catch somewhere."

Monty scanned the room again.

"I'm not seeing any hidden devices or runes," he said. "This should work."

If he didn't see anything, there was no point in my using my innersight, seeing as how he was a mage with a more developed magical sight than mine.

"It still seems too easy," I said. "But I don't have a better idea so let's give it a shot. Are you sure there are no hidden runes anywhere?"

"None that I can see, no."

"Okay then, let's do this," I said, stepping carefully into the disabled circle in front of us. "You have your shield ready?"

He nodded.

I focused and formed a dawnward.

The violet dome formed above and around us. I had to focus more than usual to make sure it remained tight and not touch any of the other circles around us.

This was harder than I expected.

"Any day now," I said, holding my focus. "My dawnward isn't usually this small. Can you put your shield up and get this party started?"

"Right way," he said, gesturing and forming a shield inside the dawnward. "That should protect us."

"You made your shield *inside* the dawnward?"

"You didn't exactly leave me any room to cast it outside

your dawnward," he said, looking down at the edge of my violet dome. "Can you bring it in even tighter?"

"Are you kidding?" I said. "I'm barely holding onto it as it is. Whatever you're going to do, now would be a good time to do it."

He formed a multitude of small orbs and tossed them out across the room, low to the floor. They spread out and landed on the majority of the circles. I think he may have missed one or two, but most of the circles were hit.

All at once his barrage of orbs detonated, changing the colors of the circles, until all of the circles I could see were red.

"Phase one done," he said with a satisfied nod. "Brace yourself, the next phase will set them all off."

"Are you sure you can't throw up another shield?" I asked. "You know, as insurance just in case my dawnward and your one shield aren't strong enough?"

"One more shield won't do much," he said. "If it makes you feel better—"

"It makes me feel better," I finished quickly. "It makes me feel a whole lot better, yes."

"Fine," he said and gestured, creating a golden lattice inside his shimmering white shield, both of which sat inside my dawnward. "Feel better?"

"Tons," I said, still nervous. "Explode away."

He formed the third barrage of small orbs.

Right away I felt something shift in the room.

"Monty..."

He tossed the orbs across the floor.

That was when red circles appeared all across the ceiling.

"Oh, shit," I said, looking up at the red circle that was directly above us. "That can't be good."

"Bloody hell," Monty said. "This must be the reaction to us trying to work around the floor pattern."

The red circles on the ceiling were beginning to glow as the orbs floated over the floor.

"Can you call the orbs back?"

He shook his head.

"I'm sor—" his words were drowned out by the explosions.

TWENTY-EIGHT

The small orbs impacted the circles on the floor, setting them off.

Once the circles on the floor went off, the ones on the ceiling began to go off in waves. We were stuck in a loop of power bouncing off the ceiling into the floor and back into the ceiling.

We didn't dare step outside my dawnward, which was getting harder and harder to maintain with every passing second.

I could feel the sweat dripping down my forehead and into my eyes. I had never really practiced holding my dawnward under this kind of attack. It felt like being crushed, and all I was doing was holding up my hand against a giant's foot.

"I don't think I can hold this for much longer, Monty," I said through gritted teeth. "The...pressure...it's too much."

"A few more seconds, Simon," he said, looking around at the explosions that were going on all around us. "I need you to hold on for a few more seconds."

"A few more seconds?" I said, nearly screaming. "I don't have a few more seconds."

"You do," he said, his voice calm. "I'm changing the shape of my shields, to deflect instead of repel."

"Let me know the instant you can't hold on any longer," he said, gesturing as he spoke. "Not a moment later."

"That was about five seconds ago," I said. "What are you doing?"

"Drop your dawnward and hold onto your creature," he said. "I'm using him as an anchor."

I dropped my dawnward and sagged to the floor, throwing my arms around Peaches. Monty crouched down and did the same, hugging my hellhound.

Several blasts were headed our way.

We moved as close to the center of the circle as we could when the blasts hit us. Monty changing the shape of his shield made it so that the blasts hit us at an angle, launching us across the floor toward the door to sub-level two.

The moment we were airborne, black beams of destruction headed our way. I turned my body to put myself in-between the beam and Peaches.

Monty gestured again and formed what looked like small blackholes in front of us. The beams shot into the blackholes and shot out on the other side of the floor.

We crashed onto the opposite side of the floor. We rolled for a short distance and slowly staggered to our feet. Only Peaches seemed unfazed by the whole trip. He landed semi-gracefully, only skidding a bit as he came to a stop near the door, and avoided getting tangled up with us.

I ached in places I didn't know I could ache. My body flushed hot as my curse worked on my injuries.

"Can we not do that again…ever?" I said with a groan as I stood. "Where did the ceiling circles come from?"

"They didn't come from anywhere," he said. "If I had to guess, they were there all along, but masked."

"They were hidden well."

"So well I couldn't sense them until it was too late."

"Ingenuity, decisive action, adaptability, and mastery of energy manipulation," Byron said as he stood next to the door and looked at us. "The reshaping of the shield to use the energy blasts in providing momentum to get you across the floor was inspired."

"Thank you," Monty said. "I don't suppose we did so well we could just head to the receptacle?"

"No," Byron said. "You did well, but not that well. You're a Montague, I expected no less."

"Glad I could live up to your expectations."

"Except for the deflection of the necrotic strikes," Byron added. "What cast did you use to redirect them?"

"Necrotic strikes?" I asked. "What were those?"

"The black beams that would have ended us had they hit while we were in midair across the floor," Monty said, glancing at me for a moment before turning to Byron. "They were temporal displacement casts."

"Were they now?" Byron said staring at Monty. "I could've sworn they felt…darker. Something with a hint of entropy added to the cast."

"I used them to catch the beams and fire them elsewhere."

"Darker?" I asked. "What does he mean—darker? Entropy?"

"I have no idea," Monty said. "I know what I used. There was nothing entropic about my casts."

"If you say so, Montague," Byron said with a small flourish and pointed to the next door. "Who am I to question your casts? The next level awaits—good luck."

He disappeared a second later.

"I'm liking Byron less by the second," I said. "Are you sure you didn't use some dark cast?"

"I'm certain," Monty said. "I'm here to secure Shadowpeak not increase my power. We need to find out what killed the monks and secure the estate. That is the entirety of our mission here. Nothing more or less."

"I think I understand this next level," I said as we headed to the door. "Shadowpeak is playing mind games, isn't it?"

"I'm afraid so," Monty said. "We have to be on our guard, because as you just saw, it plays dirty."

Monty walked over to the door and placed his hand on several sections in sequence. This door didn't swing open; it just sort of fell apart and vanished, leaving a staircase heading down in front of us.

We took the stairs down cautiously, at least I did. I kept my eyes on Monty, trying to see if there was any noticeable change in his attitude.

He was still doing grumpy mage with a side of anger management issues when we got down to the next level.

<If you sense anything different about Monty, let me know, boy.>

<Different how?>

<I don't know exactly, but if he starts to smell different, tell me right away. This place doesn't fight fair and I think it's going to attack Monty's mind next.>

<I can't smell his mind.>

<I know, but if his energy changes, tell me right away, okay?>

<I will. Are you in danger too? Will your energy change?>

<What? No. I'm not a mage or a Montague. I should be fine.>

<If your energy changes, I will help you change it back.>

<Don't know how you're going to do that, but sure, I appreciate it. Let's focus on Monty for now, okay?>

<I will focus on the both of you, because I am mighty and can focus on more than one person at a time.>

"Sub-level two?" I said when we reached another impressive door. "Maybe this won't be so bad. I mean, mages have to have amazing mental self-control. Attacking you that way would be pointless, right?"

"A mage's mind is his greatest weapon and greatest weakness," Monty said. "If you can debilitate a mage's mind, it doesn't matter how many casts he knows, he would be neutralized."

Monty traced some symbols onto the surface of the door.

The symbols flared bright yellow for a few seconds before merging into the door and vanishing.

"What did those symbols say?"

"Variations on a theme," Monty said. "As without, so within. In this case the context is referring to mind. Our minds."

Monty pushed the door and it swung inward without a sound. I heard Monty curse as we stepped inside. A second later I realized why.

We were standing in the Golden Circle.

"This is the—?"

"The Golden Circle, specifically when we went to save my father," Monty said. "Of course it would bring us here."

"This is wrong," I said. "It's going to try and screw your mind up."

"Not just me," Monty said, pointing behind me. "Those people look familiar to you?"

"What people?" I said, turning and felt my heart drop to my feet. "What the fu—?"

"You let me die, Simon," a voice said as I shook my head. "You should've taken the shot. It was easy for you. You're the Deadeye and yet you missed. You *let* me die."

"It's not that simple," I said almost in a whisper. "The target…it was a child. The target was a child. Get…out…of…my…head."

The images vanished as Connor Montague approached us.

"Oh, hell," I said, still shaken from my own memory coming to life. "He's not real, Monty. That's not your dad."

"There are no shortcuts, Tristan," Connor said. "I told you

and you still tried. You tried to use darkness, only to let it use you. Is that what my sacrifice meant to you?"

"You are not my father," Monty said. "My father knew what I had to do and gave his life, giving me that opportunity."

"An opportunity you squandered, son," Connor said gently. "Why did you do it? Why did you betray my gift?"

"I didn't betray you," Monty said, suddenly surprised. "I honored your memory. I stopped Oliver."

Connor stepped close and placed his hands on either side of Monty's head. Monty went rigid when Connor touched him.

"Monty…you need to fight this," I said. "That is not your father."

Monty's eyes had gone distant and it seemed like he couldn't hear me. I shook him, but he was unresponsive. His gaze was fixed on some point in the distance.

"Shadowpeak kills Montagues," a voice said from behind me. "It never fails. They always fall here, searching for power and losing themselves in the past."

It was Avatar Byron standing behind me.

"Let him go," I said with a growl. "Now."

"You know, at first, I thought to bring up the shot you didn't take," he said, pointing at me with a smile. "It was ripe for the taking, but then I saw it wasn't a strong enough vehicle. It seems you've made some semblance of peace with that ugly little episode of your past. I'm sure I could use it if I had more time, but this is so much more satisfying."

"Don't do this," I said. "He doesn't deserve this."

"Oh, but he does," Byron continued. "Then I realized what would be a perfect vehicle. You may not be a Montague, but I *will* treat you like one."

"What are you saying?"

"You will get to witness your bond brother lose his mind

—a mage's most precious possession—in self-pity and guilt. It will tear you apart, as you stand helpless and watch his destruction before your eyes."

"Fuck you," I spat. "You must be insane if you think I'm going to let you destroy him."

Byron laughed. It was a dark twisted sound, full of rage and hatred. I realized then what had happened in Shadowpeak. All the deaths had warped and corrupted the power of the place.

It fed on death.

"Perfect," Byron said. "What do you intend on doing? Using your firearm? By all means, please do. How about your blade? Do you think you can stab me with it? Oh, I know, how about your pitiful cast? *Ignis Vitae*, or is it *Mors Ignis* these days? Are we dabbling in darkness just a bit? No matter, it can't save you...or him."

Wits, will, and abilities. I had to use my wits and will.

"I think I get it now," I said, looking past the scene at the Golden Circle for another set of stairs. It was always a set of stairs going down. It took a few moments, but I located it. "You're scared, aren't you? You're scared Monty is going to lock you down."

"Scared?" Byron said. "Do you know who I represent? I represent the greatest mage in the Montague family. The First in the Order of Mages."

"Wrong," I said. "The greatest mage in the Montague family is standing in front of you right now. You think you have him trapped, alone in a memory, but he isn't alone."

"Are you saying he has *you*?" Byron mocked. "What can *you* possibly do to me in this place? I am a god inside Shadowpeak. Shadowpeak thrives on the power of mages—centuries worth of power and death. What threat can *you* pose, you pitiful human?"

"I had an idea it was something like that," I said, glancing at the trapped Monty and making my way to the stairs. "The receptacle in the lower level of this place needs death. The Well of Pain. Is that how you killed the monks?"

"Child's play," Byron said. "They weren't even mages, it was a simple matter to twist their minds against each other. In the end, I didn't kill them. I merely facilitated their early demise."

"You feed on power and death."

"Not just death," Byron said. "The death of beings with power." He glanced over at Monty. "His death will be delicious and it will bring other Montagues to me, and I will feed on their power and lifeforce, but you...you are different, aren't you?"

I realized that even though the essence was powerful, it couldn't read my immortal energy signature for some reason. It probably had something to do with its narrow focus on the Montague bloodline. It would explain why it didn't see my hellhound's infernal pedigree.

"Took you long enough, I was wondering when you would get to me," I said. "I have enough life to feed you forever...power too. Isn't that what you really want? Power and life?"

"Yes, but you are not a mage," he said, narrowing his eyes at me. "How did you come to have this power?"

"What does it matter?" I said, brushing aside his question. "All that matters is that you feed. This one meal of a mage can't compare to the banquet I'm offering."

"Leave the Montague to his fate," Byron said. "His cause is lost. Go down to the Well of Pain. If you please me, I will make his death swift."

<Stay with Monty, boy. When I tell you, you bite him to wake him up.>

<Where are you going? I go where you go.>

<Yes, but right now I need you to wake up Monty. Then you come get me, okay?>

<I will wake up the angry man. He doesn't smell right.>

<I know. The house has him trapped. We're going to help him escape. When I tell you, bite him and make sure he wakes up.>

"I intend to," I said, staring at Byron. "These are the stairs to the Well of Pain?"

Byron nodded.

"I have the mage's mind in my grasp," Byron warned. "Any subterfuge on your part and I make him suffer before the end."

"No subterfuge," I said and took the stairs down. "Shadowpeak is and always will be too strong for any one mage to stand against."

"You finally understand the truth," Byron said, materializing next to me as I reached the lowest level. "No mage can surpass my power."

I stood in front of the door to the third sub-level.

TWENTY-NINE

"I don't know the sequence," I said, standing in front of the immense iron door. "How do I open it?"

"Of course you don't know the sequence," Byron said, touching parts of the door in sequence. "Only a mage with power can open this door."

"You can open it?"

The runes on the door blazed with intensity as they came to life.

"I am not *one* Montague," Byron said, his voice full of arrogance. "I am the amalgam of the bloodline of Montagues mages over centuries, given form. I am the essence of Byron Montague and all who came after him, and I am…Shadowpeak."

The door swung inward slowly.

This level was smaller than the others. The room was about ten feet square and empty except for a large black marble basin in the center of the floor.

Even without entering the room, I could feel the immense power flowing out from the Well of Pain. The aura of violet and black energy around it was oppressive and thick with death.

"The Well of Pain?" I asked as I looked into the room. I took a few steps in and had to stop—the force of the power was so strong, each step forward was a struggle. "You want me to go *all* the way in there?"

"Yes," Byron said. "It is the only way."

I had a feeling that once that iron door closed behind me, all bets were off. If I was going to help Monty, it had to be now.

<*Wake Monty up now, boy. Do it now!*>

My hellhound didn't answer, and all I could do was hope he heard me and bit Monty awake, or did something that would snap him out of the nightmare trap Byron had him reliving.

I took another step forward.

I didn't want to admit it, especially not to myself, but this power felt familiar. It took me a few seconds, but then I placed it. It was power I carried deep within me, ever since Orethe had transformed Ebonsoul.

The room, or more accurately the Well of Pain in the center of the room was an oversized siphon, similar to Ebonsoul, but on an epic scale.

Is that what would happen to my blade if I siphoned centuries worth of mage power and lifeforce what would happen to me? Would I become some deranged monster, like Salya accused me of being? Would all that power destroy my mind?

I had no intention of finding out.

"Yes," Byron said. I noticed he stayed outside of the room. "You must enter the room to present yourself properly to me."

Now I understood the reason for the iron door. It wasn't there to keep mages out, it was there to keep mage victims in.

Once that door closed, I imagined the Well of Pain would siphon the lifeforce out of anyone in the room.

I figured it wasn't a painless procedure.

At least the Well was named correctly.

This was going to truly and honestly suck.

I stepped the rest of the way in and the door slammed shut behind me. Runes on the door exploded with orange and violet power.

All around the room—the floor, walls, and ceiling—I saw bright white runes grow in intensity. On the Well of Pain, I saw deep violet and black runes emerge with accents of red power.

"You made a mistake," I said as the Well began drawing lifeforce. At first the pain was bearable, but it was ratcheting up to uncomfortable with speed. "You should have never let me come in here."

"You are trapped, human," Byron said. "You can do nothing in the Well of Pain. It will drain you of power and feed off your life for as long as it remains."

I really hoped Peaches had heard me.

The pain was racing past uncomfortable and heading into excruciating territory. I took the pain and shoved it to one side as I formed Ebonsoul.

The runes on my blade shone with power as I brought it forward.

"What do you intend to do with that?" Byron mocked. "You think you can cut through the power that rests before you? With a mere blade?"

"I'm not cutting through anything," I said. "I'm going to do what someone should have done to this place long ago, before you became too strong, before you took all those lives. I'm going to stop you."

Byron laughed.

"You're going to try, and die in the process."

"One of us is," I said and gritted my teeth. "Let's find out who's the last one standing."

I thought about that for a split second, realizing I was speaking to the spirit of a house that had siphoned hundreds, if not thousands of mages over a span of three centuries.

This was a bad idea.

I took my last step forward and plunged Ebonsoul into the open space of the Well of Pain with all my strength. The power of the Well washed over me, sprinting past excruciating, and jumping headfirst into torturous agony.

"What are you doing?" Byron asked, concerned as he raised his voice. "Cease and desist this moment!"

I started laughing at that moment.

If I hadn't, I would have been howling in pain. It felt like my mind was fraying at the edges, the middle too. I caught glimpses of all of the mages who had been siphoned into the Well of Pain.

Not all of them were Montagues, but all of them were mages seeking power, not knowing that they were walking into a trap, the last one of their lives.

The power of the mages wailed and screamed in my mind, until I couldn't hear anything else besides the screams.

The screams kept rising in volume as my grip tightened around Ebonsoul. The runes along the blade shone a golden violet that blinded me with their intensity.

Orethe's words raced into my memory: *It's only pain, Simon. You should be intimately acquainted with it by now.*

I howled in agony as the first cracks started forming in the Well.

"Impossible," Byron said. "No human can withstand this much power and live."

"I...told...you...," I said through gasps. "You...made...a...mistake."

The runes on the door melted away next.

Part of my brain saw the runes disappear and made a note that it was probably a bad thing. Those runes were the only thing keeping the door intact; once they were gone, so was the door.

I really hoped Monty would get here soon.

"You fool!" Byron screamed. "Do you understand what you have done? You have unleashed the power of the Well into this plane!"

That sounded bad.

I started laughing again and I was almost certain I had lost my mind or done some major damage to what little mind I had left.

"You sound upset, Byron," I said, catching my breath. "What's the matter, no more free meals?"

"You stupid pathetic human, you've destroyed us all," Byron shot back. "For what? What is the life of one mage, a hundred mages, a thousand mages, against the balance of the entire plane? You have set us on a path of annihilation."

He did have a point.

The power I was feeling at this very moment was spiraling out of control—I barely had a grip on Ebonsoul. If I let it go, it felt like the power would explode outward into the world.

I didn't think I could hold on much longer.

"If you're out there somewhere, Monty," I whispered as my hands began to slip from Ebonsoul, "I could really use some help right about now."

Nothing but the screams of mages answered me.

<I'm here, bondmate.>

I think I nearly cried at hearing my hellhound in my head.

<Hey, boy. I think I really messed up this time. You should try and run as far away as possible from here.>

<I go where you go. The angry man too.>

<The angry man? Where are you?>

<Behind you.>

I turned my head and saw my hellhound and Monty standing behind me, wrapped in a golden lattice of energy.

"Oh, hell," I muttered. "Now I know I'm gone, I'm starting to hallucinate."

"No, you are not," Monty said and gestured. "You are, however, trying to do the impossible. You have to let go, Simon."

"Let go?" I asked. "Are you insane? If I let go, this power gets free."

"It's lying to you," Monty said as he gestured, forming several dark lattices of energy around us. "What did Byron say? Did he threaten you with Armageddon, complete destruction of the plane?"

"Yes," I said. "Don't you see the Well is breaking?"

"I do," he said. "If you don't let go—which is what Byron wants—you will keep feeding Shadowpeak. It will continue growing in power and then it *will* escape. You have to let go."

"I have to let go?" I echoed, then it hit me. "I *have* to let go."

I pried my fingers away from Ebonsoul, letting it return to silver mist, which my body absorbed a few seconds later. A few things happened then. The Well broke in half, the door exploded outward, all of the runes in the room vanished, and Byron howled.

"I will kill you, Montague!" Byron screamed. "You think you can contain me, Byron Montague? No one, nothing can contain me!"

A tremor shook all of Shadowpeak in that moment.

"I believe that is our cue," Monty said, propping me up as I nearly stumbled on my way out of the room. My legs had gone weak and one of my arms was unresponsive. "It's the effects of the Well. By all accounts, you should be dead several times over."

"That's always good news," I said, slurring some of my words. "This is not good."

"We're not out of the woods yet," Monty said. "Quite literally in fact. Shadowpeak is coming undone, but the power is still coalesced around this location, we will have to lead it away while Udolf seals this part of the Black Forest."

"Lead it away?" I asked, confused. "I understand the words, but I don't get what you mean."

"We have to lead Byron and the power of Shadowpeak away from this location," Monty said. "Udolf will seal Shadowpeak away while we do that."

"Udolf will what?"

"Less talk, more action," he said, grabbing my shoulder. "Let's go."

THIRTY

We made it to the ground floor as parts of Shadowpeak fell around us. I could still hear the screams of the mages all around me, but they were drowned out by the howls of Byron, the essence of Shadowpeak.

"He's everywhere," I said, shaking my head. "I can't get him out of my head. They're all in there—screaming."

"Hold on, Simon," Monty said, glancing at me with concern. "We just need to get to Cecil."

"To Cecil?" I asked. "He's at the airport. How are we supposed to do that?"

"We'll have help," Monty said. "Ready?"

I heard a low growl in response.

The next thing I knew, we were outside, it was morning, and I was looking up at an enormous wolf with blazing yellow eyes.

Udolf.

"How long were we down there?" I asked no one in particular. "Hey, it's morning. Did you know it was morning? Hey, when did you get so big?"

Peaches had grown to XL when I wasn't paying attention.

"Will he recover?" Udolf asked. "He was down there for two days, with the power of the Well ravaging his mind."

"He will recover," Monty said. "Can you integrate me into Simon's bond with his creature? The lattice containing Shadowpeak will only hold for so long."

"I can," Udolf said, "because he is close to my kin and you are in my domain. Once you leave my domain, the communication will cease. You may begin now."

"Peaches," Monty said. "Can you hear me?"

<OF COURSE I CAN HEAR YOU MAGE.>

"Do you recall Simon's teleportation idea?" Monty said as I stood there, looking from him to my enormous hellhound. "The one where you could teleport through the forest in phases."

<I RECALL THIS IDEA. DO YOU WISH TO IMPLEMENT THIS MODE OF TRAVEL NOW?>

"Yes, but we have to thread a fine needle," Monty said, looking back at the crumbling Shadowpeak. "We must lure the essence of Shadowpeak away from this place. Can we do that?"

<YOU REALIZE THE DENIZENS OF THE FOREST UNDER SHADOWPEAK'S CONTROL WILL GIVE PURSUIT?>

"Yes, it's a risk we must take," Monty said. "We must leave now."

<I AM READY. REMAIN IN PROXIMITY AND I WILL TAKE MY BONDMATE.>

"You're talking to Peaches?" I asked. "That's nice. Since when can you speak to Peaches?"

"Since now," Monty answered, gently pushing me closer to my hellhound and turning to the large wolf next to us. "My thanks, your majesty. I will return in the future to ensure that no stain has been left on your land."

"I will be waiting for you, Tristan Montague," Udolf said. "Go with speed. May the sun be ever at your back."

"May the moon be ever overhead," Monty said with a bow. "Now, Peaches, we must go. The lattice is breaking."

Peaches let out a low rumble and we blinked.

It wasn't really a blink, it was more like we stood still, and the world blurred past us. One moment we were standing next to Shadowpeak, the next we were in the middle of the Black Forest with growls and howls behind us, followed by some ear-splitting screeches.

"Wait," Monty said, looking behind us. "It's getting closer."

He closed his eyes while keeping one hand on Peaches' foreleg.

<IT APPROACHES.>

Monty nodded.

"Now," he said and we blinked again, arriving in more forest. "Hold a moment."

The distance from Shadowpeak must have been having a positive effect on my mind, because my thoughts were becoming clearer and the screams were dying down. They weren't completely gone, but they weren't as loud.

My arms were still numb from the elbow down.

"Ready?" Monty asked. "It's close."

I could hear the creatures of the forest giving chase, and I was worried about how many more blinks Peaches had in him. We had never done this skip teleporting before.

<WE MUST GO, NOW.>

"Do it," Monty said. "Go."

We blinked again and this time we were close to the hostel in Herrenwies. Peaches was panting by this point.

"No more blinks, boy," I said, rubbing his flank. "You can shrink down now too. I know XL takes plenty of energy to maintain."

He shrunk down to normal size and stumbled a few steps.

I held him up until he was steady.

Behind in the forest, I heard the screeches of the darkcats and the massive footfalls of the ogres, along with a deep screaming that signaled Byron was getting closer.

"We need to go now," I said. "They're getting closer."

We took off at a run, my legs feeling much better. It was amazing what the thought of dozens of monsters chasing you will do for your adrenaline production.

We made it to the garage as Elias opened the door for us.

"You made it out alive," he said. "It seems like you have some fans after you for a word or two."

I opened the door and let my hellhound jump into the Sandhog. I was about to go to the driver's side when Monty stopped me.

"Can you feel anything in your hands?"

"No," I said, shaking my arms out. "Still numb, but I'm sure I can—"

"Absolutely not," Monty said. "You get to ride with your hound, let him lick your hands. Elias, shotgun."

"I'm supposed to hold off whatever is coming from the forest," Elias said. "Those are my instructions from Mr. Fairchild."

"I don't care what Cecil told you to do," Monty said, his voice hard. "You cannot face what is coming and we cannot lead them to this town…Get in *now*. This is not a discussion."

"How bad is it?" Elias said after a moment of hesitation before jumping in the passenger side of the Sandhog. "What exactly did you two do over there?"

"We stopped an ancient siphon pretending to be my ancestor from killing any more mages and Guardian monks," Monty said. "Entities of that sort tend to get upset when you deprive them of power. Everyone strapped in?"

"Punch it," I said from the back. "Get us out of here."

"I second that," Elias said. "My team is on the Shrike and I'll contact Cecil to let him know we are coming in hot."

Monty turned on the engine and Sandy roared as we raced out of the garage and into the Black Forest.

"Are we sure this is the best route?" I asked. "Through the Forest? What about the trees and getting blocked in?"

"The Sandhog is considerably more agile than any of the vehicles Elias used," Monty said. "We can avoid getting trapped, and yes, the only way out is through."

"Do what you have to do," I said, making sure my straps were tight. "Try not to drive into a tree."

The Sandhog was a dream to drive on the open roads, but in the Forest was where it shone. It took to the uneven terrain like a fish to water. In the distance, I could still hear the howls and screeches, but Monty made sure to keep them distant.

I felt the presence of Shadowpeak getting closer, but that was to be expected. It was an essence, it didn't have to worry about running around trees or through a Forest—it just came straight for us.

What I didn't expect was that it brought some friends with it.

"Darkcats on our six," I said as Byron dropped a claw of cats right behind us. Behind the claw of darkcats, I saw three angry-looking ogres—though to be fair, ogres always looked angry. "Three ogres behind the darkcats. I strongly suggest you take evasive maneuvers with an emphasis on velocity."

"We're too heavy for velocity in the Forest," Monty said. "I can, however, execute evasive maneuvers."

Monty took the Sandhog around trees, up and down small hills, taking us airborne and then quickly switching back to change direction, always heading to the airport.

The darkcats were the most direct threat, running nearly

as fast as Monty was driving. A couple of times they clawed the Sandhog, but left no lasting damage.

A moment later, one of the ogres threw a tree.

"Tree incoming, nine o'clock," I said, raising my voice as the trunk sailed past us as Monty swerved out of the way. "Too close."

"I'd greatly appreciate those warnings if they throw any more trees, thank you," Monty said. "We're close now."

Elias leaned out of his side and gestured while whispering some words under his breath. Behind us it suddenly became dark. All of the monsters stopped giving chase, all except Shadowpeak Byron.

"Only the essence is behind us now," I said as Peaches slobbered on my hands. "It's not giving up."

"I sense it," Monty said. "With it this far out, Udolf will begin the sealing. Once Shadowpeak is sealed off, it loses access to power and will diminish in strength until it's drained completely."

"Can't happen soon enough," I said. "It's getting closer and it's… Orb, at three o'clock!"

A large black orb crashed into the ground next to the Sandhog as the airport came into view. I saw the Shrike on a runway, taking off conventionally.

"What is he doing?" Elias said. "The Shrike is a re-VTOL bird. Why is he using a runway?"

"To give us room to fly," Monty said, flipping all the switches on the dash once he got on the runway. "Hold on."

The essence of Shadowpeak was fast, but not as fast as the Sandhog on an open runway, with a supercharged SuNa-Tran engine powering it. The Shrike MKS grew before us as we closed the distance and approached the ramp Cecil had left down.

Monty swerved onto the runway and floored the gas,

jumping up the ramp and into the cargo bay of the Shrike MKS. There was no way we had enough room to decelerate in the cargo space before Monty smashed us into the far wall. Somehow, the Sandhog came to a stop inches from turning us into paste.

SuNaTran engineering was amazing.

I heard the ramp slowly close behind us as the Shrike MKS picked up speed. The roar of the engines began to drown out everything, as I felt the pressure of the acceleration push me back into my seat.

It felt like Cecil was trying to achieve supersonic flight immediately.

"What is he doing?" I asked, raising my voice as the engines grew louder. "Is that safe?"

"I think Cecil is currently more concerned with getting away from Shadowpeak and its essence as fast as humanly possible," Monty said. "Safety may not be top of mind at the moment."

"If he blows up an engine on this *prototype*, we won't be going anywhere fast."

Behind us, I heard the howls of Shadowpeak Byron fade as we left the Black Forest and Germany behind.

Later, the screams in my head died down, and slowly, they too, with every mile of distance between us and Shadowpeak diminishing the volume, vanished.

We remained in the Sandhog and let out a sigh of relief.

"That was some excellent driving," I said, laying my head back to relax against my hellhound, who proceeded to slap me in the face with his tongue. I pushed him away before he drowned me. "Stop trying to drown me."

"I'd better go check in with the boss," Elias said with a chuckle at my struggles as he stepped out of the Sandhog. "You two need anything?"

"This was a little more excitement for you than guarding

Monty in a hospital," I said. "I could use some sleep, about two months' worth. You have any of that on board?"

"Not to my knowledge," he said. "We do have a long flight ahead. I'm sure you can catch some shuteye on the way home."

I nodded as he walked off.

"I didn't know you could drive like that," I said. "Where did you learn to drive like that? Is there a mage defensive driving course I don't know about?"

"You do realize I have a large stake in SuNaTran?"

"I'm aware."

"It wouldn't do to be one of the owners of a vehicular company and not know how to drive, don't you think?"

"Monty, there's driving and then there's *driving*," I said. "You were pulling off maneuvers I didn't think were possible in the Sandhog."

"It helps to have the right vehicle," Monty said, patting the dash. "Cecil creates some extraordinary automobiles."

"That he does," I said, then became silent for a few moments. "Are you okay? Byron tried to get me with a moment of my past, a moment I thought I had put behind me, but it didn't work. Then he—"

"He blindsided me with my father," Monty said, looking straight ahead. "I didn't expect that attack. It was foolish of me to let my guard down."

"It's not foolish to be human," I said. "Your dad sacrificed everything for you. There's no way to compartmentalize that —it was your father."

"I know, but I should have been prepared...better prepared."

"I was the one who dove in the deep end," I said, shaking the numbness from my hands. "I was in the third sub-level for two days? It felt like minutes."

"I knew I was in a trap," Monty said. "I almost didn't want to leave if it meant I got to spend time with my Father again."

"He wasn't real."

"I know, which is why I ended the illusion," Monty said. "It was especially cruel to use my father and my feelings for him against me."

"How did you get out?" I asked. "I tried shaking you to snap you out of it, but you were gone."

"I had help from two sources," Monty said, raising his wrist, The Radiant Star was completely black and cracked. "Uncle Dex's gift managed to stave off the dark influences, giving me time to circumvent the trap and my other source was particularly *canine* in nature."

He glanced in the rearview mirror at my hellhound who was snoring up a storm at the moment.

"He heard me then?"

"He must have, because he gave me a solid bite in my thigh and proceeded to shake me like a rag doll until I begged for mercy."

"He's a good boy," I said, rubbing his belly. "The best. I'll make sure he gets extra portions of sausage."

"I heartily agree," Monty said. "The skip teleports were flawlessly executed."

"I didn't think he could do it," I said, glancing at my hellhound. "He surprised me."

"How are you?" Monty asked, his voice serious. "Maybe we should go see Roxanne?"

"No, thanks," I said, raising a hand. "Not before at least a week of no monsters, creatures, or world saving."

"Simon, what you did was unprecedented," Monty said, still serious. "The power in that well should have killed you, multiple times. You plunged a necrotic siphon into a greater necrotic siphon. The backlash should have melted your brain."

"I'm resilient."

"This is no joking matter," he said. "Let Roxanne examine you. I promise I won't let her keep you prisoner in Haven, unless you want her to, that is."

"That may not be a bad idea," I said, giving it thought. "I could actually get some rest in Haven."

"Or we could go to the Underworld, and ask some overdue questions of Hades about hellhounds and battleforms," Monty suggested. "In the meantime, we have a fairly long flight home. Why not catch up on some much needed sleep? I, for one, am going to get a hot cuppa and then sleep until we land. I suggest you do the same."

"I could use a few hours of sleep."

"Dex will want to speak to us when we get settled," Monty said, opening his door and stepping out. "He will not be pleased with the outcome, but I think he will understand why."

"Are you going to tell him what happened?"

"Yes, but he will know most of it by the state of the Radiant Star," he said. "It suffered a catastrophic shutdown, saving me. I didn't spend two days trapped, like you did, but it wasn't mere moments either."

"Two days," I said. "Was it *really* two days?"

"I have no reason to doubt Udolf, and time flows differently in the Black Forest," he said. "You were in Shadowpeak, which was in a stasis cast, while also immersed inside a necrotic siphon field. Situations like that tend to do strange things to time flow."

"I'm not feeling any different."

"It's too early to tell," he said. "It will be good for Dex to have a look at you, too."

"How pissed is he going to be that we destroyed Shadowpeak?" I asked. "We destroyed Shadowpeak, didn't we?"

"It's been relocated—permanently."

"Will Dex be okay with the relocation?" I asked. "He is kind of an expert at property management that way."

"I doubt he will appreciate the humor."

"Just saying, he relocated all of the Golden Circle," I said. "How will he take it?"

"He will be upset, but I think, secretly he will be relieved," Monty said. "It will be one less thing to worry about. Besides, I wouldn't put it past him to make a personal visit and speak to Udolf. He will accept it in the end."

"I'm sure he will, besides we both know you can never go home again."

"Indeed," he said and closed the door. "Rest up."

I nodded and laid my head back on my hound, the perfect pillow. He extended his sprawl and placed one of his legs across my chest in an effort to get comfortable.

I adjusted my position to give him more space. I had more questions than answers, but right now they could all wait until we landed.

They could wait...until we got home.

THE END

AUTHOR NOTES

Thank you for reading this story and jumping into the world of Monty & Strong with me.

Disclaimer:

The Author Notes are written at the very end of the writing process.

This section is not seen by the ART or my amazing Jeditor.

Any typos or errors following this disclaimer are mine and mine alone.

Come with me on a trip through the forest...the Black Forest.

What was I thinking?

Book 27 should be a little different.

It was different.

So different I nearly got lost in the forest.

The amount of research homework I had given myself with just that one idea was incredible. If you've been keeping track, you may have noticed the Trio of Destruction have been out of the city for a few books now.

It's time they go home.

We'll get to that in a minute.

MAGES & MONSTERS was scheduled to be 55k (some of you may have heard this before) it went feral and became at last count 68k+ Don't ask me why it happens, but some books stick to their scheduled word counts, and others...well, others just lose it and go wild—driving the author crazy in the process.

New characters walk in and introduce themselves (hello Obun & Udolf, who were not even in the outline for this story), events take a turn and twist around making the story longer (much longer) than it was originally planned.

It happens. You roll with it or scrap the whole thing.

I chose to roll.

Then there was the whole Shadowpeak concept and how it kills mages. Is it all mages or just Montague mages (if you're reading this, I really hope you read the story, since that was kind of a spoiler), and if so, how does that happen? How old is Byron? Is it really Byron, the spirit of Byron, an essence pretending to be Byron? Is this Byron evil or what? And if so, how evil?

Lots of fun thoughts like that.

Then we had the SuNaTran featured vehicles, a new transport, The Shrike MKS is an amazing plane designed around the very real B21 Raider a next gen stealth bomber, with a few creative liberties taken...don't tell Northrop Grumman.

Along with the plane Cecil has been working overtime with the Strongmonte line of automobiles, the Lamborghini Sterrato (the Sandhog!) and the Bugatti Galiber Strongmonte Edition. All of these vehicles needed to be researched and then submitted to the SuNaTran treatment—more homework.

I want to take this moment to thank all of the ART who found some of the discrepancies in the story and pointed them out or made the notes which brought them to my attention...it really made a difference THANK YOU. I hope I was able to resolve the conflicts and continuity snafus enough to bring clarity to the story.

It wasn't easy and your assist is greatly appreciated.

I tried, with this story to take us to a haunted forest and a haunted castle. Could I have picked either or? Sure, but why not place the haunted castle in the middle of the haunted forest and then have MS&P go through both? Wouldn't that be better?

Not for them, but for me, it was great fun, a bit more work, but still fun. At the core of this story, even though it was about a haunted, well, everything, it was also about Monty's youth and recalling his childhood.

It was also about family and how sometimes we grow apart and how sometimes that's just how life flows, but also how we should strive to remain connected to our family, those we were born into, or the one we create as we mature.

A few other points, cameos: Elias Pirn has a great cameo in this story, as does Cecil. Daniel our amazing pilot with the awesome voice has a few moments as well. Some of the more notable characters arrived as the story was being plotted, with Byron taking center stage almost immediately. At first, it was difficult to picture a castle as the antagonist. Once Byron arrived, along with the magic involved, it became easier.

For me, Shadowpeak had some excellent haunted vibes, not to mention the Black Forest around it. If you've ever been in a forest at night, when things get almost pitch black you know what I mean.

And if the forest ever gets completely silent around you that is NOT a good sign and you should be looking for the nearest exit ASAP.

I do hope you enjoyed the story.

In addition to the hauntedness of the overall story there were some esoteric ideas sprinkled here and there abut connectedness and the meaning of certain symbols that have been around for centuries and we are just recently uncovering their meanings. If I had gone deeper into that part, the book could have easily been twice as long.

What's next?

I'm currently working on STONE (John Kane) next along with PAIN EATERS (Division 13). This book upheaved my entire production schedule so I have to revamp that a bit, but the year promises to be fun. I won't go into more detail, because right now all I know for certain that there will, of course, be more M&S (DEADEYE / NEMESIS) Some Night Warden (DIVINE HELL), some romantasy (FROZEN FIRE), and plenty of novellas sprinkled in here and there.

Our next MS&P story(DEADEYE) brings us home and is focused on Simon's past coming back to shake up his life, because as he learns, sooner or later, all debts come due. If you enjoyed REQUIEM this will have a feel very close to that with Shadow Company coming back to collect.

There is still so much to explore, darkflame, darkflame Grim Whisper (which is going to cause some real headaches as a forbidden weapon), Dira the Successor, the Hidden Hand and what Simon can (and can't) do with it. Not to mention what were the effects of being in the Well of Pain for two days?

I haven't even touched on Monty's side of things but as a hint, things are getting decidedly darker, whether he wants them to be or not. Let's not forget that the Blood Hunters are still in the city and Michiko has left the Dark Council, along with all the chaos that will bring.

If you've read DUSKBLADER you heard about the Gray Council and they will be showing more power and plans in the next few stories along with some cameos from Moira.

All in all, its going to be a busy year and I hope you join me for the ride!

Through it all, I want to thank you for hanging in there

and reading all these amazing adventures I create, which leads me to this next part:

This next section I repeat often because I find it to be profoundly true. Please forgive me for stating it again and know that I mean it all.
You are totally amazing

As always, I couldn't do this incredibly insane adventure without you (really I couldn't), my amazing reader. You jump into these adventures with me, when I say "WHAT IF?" you say: "Hmmm what if indeed! LET's GO FIND OUT!
For that, I humbly and deeply thank you.

I consider myself deeply fortunate to have the most amazing readers that are willing to leap into these worlds with the same reckless abandon I have in writing them.

You truly spoil me.

Few writers I know have such incredible readers that make it possible to explore creating new worlds, introducing different characters, with an incredible group of readers willing to give the new world and characters a chance.

Thank you so much for joining me as we load up the extra thermos (better bring three or six of them—industrial-sized) filled with the delicious inky Death Wish Javambrosia, some of you can call shotgun, but a few of you are going to have to shove the enormous hellhound in the back of the Dark Goat (or the Sandhog) over if you want a seat (bring plenty of sausage/pastrami-for a guaranteed seat!), as we strap in to jump into all sorts of adventures!

There's a long way to go and a short time to get there, we have plans to disrupt, powers to learn, people to rescue, mages to anger, and property to aggressively renovate!

Again, I want you to know that this adventure is incredible, but it's made even more incredible by having you on it with me.

I humbly, deeply, and profoundly thank you.

In the immortal sage words of our resident Zen Hellhound Master...

Meat is Life!

gratias tibi ago

JOIN US

Facebook
Montague & Strong Case Files

Youtube
Bitten Peaches Publishing Storyteller

Instagram
bittenpeaches

Email
orlando@orlandoasanchez.com

M&S World Store
Emandes

SUPPORT US

Patreon
The Magick Squad

Website/Newsletter
www.orlandoasanchez.com

BITTEN PEACHES PUBLISHING

Thanks for Reading!
If you enjoyed this book, would you please **leave a review** at the site you purchased it from? It doesn't have to be long… just a line or two would be fantastic and it would really help me out.

Bitten Peaches Publishing offers more books and audiobooks
across various genres including: urban fantasy, science fiction, adventure, & mystery!

www.BittenPeachesPublishing.com

More books by Orlando A. Sanchez

Montague & Strong Detective Agency Novels
Tombyards & Butterflies•Full Moon Howl•Blood is Thicker•Silver Clouds Dirty Sky•Homecoming•Dragons & Demigods•Bullets & Blades•Hell Hath No Fury•Reaping

Wind•The Golem•Dark Glass•Walking the Razor•Requiem•Divine Intervention•Storm Blood•Revenant•Blood Lessons•Broken Magic•Lost Runes•Archmage•Entropy•Corpse Road•Immortal•Outcast•Shieldbearer•Saints & Monks•Mages & Monsters

Montague & Strong Detective Agency Stories
No God is Safe•The Date•The War Mage•A Proper Hellhound•The Perfect Cup•Saving Mr. K

Night Warden Novels
Wander•ShadowStrut•Nocturne Melody

Rule of the Council
Blood Ascension•Blood Betrayal•Blood Rule

The Warriors of the Way
The Karashihan•The Spiritual Warriors•The Ascendants•The Fallen Warrior•The Warrior Ascendant•The Master Warrior

John Kane
The Deepest Cut•Blur•Stone

Sepia Blue
The Last Dance•Rise of the Night•Sisters•Nightmare•Nameless•Demon

Chronicles of the Modern Mystics
The Dark Flame•A Dream of Ashes

The Treadwell Supernatural Directive
The Stray Dogs•Shadow Queen•Endgame Tango

Brew & Chew Adventures
Hellhound Blues

Bangers & Mash
Bangers & Mash

Tales of the Gatekeepers
Bullet Ballet•The Way of Bug•Blood Bond

Division 13
The Operative•The Magekiller•Pain Eaters

Blackjack Chronicles
The Dread Warlock•Deathdancers

The Assassin's Apprentice
The Birth of Death

Gideon Shepherd Thrillers
Sheepdog

DAMNED
Aftermath

Nyxia White
They Bite•They Rend•They Kill

Iker the Cleaner
Iker the Unseen•Daystrider•Nightwalker

Fate of the Darkmages
Fated Fury•Cold Front

Nightingale the Duskblader
Duskblader

Stay up to date with new releases!
Shop www.orlandoasanchez.com for more books and audiobooks!

ART SHREDDERS

I want to take a moment to extend a special thanks to the ART SHREDDERS.

No book is the work of one person. I am fortunate enough to have an amazing team of advance readers and shredders.

Thank you for giving of your time and keen eyes to provide notes, insights, answers to the questions, and corrections (dealing wonderfully with my extreme dreaded comma allergy). You help make every book and story go from good to great. Each and every one of you helped make this book fantastic, and I couldn't do this without each of you.

THANK YOU

ART SHREDDERS

Amber, Audrey Cienki
    Chris Christman II
    Diane Craig, Dolly, Donna Young Hatridge
    Hal Bass

Jasmine Breeden, Jeanette Auer, Joy Kiili, Julie Peckett
Karen Hollyhead
Laura Tallman I
RC Battels, Rohan Gandhy
Tami Cowles, Terri Adkisson
Vikki
Wendy Schindler

PATREON SUPPORTERS

Exclusive short stories
Premium Access to works in progress
Free Ebooks for select tiers

Join here
The Magick Squad

THANK YOU

Aaron Matthews, Alisha Harper, Amber Dawn Sessler, Angela Tapping, Anne Englehart, Anne Morando, Annette Spicer, Annie, Anthony Bock, Anthony Hudson, ASH, Ashley Britt

Becky Gambill, Bethany Showell, Bob Morrissey, Bradley Herrup, Brenda French, Brent Lowe, Brett Morse

Carl Skoll, Carolyn J. Evans, Carrie O'Leary, Chris Christman, Cindy Deporter, Connie Cleary, Cooper Walls

Dan Bergemann, Dan Fong, Daniel Harkavy, Davis Johnson, Dawn Bender, Di Hara,

Diane Garcia, Diane Jackson, Dorothy Phillips

E.A., Enid Rodriguez, Eric Maldonado, Ernie Martinez, Eve Bartlet, Ewan Mollison

Federica De Dominicis, Fluff Chick Productions, Fred Westfall

Gail Ketcham Hermann, Gary McVicar, Groove72

Howy

Ingrid Schijven

James Burns, Jasmine Breeden, Jasmine Davis, Jeffrey Juchau, JF, Jim Couger, Joe Durham, John Fauver(*in memoriam*), Joy Kiili, Joyce Casement, Just Jeanette

Kat Wilson, Krista Fox

Leona Jackson, Lisa Simpson, Lizzette Piltch

M. Morgan, Maggie, Malcolm Robertson, Marie Stein, Mark Morgan, Mark Price, Mary Beth Wright, MaryAnn Sims, Marydot Pinto, Maureen McCallan, Mel Brown, Melissa Miller, Meri, Duncanson

Paige Guido, Patricia Pearson, Patrick Hurley, Peter Griffin, Pete Peters, Peter Griffin

Rachel Buchanan, Ralph Kroll, Renee Penn, Robert Walters, Robert Walters, Rohan Gandhy, Ronn Branton

Samantha Rense, Sara M Branson, Sara N Morgan, Sarah Sofianos, Sassy Bear, Sharon Elliott, Shelby, Sherry, Sonyia Roy, Stacey Stein, Steve Scott, Steven Huber, Stuart Jay Stuple, Susan Bowin, Susan Spry

Tami Cowles, Terri Adkisson, Tommy, Trish Brown

Valerie Jondahl, Van Nebedum, Vicki Coppock, Vickie Grider

W S Dawkins, Wendy Schindler, William Haught

***

I want to extend a special note of gratitude to all of our
Patrons in
The Magick Squad.

Your generous support helps me to continue on this amazing adventure called 'being an author'.
I deeply and truly appreciate each of you for your selfless act of patronage.

You are all amazing beyond belief.

THANK YOU

ACKNOWLEDGEMENTS

With each book, I realize that every time I learn something about this craft, it highlights so many things I still have to learn. Each book, each creative expression, has a large group of people behind it.

This book is no different.

Even though you see one name on the cover, it is with the knowledge that I am standing on the shoulders of the literary giants that informed my youth, and am supported by my generous readers who give of their time to jump into the adventures of my overactive imagination.

I would like to take a moment to express my most sincere thanks:

To Dolly: My wife and greatest support. You make all this possible each and every day. You keep me grounded when I get lost in the forest of ideas. Thank you for asking the right questions when needed, and listening intently when I go off on tangents. Thank you for who you are and the space you create—I love you.

To my Tribe: You are the reason I have stories to tell. You cannot possibly fathom how much and how deeply I love you all.

To Lee: Because you were the first audience I ever had. I love you, sis.

To the Logsdon Family: The words *thank you* are insufficient to describe the gratitude in my heart for each of you. JL, your support always demands I bring my best, my A-game, and produce the best story I can. Both you and Lorelei, along with Audrey, are the reason I am where I am today. My thank you for the notes, challenges, corrections, advice, and laughter. Your patience is truly infinite. *Arigatogozaimasu*.

To The Montague & Strong Case Files Group—AKA The MoB (Mages of Badassery): When I wrote T&B there were fifty-five members in The MoB. As of this release, there are over one thousand seven hundred members in the MoB. I am honored to be able to call you my MoB Family. Thank you for being part of this group and M&S.

You make this possible. **THANK YOU.**

To the ever-vigilant PACK: You help make the MoB...the MoB. Keeping it a safe place for us to share and just...be. Thank you for your selfless vigilance. You truly are the Sentries of Sanity.

Chris Christman II: A real-life technomancer who makes the **MoB Kaffeeklatsch** on **YouTube & Facebook** amazing. Thank you for your tireless work and wisdom. Everything is connected...you totally rock!

To my fellow Indie Authors: I want to thank each of you for creating a space where authors can feel listened to, and encouraged to continue on this path. A rising tide lifts all the ships indeed.

To The MoB English Advisory: Aaron, Penny, Carrie, Davina, and all of the UK MoB. For all things English… thank you.

To DEATH WISH COFFEE: This book (and every book I write) has been fueled by generous amounts of the only coffee on the planet (and space) strong enough to power my very twisted imagination. Is there any other coffee that can compare? I think not. DEATH WISH—thank you!

To Deranged Doctor Design: Kim, Darja, Tanja, Jovana, and Milo (Designer Extraordinaire).

If you've seen the covers of my books and been amazed, you can thank the very talented and gifted creative team at DDD. They take the rough ideas I give them, and produce incredible covers that continue to surprise and amaze me. Each time, I find myself striving to write a story worthy of the covers they produce. DDD, you embody professionalism and creativity. Thank you for the great service and spectacular covers. **YOU GUYS RULE!**

To you, the reader: I was always taught to save the best for last. I write these stories for **you**. Thank you for jumping down the rabbit holes of ***what if?*** with me. You are the reason I write the stories I do.

You keep reading…I'll keep writing.

Thank you for your support and encouragement.

SPECIAL MENTIONS

To Dolly: my rock, anchor, and inspiration. Thank you...always.

Larry & Tammy—The WOUF: Because even when you aren't there...you're there.

To Dolly Sanchez: For the re-VTOL design. Because everything is better with runes :).

Orlando A. Sanchez
www.orlandoasanchez.com

Orlando has been writing ever since his teens when he was immersed in creating scenarios for playing Dungeons and Dragons with his friends every weekend.

The worlds of his books are urban settings with a twist of the paranormal lurking just behind the scenes and with generous doses of magic, martial arts, and mayhem.

He currently resides in NYC with his wife and children.

CONTACT ME

I really do appreciate your feedback. You can let me know what you thought of the story by emailing me at:
orlando@orlandoasanchez.com

To get **FREE** stories please visit my page at:
www.orlandoasanchez.com

For more information on the M&S World...come join the MoB Family on Facebook!
You can find us at:
Montague & Strong Case Files

Visit our online M&S World Swag Store located at:
Emandes

If you enjoyed the book, **please leave a review**. Reviews help the book, and also help other readers find good stories to read.
THANK YOU!

__Thanks for Reading!__

If you enjoyed this book
Please leave a review & share!
(with everyone you know)

It would really help us out!

Printed in Great Britain
by Amazon